The critics acclaim the Eddathorpe mysteries

‘A solution as clever as any I’ve read this year. D.I. Graham, with his homicidal Lakeland terrier, is an unconventional copper from the same breed as Frost and Morse. On this form, he should win fans and keep them.’ *Val McDermid, Manchester Evening News*

‘Flynn has created an excellent detective and a memorable setting ... extremely talented.’ *Yorkshire Post*

‘Expertly done ... Some very satisfactory policing set against acridly detailed background of out-of-season holiday town.’ *Literary Review*

‘A welcome addition to the fictional police ranks.’ *Sunday Telegraph*

‘He gives the police procedural an insider’s expertise, including in-jokes ... Flynn is the former head of Notts Fraud Squad. But his first book proves he’s no PC Plod in the art of writing.’ *Sunday Express*

New English Library paperbacks by Raymond Flynn

Seascape with Body
A Public Body
A Fine Body of Men
Busy Body
The Body Beautiful

About the author

Raymond Flynn spent twenty-six years with the Nottinghamshire Constabulary. Starting as a uniformed constable, he later moved to the CID and then served for twelve years as the detective inspector in charge of the Fraud Squad in Nottingham, where he still lives. He turned to writing after taking medical retirement. He was a finalist in the 1992 Ian St James Short Story competition and won the Gooding Prize for short stories in 1994.

Over My Dead Body

Raymond Flynn

NEW ENGLISH LIBRARY
Hodder & Stoughton

First published in Great Britain in 2000
by Hodder and Stoughton
First published in paperback in 2000
by Hodder and Stoughton
A division of Hodder Headline

A New English Library Paperback

10 9 8 7 6 5 4 3 2 1

A CIP catalogue record for this title is available
from the British Library.

ISBN 0 340 71226 0

Printed and bound in Great Britain by
Caledonian Book Manufacturing Ltd, Glasgow

Hodder and Stoughton
A division of Hodder Headline
338 Euston Road
London NW1 3BH

In memory of my father, William Flynn D.C.M.

The North Central Area of the National Crime Squad does not exist. Nottingham is not one of the three Area centres of this organisation and it therefore follows that the offices and personnel I have described are figments of my diseased imagination. I have also taken some liberties with the rank structure, and [dare I say it?] the working practices of the genuine National outfit for the purposes of this book.

Chapter One

'There's some joy in your life!'

Detective Chief Inspector Colin Templeton took a long, satisfying pull at his pint. I followed suit, and waited, a trifle warily, while he prepared to expand his theme.

'Sun, and sand, sex and sea; no stress to speak of and a quiet place to work. I tell you Robert, old son, you don't know when you're well off; it's a Bobby's job around here!'

'Eddathorpe,' I said cheerfully, 'is the arsehole of the world; just like Hyson Green on a Saturday night one minute, and about as exciting as a cemetery in the rain the next.'

'Some people never know when they're well off.' Colin, Nottingham born and bred, had a more than passing acquaintance with the delights of Hyson Green and the fortress on Radford Road, which passed for the local nick.

'Tell me about it,' I said.

Colin hesitated for a moment before staring the length of the bar of the Links Hotel where Keith Baker, the landlord, half bent across his glass washer, and with one ear cocked, was meticulously washing and rewashing a solitary pint glass. If he didn't wear it away first, he was well on the way to achieving the prize for the most sterile drinking container in the world.

'He's earwigging!' Without waiting for my reaction, he turned and made his way to one of the booths at the rear of the room. The landlord twitched, and then he turned slowly prior to glancing towards me with reproachful oyster eyes. I winked placatingly: Keith was harmless, but absolutely typical of Colin Templeton, was that. Old friend, good copper, but a man with one all too frequent motto: leap before you look. I threw a reassuring smile in the direction of Keith's bulky, disappointed figure before turning and playing follow my leader in the direction of a more secluded part of the room.

'Ears like Dumbo the flying elephant,' muttered Colin unforgivingly as he sat down. 'Probably alchy, too; I wouldn't be a bit surprised.'

'He's bound to be curious,' I murmured soothingly. 'He's an ex-cop, after all; even though it was thirty years ago.'

'They're always the worst.' He took another swig of his pint and I sighed. Another set of native feelings to soothe once he'd gone. Newly promoted, he was, I decided, feeling his feet, and old friend or not I was beginning to pick up on one or two of Colin's faults. Especially his tendency to leave a few bruises, not all of them metaphorical, in his wake from time to time.

'How's it going then, Col?'

He took another slurp of his pint and grinned, 'Not so dusty, thanks. New job, new wife, clean sweep.'

He lifted his left hand and smoothed the cowlick of dark red hair threatening to fall down across his eyes. At forty-two he was a year older than me, but he could easily have been almost ten years younger; still slim, still chipper, with a smooth, unlined face, a four-hundred-pound suit, and the same, occasionally wearing line in cynical chat.

'What happened?'

'I was traded in for a later model,' he said brusquely, 'so I took the hint, and decided to do the same.'

'Oh.' Nothing much else I could say. I was still stuck with the old, outdated image of Colin and his first wife, Sandra; he'd taken the wind completely out of my sails.

'CID marriages,' he said airily, 'you know how it is. Angie and the baby all right?'

'Fine, thanks.'

Nice one, Colin. A dig in the general direction of the circumstances of the temporary Angie-versus-Robert Graham bust-up that had led to a brawl with a senior officer, and my abrupt transfer to the East Coast nearly four years before. And, just in case I was thinking about it, a reminder that those who live in gossipy glass police stations should avoid hasty judgements, and refrain from throwing moral bricks.

'OK,' he said ironically, 'now we've caught up with our domestic lives, we might as well get on.'

'I assume it's something too hot for the office; all this super-security and a meeting in the local pub?' I smiled at him guilelessly: I can do sarcasm, too. He didn't take it up.

'Yeah,' he contemplated his half-empty glass for a few moments. 'I'm serious, Bob; there's a lot of money involved here, and this could turn very nasty if it gets out; I kid you not.'

'What is it, then? Some sort of fraud?'

'Fraud? This is the all-singing, all-dancing National Crime Squad, mate. The boring bits are nothing to do with us!'

'The all-British FBI, huh? Step aside J Edgar Hoover, let's hear a very big welcome for Jolly Jack Straw!'

'OK, OK, spare me, I've heard all the jokes. It was more than time we had a national investigative service, anyway. And part of our remit is corporate blackmail, and we've certainly got one here.'

'Anybody I know?'

'Cary's supermarkets,' he said.

'You call that corporate; one store in Eddathorpe and one in Aylfleet?' I groaned. I had, I decided, already read this particular script. The Big City superintendent sends one of his minions on a flying visit to a small seaside town to chat up a fellow detective chief inspector in the sticks. The dogsbody tells his story, unloads the dirt and departs smiling, leaving the local bumpkin to sort out the resultant mess. I too had once worked on a Crime Squad, if only as a relatively humble DI.

He stared at me shrewdly. Been there, done that, bought the T-shirt; it didn't take a genius to read what was going on in my mind.

'Now would I do a thing like that to you, old son?'

'Yes.'

'Too bloody right,' he admitted. 'Given half a chance, but this isn't the old Regional Crime Squad any more. Besides, this Cary outfit is a lot bigger than you seem to think.'

'Family firm, isn't it? I know that when they first opened they undercut every local shop in sight, but they're far from being a national company, although they caused a lot of heartburn among the smaller shopkeepers around here.'

'They're a Nottingham company, one of ours. Fourteen branches in the Midlands and the North, and they run a couple of cash-and-carry wholesalers on the side. Not exactly Sainsbury's mate, but Maurice Cary, the old man, thinks he's God.'

'And he's given your boss a hard time?'

'Currently, he's giving *everybody* a hard time, including our boss, Detective bloody Superintendent Frank Purcell. I can't say I blame him much. Forty years building the business, and then some toerag comes along and tries to milk him for half a million quid.'

'How?'

Colin glanced briefly over one shoulder; three or four other lunchtime customers at the other end of the bar, and Keith Baker well out of earshot, still licking his wounds.

'Food contamination,' he murmured softly. 'They thought it was some sort of nutter at first; a spate of crank letters addressed to their MD. Then this bugger turned nasty and planted a few jars of contaminated baby food on their shelves in and around our city, just to show he meant business.'

'Anybody hurt?'

'Not yet,' he said grimly. 'He planted the gear in three separate stores at the back of the shelves, but he took care to let the store managers know straight away. No harm done, but he scared 'em shitless, mate.'

'So they called the police?'

'Not at first, no. Me laddo wanted payment through various bank and building society accounts he'd opened. He intended getting his payments via the cash machines; not exactly a new idea, but it was pretty sound from his point of view.

'Anyway, the Managing Director arranged to seed the accounts – nowhere near half a million quid, of course, and then they employed this ruddy private detective agency to liaise with the banks, and try to track him down. They thought they had a chance of catching him on the job, after all the cash limit on an individual account is only around five hundred a day.'

'Description of the offender?'

'One head, two arms, two legs. They hardly remember him at the banks, one girl thought she might recall the man who obtained one of the banker's cards, if it was the right man in the first place. He struck her as being a bit of a pouf. I have not widely circulated that little gem as a possible description, you can imagine how that would go down for political correctness in this day and age.'

Colin cocked one ironic eye in my direction. The roughie toughie copper with the Rugby Club mouth. I think he was patting me down for signs of incipient humanity or even orthodox PC. Apparently satisfied, he continued. 'Anyway, the bank and building society accounts were opened anything up to eighteen months ago.'

I whistled appreciatively, a high degree of planning had gone into this.

'What happened with the original private eye?'

'Nothing worthwhile, apart from laughing boy collecting around twenty thousand quid in less than a week; the so-called investigators were running from machine to machine like scalded cats.' He paused for a brief pleasurable smirk. 'That's when they called us in.'

'These banks and building societies . . .' I started.

'He used real people with decent credit ratings, mostly, but the bastard had given them a new address whenever he opened an account. Lodging houses, places up for sale, empty flats. He'd obviously copied one or two estate agents' keys so he could pop in and collect the mail whenever it arrived. Clever sod.'

'Says a lot for the estate agents, does that.'

'Oh he's cunning; he usually made a supervised visit with a junior employee at first, he talked serious interest and so on. Then he'd go back to the agent later, and con them into handing over a key – checking for problems, measuring up; stuff like that.'

'No description again?'

Colin raised his eyes heavenwards, 'One. They think it was a businessman, stoutish, middle aged. Know something? The bugger's got a sense of humour, too; he even filled in one application form in the name of a Probation Officer in Notts!'

'You didn't, er, do anything drastic, I take it?'

'Not funny, Bob; people can get very uptight about a thing like that. Our Frank handled that one as though he was treading on eggs.'

'Personally,' I said, 'I've always had this yen to arrest a Member of Parliament, or a QC.'

'That,' said Colin Templeton briefly, 'is one of the reasons why Frank Purcell is a detective superintendent, and you're not.'

'Smile when you say that.'

He smiled.

'OK, whose job is it then; yours, or this mysterious Frank Purcell?'

He looked at me boldly, but he hesitated for that moment too long, 'Mine.'

'But?'

'I've got this nasty feeling, Bob. It's probably his if there's any credit going and mine if we all fall down in the mire.'

'OK, Colin, now I know you're serious; what is it you want?'

'Cooperation.'

'You've got it.'

'Thanks, but I was thinking more along the lines of Peter Fairfield, your boss.'

'Problems?'

'Not so you'd notice.' He gave a harsh imitation of a laugh, 'Apart from his general desire to erect a twenty-foot barbed wire fence around his bailiwick, complete with armed guards. Not to mention the feud he's had running for something like twenty years with Frankie Purcell, my current wanker-in-chief.' Never one to hide his feelings, Colin, there was a note of real bitterness in his voice.

'Peter still outranks him, huh?'

'Only nominally, according to Frank. It's this new bloody grading system, matey: two grades of superintendent in most forces these days, although the Squad holds on to the chief super rank. According to Frank, you're a dinosaur if you're still a chief, and you ought to be on your way to the old folks' home. Still,' he sniffed, 'that doesn't mean that Frankie's prepared to come here and talk to your guy himself.'

I turned my mind to Chief Superintendent Peter Fairfield, my CID head. If he was any sort of dinosaur, he was probably a Tyrannosaurus Rex, and obviously, this Purcell character must think the same. Not a man to cross, despite his smiling boozer's face, and his carefully promoted image; the lumbering wide-eyed ploughboy at the Fair.

Good at feuds was Peter. Like the grey-suited, crumpled, untidy elephant he somewhat resembled, he seldom forgot.

'Something serious, was it?' I murmured; it was always as well to know the details of Peter's loves and hates.

Colin shrugged, 'They were both Regional Crime Squad men,' he said offhandedly. 'Detective sergeants, apparently; way back in the days before Adam was a lad. They were rivals, and they both wanted to get made.'

'And?'

'Oh, you know how it is; Frank Purcell's well known for it, even now. He had something on your man, so he dished the dirt.' He paused deliberately, gauging the level of my interest, 'Nothing terminal, but things were a bit different then. Policewoman trouble; she got posted, and they gave your man the choice.'

'Let me guess; he was married, so they told him it was a case of his career prospects, or a life of poverty, professional obscurity and eternal love?'

'Something like that. You're a failed romantic, Bob. I wouldn't have put it that way myself.'

'Fairfield might,' I said tersely, 'and he's not the forgiving and forgetting type.' I left it at that. If Peter was still feeling sore over some dim and distant affair, I didn't intend sticking my head above the parapet by making an educated guess as to the identity of the policewoman involved. He was rumoured, however, to have once had a close, even intimate relationship with the female divisional commander at Aylfleet, the other half of my patch. As a comparative newcomer to the force I didn't know the full, and presumably juicy details of the ancient scandal, but it was remarkable how warily Peter trod whenever he had dealings with Superintendent Dorothea Spinks.

'This Fairfield character; you'll give me a bit of a leg-up, Robert, eh?'

I gave Colin the once over. Tall, svelte, silk shirt, important-looking tightly knotted tie, a flash of gold beneath a well-pressed double cuff. A touch of the super salesman about him, too, and not, I would have thought, the natural Fairfield type. He might do better in his gardening kit; less glitz, a shabby jacket and a pair of creaseless cords, perhaps.

'Why me?'

'For one thing, I know you. For another he rates you, Bob.'

'News to me, mate. He usually behaves as if he wishes I'd go away and make life impossible for somebody else.'

'Modesty will get you nowhere, Bob; you're covering two divisions. In any other force you'd be holding down a superintendent's job.'

'It's a rural area,' I muttered, 'with a relatively low population, so they've utilised the detective chief inspector rank to cover a lot of ground; they're running a very low-budget CID.'

'They're running,' he said acidly, 'a very low-budget, not to mention a very low-talent force. Present company excepted,' he added hastily, 'naturally.'

'You've spoken to Peter Fairfield already?'

'Only on the phone: don't know how anybody manages to put up with him. I get the impression he's far from keen on all these new-fangled squads. He can't refuse, exactly, but he ended up wanting everything in writing. The man's autocratic, bull-headed, and reactionary. Living in the past.'

'With an attitude like yours, Colin, I can well understand how much you managed to impress.'

'Sarcastic bastard! How's about a spot of respect for the representative of the new-born National CID?'

'Not once you step across this boundary, friend. And not when you're asking me to beg for favours from somebody you've already managed to upset.' He might be joking; on the other hand it was a worthwhile moment to lay down a few ground rules, to tell the cocky bugger exactly how he stood.

'Okay, okay,' he held up his hands in mock surrender. 'I just want to talk to the feller, right? There are four supermarkets belonging to this outfit in your county. You'd think the sour old bugger could be persuaded to take some sort of interest in the problem, OK?

'All I'm asking for is a bit of help; I'd sooner do it the nice way, but if your head of CID wants to treat me as if I'm carrying typhoid, I can always bring a spot of pressure to bear, and that won't do Mr High-and-mighty Fairfield any good.'

'Via our Chief?'

'Via your Chief, via our National Director, via the Home Office, if necessary. You'd be doing Fairfield himself the favour, if you could only make him see sense.'

Colin, doing a spot of one of the things he did best; the old CID stand-by, threats, cunningly mixed with a touch of the pseudo-sincere. Here was a man, I remembered, who had the knack of persuading some fairly intelligent criminals that it was in their own best interests to open their mouths and talk their way into a nice cosy cell from time to time.

'Yeah, all right, I understand.' I took another cautious sample from my rapidly diminishing pint. Politeness dictated that I should keep a nominal sup in the bottom of my glass, draining it indicated the end of the game. 'You're just a passing altruist, and whatever we end up doing, it's all for our own good. There's only one thing you haven't told me, so far; what exactly do you want from us hicks from the sticks, anyway?'

'Ah,' Colin examined his drink, supplies were definitely running out. 'In a word, manpower. Women power too, if you like.' He spared a moment for a lascivious grin. 'Blackmailers, if they come unstuck, frequently get caught at the point of collection, right?

'This particular clever Dick thinks he's got it all worked out: open several bank or building society accounts, collect the cash cards from empty properties, and employ the holes in the walls to get the money out. Nice work if you can get it, but his problem is the daily cash limit on each account.

'He's going round and round like a mouse on a wheel, making withdrawals in town after town. We're not some little, under-resourced private detective agency, so that's when we score.'

'Now hang on a minute,' I thought I was beginning to catch his drift. 'If you think that you can persuade every copper from Lands End to John o'Groats to keep obs on bank and building society cash points from now to evermore, you're out of your mind.'

'Not quite,' Colin Templeton looked smug. 'For some reason known best to himself, he's keeping to a regular beat. Notts, Derbyshire, Leicestershire, and a couple of forays into South Yorks, so far.'

'Towns with Cary's supermarkets?'

'Not invariably, but generally speaking, yes. Personally, I think he feels comfortable with the areas, OK? Anyway, we're setting up an arrangement with the service providers; they monitor their machines, they phone the local police stations whenever there's a hit, and—'

'The police arrive just in time to arrest the next granny using the hole in the wall,' I finished.

'Not quite.' Colin favoured me with his pitying look. 'He usually chooses market towns; three or four bank or building society cash points, at least. He does the rounds, OK; then he moves on.

'Listen to this,' he produced a list from the inside pocket of his coat. 'Take last week, for example: Saturday, one of his favourite days. He started in Notts: Beeston, Stapleford, then Sandiacre, Derby, and on up to Matlock Bath. We were just getting ready to jump on him at Matlock itself when he packed it up.'

'So, you're gathering more men, but you've pinched the basic concept from some scrubby private eye. Second-guess your offender by getting ahead of him to a cash point, or hope he follows a particular route while you wait for him in the next town?'

'Yes, but there's a bit of a snag. There's no worthwhile description of the offender, right? He visited the empty addresses and set up the accounts months ago, so neither the banks nor the estate agents have got a clue.'

I weighed up the odds, no better suggestions myself, but it sounded like a crazy idea to me. Lots of policemen on lots of streets conducting observations and rushing around. They might, of course, secure the prize in the end. In my mind's eye, however, I could see them all out there, cursing Colin Templeton and achieving nothing. Probably getting wet.

'May I,' I said elaborately, 'congratulate you on your unbridled optimism, and sincerely wish you the best of British luck!' In pursuit of additional well-deserved refreshment, I drained my glass.

'Thanks,' said Colin, following suit. 'I know you mean that.' He collected the glasses, 'Fancy the other half?'

He stood up, and under the wary eye of mine host he made his self-confident way towards the bar. Keith bent forward, his head disappearing beneath the counter. Suddenly, I had a very uneasy feeling about all this.

When he reappeared, the landlord was clutching a handful

of tea towels, which he proceeded to drape over the pumps the moment Colin arrived at the counter.

'Sorry,' Keith's voice carried, and he sounded anything but; 'we don't do all day opening. Next drinks are at six o'clock; we're closed.'

Chapter Two

'Daddy, daddy, daddy!' three-year-old Laura shrieked, deliberately hurling herself at me via a sliding rug in the over-polished hall. Joe, my Lakeland terrier, jumped and bounced and barked. I gathered her up, and attempted, awkwardly, to both pat and fend off a small, overenthusiastic dog at the same time.

It's nice to be so instantly popular; builds up the ego, does that. Nevertheless, a vague suspicion stirred; there was usually a good and sufficient reason for such extreme demonstrations of love and affection the moment I stepped through the door.

Sure enough, a significant clattering of pots and pans echoed from the kitchen. 'Thank God you're home!' called Angie, 'you can look after the pair of them. I'm thoroughly fed up!'

'Had a nice day, darling?' I murmured to myself, *sotto voce*, kissing Laura, 'yes thank you, darling; disarmed a dangerous gunman on the Promenade, and recovered a stolen elephant from the zoo.'

'Mummy!' yelled Laura before I could stop her, wriggling out of my arms, 'Daddy caught a bad man with a gun!'

Angela, her hands encased in flour, was out of the kitchen and upon me even as I opened my mouth to protest.

'It was a joke, just a joke!' I protested weakly.

'I can't believe it! How could you even dream of going around frightening a child like that?' Not to mention, I gathered, my busy, fed-up wife.

The terror-stricken child looked up at me wistfully, 'Was it a nice elephant?' she said.

'What elephant?'

'The one the bad man stole from the zoo.'

'Oh,' said Angie, back-pedalling rapidly, and jumping to unwarranted conclusions, 'daddy was just telling you a story, then?' Wifely embarrassment became an additional feature of Angela's bad day.

Laura, with wisdom beyond her years, stared at me knowingly. A story it became; my name was no longer mud.

'I'm sorry, darling,' said Angie contritely, 'but it's been a hell of a day; they were both playing up all morning, and while Val took her to the playgroup when I went to work, she apparently hit Daniel with his little red engine, and his mother came round afterwards and said . . .'

'Oh dear,' I stared down at the miscreant and tried to look severe. Valerie Todd, a near neighbour, was Angela's child minder and port of refuge in the not-infrequent storms associated with Angie's part-time teaching job. Daniel, not to mention Daniel's mother, was unknown to me. My daughter was obviously innocent, however, and first reports suggested that Daniel might be a bit of a wimp.

It's amazing how you can deliberately distort the truth in favour of a pretty, blond-haired, blue-eyed suspect, especially when she keeps her mouth shut and hands you twenty-five undeserved Brownie points in the battle of domestic life.

Peace having been declared, I listened to Angie's catalogue of minor disasters. Dog chews leg of kitchen stool, Laura spills a particularly virulent mixture of play-paints and water on the dining room rug; both of 'em plaguing the life out of her while lesson plans were being prepared, and as for her class at school . . . I listened, less than entranced, as she developed her lengthy thesis on child psychology in general with particular reference to Juniors behaving badly on a windy day.

Eventually, having drawn the heavy living-room drapes against the sea, the esplanade traffic and the chill offshore breezes of an early autumn evening, I managed to pour two large malts, sit her down, and, in true male chauvinistic fashion, turn the conversation around. No elephants, no gunmen, it was true, but my day hadn't been entirely devoid of incident either, so what about me?

'Colin Templeton,' she muttered thoughtfully when I told her, 'fancy him turning up.'

'You don't sound altogether pleased.'

'Another one who never seemed to want to go home.' Still a sore point, I understood. Angie had always been able to do without the police force as an institution, especially the CID. A gang of boozers, womanisers, and selfish workaholics according to her, an attitude which had made her brief affair with Clive Jones, a whiz-kid superintendent in my old force all the more difficult to stomach from my point of view.

Clive, a smooth nine-to-five administrator with every weekend off, had moved in while I was out there making the world safe for democracy fourteen hours every day. Not to mention living off pork pies, leaving the home-cooked dinners to spoil in the oven and knocking it back with Colin, among others, in a series of unofficial, all-night pubs.

Over four years now, since, as a lowly inspector, I'd hammered Clive, laying him stiff and stark on the dance floor during the Senior Officers' Summer Ball. Angie had left me after that, and the police, following up on the grand old tradition that everything, always, is invariably the fault of the junior man, had arranged for my rapid transfer to the East Coast. And lucky to get it, you might say; Eddathorpe, with all its little foibles and eccentricities, was obviously preferable to the big disciplinary chop.

Angie had, of course, eventually returned, leaving Superintendent Jones to continue his onwards-and-upwards career. For those among the gossips who can count, six months after our reunion Laura had been born. It had all happened in what we now both wanted to regard as another country, another life. Still, old friends, old times, and uncomfortable reminders. Angie could probably do without 'em: she was definitely feeling sore.

'What does he want this time?' Again, that slight wary, possibly unfriendly edge to her voice.

'I thought you liked him?' Ignore the obvious answer to the question and go for the underlying warning in her voice.

'I did – do, but Colin is always on the lookout for Colin, first and last, and we haven't had so much as a Christmas card from either of them for the last couple of years.'

'Ah, well,' momentarily, I paused. 'He's got a new wife; Sandra left him, that's probably why he lost touch. He didn't seem inclined to, er—'

'Share the grisly details? I'm not surprised.'

'And what's that supposed to mean?'

'Nothing; nothing at all. Except,' she leaned forward in her chair, drink poised, 'you know Colin just as well as me. One, he keeps his private life very much to himself, and two, he wouldn't like anybody to be in a position to have anything even slightly discreditable to hold against him, even an old friend.'

'And that's liking, huh?'

'Liking people doesn't mean you have to go around with your eyes shut. Men,' she added significantly, 'can be so naive.'

'I haven't seen all that much simple-minded good will lying around,' I said. 'Not in this particular job.'

'Macho man,' said Angie affectionately, 'you're all the same. About ten years old inside, going around flexing your muscles and saying, *"Look at me, mummy, I'm a big tough cynical cop!"*'

'It's nice to know what you think of me on the quiet. Now you can't say I haven't done my bit, I poured you a drink, I even let you sit down and share your troubles with me for a while. So why don't you leave the head of the household to relax, while you trot about your household tasks like a good little spouse?'

'Not until I've finished it,' said Angie comfortably, 'and given due consideration to the thought of wrapping a hot meat and potato pie right around your neck. In the meantime, you can tell me exactly what Colin Templeton wants you to do on his behalf.'

'Grown-ups' business, ducks.'

'Seriously,' said Angela.

'He's got a nasty case of corporate blackmail on his hands, and at this stage, in my opinion, he's clutching at straws. He needs a spot of inter-force cooperation, and he wants me to soothe the way for him with Peter Fairfield, that's all.'

'And why can't he go and ask for this, er, fraternal assistance all by himself?'

'Fairfield can be a bit parochial from time to time,' I admitted casually, 'and he doesn't altogether get on with Colin Templeton's boss.' Not the moment to disclose all the vulgar details; unfortunate parallels might be drawn.

'And?'

'We're seeing Peter first thing tomorrow morning. In the meantime,' I added grandly, 'detailed plans are being drawn.'

'You're beginning to sound,' said Angie doubtfully, 'like some sort of Civil Servant; if it's all so hush-hush and important, why didn't you arrange to go today?'

'Fairfield says he doesn't know what all the bother is about; he's already said he's going to help in principle, and if anything happens in our force area we'll do our bit. He just wants to ensure that the necessary protocols are observed, and anyway, all this fussing and moaning is absolutely typical of Colin Templeton's boss.'

'I was right,' said Angie maliciously, 'it's beginning to sound less like a police force, and more and more like the Ministry of Funny Walks.'

I didn't want to disabuse her, she genuinely thought that she'd discovered something new.

I suppose I should have known; Peter Fairfield was hardly the type to fail to cover his back. Irritating an old enemy was one thing, failing to take due note of an inter-force request for assistance was quite another.

At 10 a.m., unwisely dressed in another expensive version of the top detective's suit, Colin Templeton presented himself at our HQ to make his plea. By twenty past, Colin, with me in tow, had been briefed on Peter's carefully prepared operational order and action plan.

'Just in case,' as he delicately put it, 'the man *does* come our way, and you and Faithless Frankie, by some stretch of your collective imagination, do turn out to be right.'

Colin twitched while our head of CID openly examined this unexpected vision of sartorial elegance, eased his own semi-creaseless trousers at the crotch, belched, and treated his guest to a slow, thick-lipped farmboy's grin.

'Manners!' he said, beaming, momentarily covering his mouth. Even for Peter, it was going pretty far. Not the actions of an officer and a gent; not, come to think of it, the sort of display you'd expect from anybody of or above the rank of lance corporal in the Pioneers. Nevertheless, he was making his point; experienced thief-takers and smart-arse tailor's dummies, he seemed to be saying, were worlds apart.

'Well,' he said, having conducted the business entirely to his own satisfaction, 'you'll see from the confidential draft operational order that we're all prepared, Chief Inspector. We'll distribute it on a strictly need-to-know basis, of course.

'In the meantime, if your offender enters our county, and if either you or the, ah, various financial institutions notify us in time, we'll do our best to put officers out at the appropriate cash points.' We both noticed it, the operative expression was *if*.

'Yes, sir,' muttered Colin Templeton doubtfully, 'thanks.'

'And,' a final twist of the rusty knife, 'you can assure Superintendent Purcell of our continuing interest and support. Tell him that we'll do our very best to arrest his offender for him, hum?' He paused for a few pregnant moments and added, 'Speculative, though; slightly nonsensical, even, wouldn't you say?'

Colin wouldn't: Colin, prepared to leave, and, however long ago the cause for offence, Colin had just been treated to a petty sample of east-coast peasant's revenge. Nothing he could do about it, but I could tell he was not impressed.

I muttered something neutral, and we both stood up, 'Thank you Mr Templeton, er, Colin, for letting me know.' He waited until I had one hand wrapped around the doorknob before he added, 'Perhaps you could give me another couple of minutes, Bob, before you go?'

I opened the door, and Colin passed through it with a flat, 'Good morning,' and a single expressive glance. What with one thing and another, I decided, he had a fairly unenviable job.

'He's young,' said Peter smugly as I resumed my seat in front of his huge, untidy desk, 'but no doubt he'll learn, in time.'

'Learn what?' I asked. It was not the moment for an idle chat about Colin's youthful appearance and proper age.

'To stop playing errand-boy for Faithless Frank,' he replied disparagingly. 'I suppose the old bastard hasn't got the guts to come here himself!'

'Sir . . .' I started indignantly.

'Never mind, Bob,' he waved one airy, forgiving hand. 'You weren't to know, devious old bugger is Frank. Started out somewhere in Yorkshire damn near thirty years ago, and he's been shunting himself backwards and forwards from force to force ever since. National Crime Squad, hah! Only way he could get further promotion, once they'd found him out, I reckon.'

'I understand—' I started, but Fairfield shook his head.

'No need for you to get involved, Robert. Leave him to me, Frankie and I go back a long way. He must be losing what's left of his marbles if he thinks that I can't smell him out!'

'As I understand it,' I said quickly, interrupting any further touches of slander, interspersed with snippets of personal reminiscence, 'this is exclusively Colin Templeton's job.' Not the plain and unadulterated truth, mind you, but anything Peter didn't know at this stage wouldn't hurt him. It's called sticking by your mate.

'Of course, of course,' the beam was back. 'And that's how we'll play it laddie. Give your pal Colin all the help and cooperation you like, and I'll instruct the rest of the CID to do the same.

'Personally, with the whole United Kingdom to choose from, I don't buy this sticking to one area stuff. And as for catching this offender by snooping around cash points twenty-four hours a day, I don't think they've got a snowball's chance in hell.'

'It's a bit thin,' I admitted, 'but—'

'You think he might be right, then?'

'It's a possibility, sir, at least. If this is an inside job, and somebody from the company itself has decided to screw the boss, it's just possible that they'll stick to areas they feel comfortable visiting, places with stores, towns they know.'

'Then they must be barmy,' said Detective Chief Superintendent Fairfield, a flexible sort of chap. 'And if this is an internal job, laddie, you'd think they'd do something more positive back in Nottingham than getting us to arse around outside the Natwest Bank. Among others,' he murmured swiftly as I began to open my mouth.

He rocked back in his chair and stared thoughtfully at the ceiling for a few moments, 'Stiiillll,' he drawled eventually, 'there just might be something worthwhile in it, as you say. Reckon these banks and other – other financial institutions could get on the blower in time?'

'They might: not fast enough to get us to the first, or even the second cash point in a town in time. After all, it only takes a couple of minutes to make a withdrawal from a machine. But town-centre cash points are pretty close, somebody could be out there by the third or fourth touch.

'Besides, if they spotted a pattern developing, a route from town to town . . .'

'Point taken, Bob.' He paused again, 'OK, this is what we do. I'll circulate the operational order, right? And if this merchant ever enters our county, we'll jump. Then, when it happens, *if* it ever does, it's our capture. We'll get an admission, lock the bugger up for whatever he's done to us, and after, only after we've got it all sorted, I'll get on the blower to Frank.'

Angie had been wrong, I decided, as I stared almost incredulously at his elderly, reddening, crumpled face. Only a year or two short of sixty was Peter, the magic age at which even detective chief superintendents have to retire. But on this occasion, at least, she'd have been seriously overstating his emotional maturity by setting it at anything even approaching ten.

Chapter Three

Nothing happened for something over a week; nothing about Cary's, or Colin Templeton, Peter Fairfield, Dorothea Spinks or even Frank Purcell, that is. Not directly, anyway. The rumour factory had been busy, however, and I didn't much like the sound of the things that had gone before.

According to George Caunt, the Eddathorpe detective sergeant, whose encyclopaedic knowledge of police personalities and scandals went far back into the mists of time, Detective Superintendent (Lower Grade) Frank Purcell was bad news.

'He was a PC in the old Dewsbury Borough,' said George gloomily, 'and as a Probationer they called him Boots.'

'Boots Purcell?' said Paula Spriggs, the Borough DI, looking up from the pile of Crime Reports half scattered across her desk, 'Why was that?'

'Because,' said George with relish, 'he used to polish 'em until they shone like glass. Thought it was his way to fame an' fortune in those days, or so people said.'

'Sounds like a harmless enough delusion,' she said, returning to her task.

'Then,' said George remorselessly, 'Dewsbury amalgamated with the old West Riding back in 1968, and eventually he went back to the training school as acting sergeant. That's when they started calling him Brown Nose Frank.'

'No thank you, George,' murmured Paula fastidiously,

'that one you can keep all to yourself, I no longer wish to know.'

'After that,' continued George, 'he was a uniformed sergeant in South Yorks, but they went and inflicted him on the CID after a couple of years. Next they shuffled him off to the Crime Squad, then he was a DI with us for a while, and when *we* got rid he was made uniform chief inspector in Derbyshire, a consolation prize, I suppose.

'He must have known something pretty awful about somebody senior after that, because he obtained a job as a uniform superintendent somewhere down South, and every single copper in five Forces was hoping that's where he'd stay!'

'George,' I said, torn between laughter and disapproval, 'that is undoubtedly one of the most damning examples of a CV I've ever heard. I hope I'm not around to hear it when you're slagging me off.'

'No chance,' said George comfortingly, 'I always go somewhere nice and quiet when it's your turn and shut the door.'

'That's really nice to know; but so long as you're on the subject, with all these other nicknames, why does Peter Fairfield call him Faithless Frank?'

'Oh,' said George slowly, 'that's Peter for you; but it's a long time ago.'

'Yes?'

'Purcell came here as a detective inspector, sometime after the trouble involving Peter and Thea, you know about that?' He paused, and then he nodded, satisfied, and went on. 'Anyway, he was stationed well away from those two, somewhere up north in the county, and this uniformed lad caught a burglar one night, OK?'

'Yep.'

'The lad had him bang to rights, the burglar knew it, and he made a voluntary statement admitting the lot. In those days individuals were responsible for keeping their own original documents for production in court.

'Unfortunately, this kid lost the VS, so Frank told him, never mind, son, these things happen, just write out another and sign it, no need to worry, you know it's going to be a guilty plea. And then it wasn't,' he added simply. 'He had to enter it as evidence in court.'

'And?' Paula sounded puzzled.

'The kid got charged with perjury, Frank denied everything, and the youngster ended up getting nine months: Peter's not the sort to forget a thing like that, so it's always been Faithless Frank.'

'I can see why the bugger had to keep moving,' I said.

'Yeah.' There wasn't much humour in it, but George grinned. 'Bet there's a story behind him coming back to the Midlands, boss. He might be calling himself a Crime Squad superintendent, but it looks like another sideways move.'

'Miaow!' said Paula.

'You don't have to put up with the bugger, begging your pardon, *Ma'am*,' murmured George ironically, knowing exactly how far he could go.

'It couldn't possibly,' replied his superior officer brightly, 'be any worse than putting up with you.'

A soft, bright October Sunday morning, officially out of season, so I could afford to ignore the warning on the Council notice board; dog-walking on the town beach was now allowed. One happy Lakeland terrier, one large, cholesterol-packed breakfast, and I was on my way to work.

Brimming over with self-congratulatory virtue as well, a volunteer, you understand. I could, had I been mean enough, have claimed far more weekends off. Senior enough to be free, apart from the force-wide CID call-out rota that is, and my personal call-out list only covered serious crime. Instead of taking advantage, I shared weekend CID duties with both Paula and Harry Wake, the Aylfleet detective inspector, so the supervisories in my area all enjoyed two out of three weekends off.

Paula Spriggs, in particular, was grateful; married to Andy, one of my former detective constables, she had a year-old baby to run. Harry Wake, the stolid, marginally miserable Aylfleet DI who was drawing gently towards the end of his service, took whatever he was offered in silence. He was the phlegmatic type; head down, mouth shut both in good times and bad. Just the sort to suit Superintendent Dorothea Spinks, whose own virtues did not include what might be termed a gushing attitude towards the CID. Not a bad sort in her way; widely known as the Boudicca of the East Coast.

Sunday, an odd sort of day to be at work, a minimum of staff, largely empty offices and no canteen. I sat in solitary splendour for a while and stared at the silent telephone, the new and slightly frightening computer terminal and the wodges of largely inessential paper littering my desk.

Idly, I checked the daily state: George and two DCs on duty at Eddathorpe, Detective Constable Patrick Goodall all by himself at Retton, five miles down the road. A solitary burglary, he'd already reported, overnight.

Eddathorpe, the thriving metropolis of crime, had three, and the detective constables were already out there taking a look.

'Real big crime,' said George sarcastically, as he entered my office, staring contemptuously at the illuminated computer screen. 'Three terraced houses, entries through cellar grates; one video recorder, one watch, one wallet and a load of change from jackets left downstairs.

'Scenes of Crime reckon they're busy, they don't like pratting about with piddling little burglaries way out here in the sticks, an' it's going to be two or three hours before they come.'

'They tell you that?'

'Not in so many words, but—'

Oh, dear, George was in one of his elaborately explanatory moods, 'Coffee,' I said firmly, 'and it's your turn to be Mum.' And what, I asked myself as he shuffled out, are you going to do with yourself for the next seven-and-a-half hours, Chief Inspector, on this really exciting autumn day?

Casually, I opened Colin Templeton's Food Contamination file and went through it once again. It was possible that, with the whole of the British Isles to choose from, our greedy extortionist would never come our way. On the other hand . . .

From what we knew already it was perfectly obvious that our blackmailer had spent considerable time and trouble setting this one up. Ingenious, to say the least. For a start he hadn't tried to open any accounts with a fictitious name and address. The banks and building societies were wise to that. He'd used real people with real credit ratings and homes; he'd simply arranged for them to move house so far as the account applications were concerned, prior to collecting the resultant mail from the empty 'new' address. Eight bogus accounts, covering a fair selection of the major building societies and banks. With something like six thousand individual cash points to choose from throughout the country, he was giving his pursuers a pretty horrendous task.

Not that Chummy was engaging in something entirely new; the false address/false account trick must have whiskers on it by now. It had been used in the early seventies to open bank accounts, and shortly afterwards some genius had used the same scam to obtain loans from finance houses. Credit sale agreements on cars had been a favourite target, and the offenders had seldom been caught.

Afterwards, things turned nasty in the eighties and early nineties when at least two extortionists used holes in the wall to collect their loot. Both of them, after massive police operations, were caught, but the cost in police resources was estimated at something like a million pounds a week, and on top of that the food manufacturers had spent a fortune on sealed, hopefully tamper-proof packaging for their products afterwards.

Not much wonder that Colin Templeton was resting his current hopes on the CID equivalent of a crude, relatively inexpensive game of kick and rush. And why, I wondered, was our latest candidate for a sixteen-year stretch confining his activities to a relatively small geographical area, and a family firm? Personally, I'd have placed my bets on an employee, or a disgruntled former employee of the company. Not that it helped a lot; fourteen branches, all employing everything from trolley-boys through checkout girls to underpaid managers. A high staff turnover, probably: sort that!

Colin wasn't stupid; surely he was thinking along similar lines, making other enquiries? He'd never let a greedy, arrogant offender call the shots. Then again, was he really running the job, or was Detective Superintendent Frank Purcell, his wholly unlovable boss, tweaking his strings . . .

One cup of coffee and two bourbon biscuits later the phone rang.

'Colin? Speak of the devil,' I said.

'I'm glad,' he said dryly, 'that you had me in mind. I hope you're feeling energetic this morning, mate, because he could be coming your way.'

'You reckon?'

'Quiet day, Sunday; not very many coppers on the streets. He might be counting on that.'

'He's got wind of your surveillance, then?'

'Not so far as I know; he hasn't reacted, anyway. But he's just begun his Cook's tour – he's started again in our city this morning, but this time he's heading north-east.'

'OK.'

'He's changed tactics, too. Recently, he's only been doing 'em at night. Now listen, my lads are circulating the remainder of your force by fax, the banks and so on will contact towns direct as soon as the fun starts, and we've managed to persuade them to alter the computer programmes slightly to slow down the cash machine responses. Gives you all a better chance, OK?'

'If you say so. I still wonder why you're so convinced that he might be coming here.'

'I feel it in my water, Bob.'

'Fine,' I said cynically, 'and what's more it's cheaper than putting men out on the street observing cash machines, and running up a massive overtime bill.'

There was a short, pregnant silence at the other end of the line. 'You've been reading my mail,' he accused me finally, before he put down the phone.

* * *

It was, as I never tire of saying, still Sunday morning, and we weren't exactly overwhelmed with men, and it was definitely not a uniformed job. If ever it even got off the ground, that is.

'I've already got the fax,' grunted Roger Prentice, the Aylfleet detective sergeant when I phoned him with the news. 'What am I supposed to do about it, there's five cash machines around the town centre, and only two of us here.'

'Two CID cars,' I suggested, 'split up, borrow a couple of uniforms, one to each vehicle and instruct them to put a civvy coat on top. Make sure you've got a radio, and a mobile phone.'

'A *couple* of uniforms,' he howled, 'apart from the duty sergeant and the team in the cellblock, that's about all we've got on the streets! Besides,' he added resentfully, 'we've got our own work to do.'

It can be unbelievably tough at times, out here in the sticks.

'There's only me on, this morning,' said Detective Constable Goodall at Retton, Eddathorpe's out-station, five miles down the road. 'And two woodentops,' he said disparagingly as an afterthought, breathing heavily down the phone. 'Mind you, boss, we're not entirely overwhelmed with cash machines around here.'

'How many?'

'One.' Long pause, 'I think.'

'Well go out and count them again.'

'OK, boss. Shall I let you know?'

One of my problems with Patrick, I'm never quite sure at any one time whether he's opted for outright insolence, or if he's simply the unfortunate victim of a very literal mind.

'No,' I snapped, provoked, descending to sarcasm straight away. 'Once you've located them all, I want you to stand beside each of them in turn and see if they're going to hatch.'

'Yes, sir,' he said calmly. Another successful senior officer wind-up completed, he put down the phone.

Eddathorpe, a town of forty-five thousand people out of season, swelling to something like a hundred thousand when the sun shone, had eight machines; one each at the branches of the four major banks, and four situated outside building societies. Two CID cars, with the occupants keeping observations in our less than lavish town centre, would, I figured, be enough.

It was still a bright, if somewhat blustery October day. George drove, criss-crossing the town, looking out at the small clusters of people, mainly elderly, taking advantage of the out of season prices at the guest houses and hotels. A couple of amusement arcades were open, and about twenty-five percent of the shops. The wrinklies could, if so inclined, still play bowls, and a single ice cream vendor had parked his van on the concrete slope leading to the beach at the bottom of our euphemistically titled Grand Esplanade. The scattering of shelters provided by our thoughtful Borough council each contained its complement of Sunday paper readers each avidly pursuing their choice of scandal in the *Sunday Mirror*, *People* or *The News of The World*. Few of the elderly and infirm, I was pleased to notice, were over-extending their cardiovascular systems with the *Sunday Sport*, and the pubs, naturally, would not be open until twelve o'clock.

'And what more,' said George with a regal, all-embracing gesture as we toured the town where he'd served for something over twenty years, 'could anybody want?'

'See Eddathorpe, and—'

'Die,' he finished reproachfully. 'You've used that joke before, boss.'

'But it's the way I tell 'em,' I said.

We crossed and criss-crossed the town centre, exchanging waves and the occasional shouted comment as the other CID car came in sight. Sometimes, we got out for a walk and hung around in doorways near cash machines, window-shopped and stared at the huge variety of seaside tat that we were definitely not going to buy. We, that is to say George, also played this male chauvinist game; see how many good-looking (i.e. beddable) women you can spot in any given street. Not, according to the same source, a lot, at least at this time of year.

Amazing, how short of men we are in the summer, how much there is for both the uniforms and the CID to do. Thieving and fighting, mostly, burglaries and the occasional case of non-consensual sex. Then, once the season closes down, it's like policing a ghost town, and we have this terrible problem with the residual holiday-making wrinklies, crime-wise they just don't want to know. The Traffic division reckon they had this problem with a foul-mouthed, ton-up granny on a Harley Davidson once, but I reckon the whole story was much more likely to have been a canteen myth. The whole dreary effort seemed to last for hours; boredom set in.

Eventually, Colin rang me on my mobile phone, 'He's probably coming your way!' He sounded quite excited, he could afford to, he hadn't been doing the special tour of Eddathorpe for the past hour and a half.

'He made two withdrawals north of our town, then one at Southwell, and two more in Newark; we only just missed him there.'

'Where is he now?'

'Well,' he admitted, 'I don't exactly know, but if he is coming your way, he's got a choice. He could go via Lincoln; plenty of cash points there, or he could try Sleaford on the A17 and then head for the coast.'

'Or he could,' I suggested maliciously, 'take a trip either north or south on the A1. Maybe he doesn't fancy a trip to the seaside at all.'

'Doncaster,' muttered George sourly, following the conversation, 'and York's pleasant for a nice day out.'

'Perhaps we won't need you, after all,' continued Colin blithely, 'I've got a really big surprise party waiting for him at Lincoln, Crime Squad men watching machines in the city centre, the lot.'

'Good luck.'

'And as for Sleaford, well, it's a one-eyed hole at best.

It's the biggest event since World War Two so far as they're concerned,' he added smugly, 'and the yokels are out in force.'

Lovely fellow. Yokels, just like me, huh? Any sympathy for Colin and his problems oozed slowly down the pan. Soon, very, very soon, I was going to suggest the Market Café for a big sausage sandwich, followed by one more conscience-saving bat around town, and then home for an early lunch. Not much wonder I was putting on weight.

The morning crawled by; a few of the faces in the streets became familiar as elderly wives drove reluctant husbands from shop to shop. Almost invariably, the ones they were the most interested in were closed. We became quite familiar with a fair sample of women in pastel-coloured raincoats (just in case) pointing out inaccessible treasures to gloomy men in caps.

'Bugger this for a comic song,' said George, 'he could be halfway to Scotland by now.'

Coincidentally, the mobile rang again as he spoke. 'The magic incantation,' I said approvingly, 'well done, George.'

'We gotta touch in Newark,' Colin sounded jubilant, 'he doubled back into our area. We caught him right outside the National Westminster Bank.'

'You mean you've made an arrest?' It had been a long morning; deliberately, I used my cool, correct, slightly distant voice.

'Yep, middle-aged chap named Andrews; they're fetching him back to Nottingham now.'

Bringing, fetching? A very limited lot grammatically speaking, these Crime Squad cops.

'Does that mean we can stand down?'

'Oh, yes, sorry, Bob. You can call off the dogs, now, and thanks very much.'

'Peter Fairfield,' murmured George sardonically as he reached for the radio handset, '*will* be pleased.'

Not, as it happened, entirely true. Not with Detective Constable Patrick Goodall of Retton CID about.

Chapter Four

Between twenty-five and thirty so far as I could judge, five foot two or three with glasses and fluffy brown hair. Still, she was doing her best, poor lass, with a smidgen too much make up, a smart suede coat and a micro skirt. Pat Goodall, big, muscular and very blond loomed over her, an unfortunate resemblance to the cinematic version of your typical Gestapo pig.

'OK,' sighed the custody sergeant distantly, he didn't like Pat. 'What are you supposed to have got this time?' He pulled the custody record closer towards him and waited, biro poised, with the air of a man who would need lots of time to be convinced.

'This, Sarge,' said Patrick winningly, 'is Rachel Foster, and I have arrested her on suspicion of demanding money with menaces, contrary to Section 21(1) of the Theft Act, 1968. Alternatively—'

'Never mind the alternatively,' growled his big-bellied opponent ungraciously, 'just tell me what happened first. If ever we get to that stage,' he added, with one eye on Patrick and the other on the faintly dowdy, distinctly downtrodden figure of the captive standing in front of his desk.

'At 11.57 a.m.,' recited Pat, unabashed, 'following observations on a locally situated cash machine on behalf of the Nottinghamshire Crime Squad branch, I received radio instructions to stand down.' He paused impressively, but receiving no encouragement from the assembled ranks of the CID, he continued. 'Anyway,' he muttered, with slightly less self-confidence, 'at 12.02 p.m., a Mr Alan Stevens, a computer operations manager of the Kettering and Eastern Building Society, called me up on my mobile to inform me that a payment had been made on a suspect account at their Retton town-centre machine. I immediately returned—'

'Yes,' said the sergeant impatiently, 'in what way suspect? Tell me that first.'

'It's one of a number of accounts set up by a blackmailer to extort money from a supermarket chain,' muttered Pat, aggrieved.

'Huh!'

'Anyway, I went back to the machine where I saw this woman, I challenged her, and after a short chase I caught her running away.'

'I wasn't running away from the machine, sergeant, I was running away from him.'

The uniform man stared at his prisoner almost benevolently. He opened his mouth to reply, sneaked a glance at the expression on my face and hurriedly changed his mind. 'One moment, Miss, er, Foster,' he murmured, instead, 'let me hear what this officer has to say, first.'

'She,' said Pat sullenly, receiving the unstated message loud and clear, 'was still at the cash point when I arrived. She was putting something away in that zip-up bag.' He indicated a red straw shopping bag he'd placed on the counter. 'I watched her, then I called to her and told her who I was. She was off around the corner like a shot, in the end it took me all my time to catch her up.'

Lightly built, and impeded by a tightish skirt, she was however, wearing flat-heeled pumps. I looked at the latest Goodall victim with a degree of respect; no mean athlete himself, was Pat.

'Then what?' The custody sergeant was determined to have his pound of flesh.

'I identified myself again, I told her that she was suspected of obtaining money from an account set up by an extortionist from the machine, and told her that she was under arrest.'

'And you cautioned her?'

'Yes.' Pat handed him a look that would probably have soured milk.

'And what did she say?'

'Nothing.' This with some degree of satisfaction, 'She was too out of breath. Afterwards, she said she was only getting a balance on her own account at the machine.'

'Have you searched her bag?'

'I've not had a chance; not yet.'

His opponent raised his eyes heavenwards for an instant before turning to the prisoner; he looked almost fatherly, benign.

'I suppose—' he started.

'My name is Rachel Foster, I live at Flat 2, Hampton House, All Saint's Street, Nottingham, and I want to make an official complaint about this big oaf, here.'

'Yes,' he replied comfortably, 'I thought you might.'

Pat could be trouble, and Pat could frequently be a pain; nevertheless, he'd made a capture, he'd answered a genuine call. Besides, I thought I knew more about this particular business than a fat, anti-CID bigot with shiny buttons and a black barathea suit. Right town for starters, and a flat in the middle of drifting, scruffy, bed-sit land: a pretty good address from our point of view.

Search the bag, phone the building society, then ask some pertinent questions. Whatever her brand-new ally thought about her, she was definitely worth a whirl, whatever she said. We might even succeed in making Peter Fairfield a happy man. Not an entirely unproductive Sunday morning, after all. For once, I was inclined to look favourably on Pat: my spirits rose.

'Nothing,' said Sylvia Doyle, our uniformed policewoman, fresh from searching the suspect.

'Nothing?' echoed Pat, staring at the closed interview room door with the air of a man who suspects that some traitor has flushed his vital evidence down the loo.

'Like to take a look for yourself?' she asked cheekily. She paused momentarily, and decided she had gone too far. 'Sorry, sir,' she said.

I smiled non-committally. I knew how she felt. With his hopes frustrated, chief inspectors were far from immune from criticism from Pat.

'She's got her own cash card, Kettering and Eastern Building Society, it was in the left-hand pocket of her coat.'

'And that's it? One lousy card, and that's it?' His voice rose, Rachel Foster, safely ensconced on the other side of the door could take comfort from knowing exactly how he felt.

'Well, there's the bag itself, one handkerchief, one lipstick, one compact,' recited Sylvia, stung. 'One brown leather purse, two compartments, containing one gold-coloured lucky charm, a couple of old car park tickets and thirty-eight pounds forty in cash. Oh, yes, she also had two packaged you-know-whats, one partly used cheque book, also in a brown leather case and complete with a cheque guarantee card from the Midland Bank, and a spare pair of tights.'

'Condoms?' He asked unwisely.

'Tampons,' she said.

'Oh.'

And that, according to my calculations, was something like game, set and match to the female member of our uniformed staff.

'What about the banker's card?' Nothing if not persistent, Patrick Goodall was never a man to leave ill alone.

'It's in her name, if that's what you mean.'

More than time, I decided, to rescue the remnant of my troops, 'Would you, er . . .'

'Look after her for a bit, sir? Of course.' The victor awarded me a brisk, business-like smile, and disappeared back behind the interview room door, leaving us to the cold, cream-painted corridor outside.

'When she shot off round the corner she was out of sight for a few seconds, she must have dumped the gear,' said Pat.

'Great, now you tell me. Why didn't you say so before?'

'Sorry, boss.'

'You searched the car you brought her in, I suppose?'

'Not yet.'

'You come haring over here with a prisoner,' I scolded, 'and you fail to search the CID car, and you even fail to search the scene.'

'I brought her over because there aren't any certified cells at Retton,' the hint of a very satisfactory whine entered his voice, 'and there's nobody else on duty. I was all by myself.'

'There are,' I said sarcastically, 'at least a couple of those woodentops you're so fond of maligning, hanging about.'

'Sorry, boss,' he reiterated. So was I.

'How long do you reckon she was out of sight?'

'Only a matter of seconds,' he said eagerly, then he paused, considering. 'Five, maybe; ten at the most.'

'Long enough to dump the gear though, as you say.'

'I suppose I'd better take a look at the CID car,' he muttered in a vain attempt to divert my fire.

'And get somebody at Retton to take a look around at the scene. Mind you,' I told him kindly, 'if she did get rid of the money and cards in the first place, some passing old age pensioner has probably picked them up by now. Probably thinks it's his birthday, huh?'

It was beginning to look more like another grand Keystone Cock-up with every moment that passed. I was already turning away, en-route to the CID office, a quick telephone call to the building society computer centre and consultations with George, when I was struck by a sudden thought.

'Where was she going when she ran?'

'Away?' He stopped suddenly, gauged my likely reaction to funnies at this particular stage, and rapidly changed his mind. 'Nowhere in particular, I expect.'

It was obvious, however, that Patrick, persecuted by an unfeeling senior, was rapidly coming to the end of his rope.

'Walked all the way from Nottingham, did she?'

Another pregnant pause.

'Oh my God!'

It's the closest he ever gets to despair.

Three of us were arranged around the table, with Police Constable Doyle sitting quietly behind the tape machine at the back. Present, theoretically, in the cause of feminine solidarity and the protection of prisoner's rights, she wore the anticipatory expression of a paying customer at the racetrack whose least favourite driver is about to come unstuck at ninety in his Formula One car.

'I was on my way to the seaside, right?' Rachel Foster had her eyes boldly fixed on Pat. 'I wanted a cup of coffee so I parked my car and stopped. It's not my fault that the entire place is shut up tight on a Sunday.'

'You told us you stopped to check your building society balance a moment ago.'

'I stopped to find a cup of coffee, I saw the cash machine, so I thought I'd check my account.'

'Just for a balance?'

'I've already told you, I might have withdrawn a few pounds, but it's getting towards the end of the month, I might still have a few bills to pay, and when I checked I realised that things were getting a bit tight.'

'So, for no particular reason, all by yourself, you decide to drive all the way from Nottingham to Eddathorpe on a Sunday, out of season?'

'No.'

Pat took no notice of the reply, one idea in his head at any one time; he failed to take her up.

'And a mere five miles from your destination, you stop to look for a coffee shop?'

'Congratulations, at least you've managed to get that right.'

'And,' an entirely genuine tone of antipathy etched his voice, 'finding to your surprise that all the shops were closed, you decide to sort out your finances at a cash machine, where, moments before, somebody had used a duff account to withdraw five hundred pounds?'

'That's hardly my fault, is it?'

'It all sounds like a very lame excuse to me.'

'Coming from you, that sounds pretty rich. You suddenly appear near a cash machine in an otherwise empty street. You watch me, then you make a dive at me, bawling your head off in a very threatening way. I thought you were a mugger, that's all.'

'But you hadn't taken anything from the machine to mug!'

'I don't suppose a mugger would know that. Besides, I've got nearly forty pounds in my purse.'

'Not exactly a fortune, is it?'

'People have been beaten up and robbed for a lot less than that.'

'And you don't know anybody who works at Cary's supermarket?'

'No.'

'No relations?'

'No.'

'You've never worked for Cary's yourself?'

'I'm a schoolteacher; I told the sergeant that.'

I wasn't about to let it show, but somewhere deep inside I winced. Innocent young single woman, bored with life in the big city, takes her Mini to the seaside for the day. Respectable professional type; a schoolteacher, to boot. En route, she stops for a coffee, finds the shops closed, and coincidentally she decides to check up on her dwindling cash. A nice touch, that: innocent, flat-dwelling young schoolteachers, as any jury looking at the damages would know, do not earn a lot.

In the midst of her penury, she is leapt upon by some great blond fascist beast. Then she's chased through deserted streets, arrested and dragged off to a distant police station, there to be accused of participating in a vicious, heartless scam. What's more, her persecutor had failed to call up so much as a female escort for the journey to Eddathorpe nick. The only flaw in an otherwise watertight case for damages so far, appeared to be her unaccountable failure to make allegations of indecent assault.

'Which route did you take this morning?'

'From where?'

'Nottingham,' snarled Pat. It was his interview, and for the moment, I kept quiet, but I was beginning to think that a spot of conciliation might be the order of the day.

'A52, A46, A17,' she replied briskly. 'Why?'

'You didn't withdraw any cash from any other machines, by any chance? Or maybe you stopped to check your balance there, too?'

'Where? Now you're just being silly,' she said.

Sylvia Doyle looked across at me and smiled sadly. It's a shame when police officers become so hypocritical, so young.

'OK,' nothing if not persistent, he tried again. 'You arrive in Retton, you park your car, and you take a walk around looking for a place to have coffee. You fail to find one, and then, completely out of the blue, you decide to check your balance at the cash machine?'

'I don't like the way you put that, but it's true.'

'And did you see anybody when you decided to use this particular hole in the wall?'

'No.'

'So the street was completely deserted, right?'

She hesitated, 'Well, yes, I suppose . . . A car came past me. It might have been drawing away.'

'From the machine?'

'Yes.'

'How very convenient.'

'I just said it might have been; I don't really remember, I wasn't taking much notice. Why should I?' she said.

Why should she, indeed?

'Tell me,' I asked mildly, 'why did you deny that you were travelling here for no particular reason, a few minutes ago?'

'Because I did have a reason; I occasionally pop over to Eddathorpe to see my aunt. She keeps the Britannia Hotel on Clarence Parade.'

Pat Goodall pulled a face: hotel by courtesy. Clarence Parade; big, early Victorian houses, three stories, an attic and a basement. The lower end of the market; bed and breakfast havens and social security flops.

'Fond of your aunt, huh?' Nothing tactful or conciliatory about Patrick, aggression was his middle name.

'Not especially, no.' She waited until his face began to light up before she added, 'But she brought me up, and she's the nearest thing to a family I've got.'

Oh Lord, what a magnificent capture! A lone woman schoolteacher, a former resident of the borough with every reason to visit, and an orphan, too.

'This, er, car you say you saw,' I asked hopefully. 'Any idea of the colour and make?'

'Blue, sort of royal blue.'

'Anything else?'

'I'm not good at cars,' she shrugged. 'A smallish hatchback, I think. That's all.'

'Well, I didn't see it.' Sulky, disgruntled Pat.

'I'm not saying that it was anything to do with anything,' she said coldly. 'And it was well before you arrived.'

I stood up slowly; have a word with Colin Templeton, see whether he wanted to collect our very dubious prisoner. But first, prior to passing the buck, talk to Peter Fairfield at home. As I made for the door my eyes met those of Sylvia Doyle: nothing against me, but she wasn't exactly devastated by the discomfiture of Pat.

'Hey!' Rachel Foster's voice was loud and clear behind me. 'To whom,' she asked deliberately, 'do I make the police complaint?'

Chapter Five

Tuesday morning at eleven o'clock; Fairfield had bided his time and, for a man who'd driven all the way from Headquarters to distribute a swift round of applause to a subordinate, he looked remarkably chuffed. Come to think of it, why drive all the way over to Eddathorpe simply to bawl me out?

Inferiors could be summoned to the presence any time he liked; a cross-country trek, a good hour of worry, keep 'em waiting in the outer office while his supercilious secretary clattered and typed her way through something nasty to add to the offender's personal file. Then, after the statutory twenty minutes of increasing tension, he could haul the miscreant into his office before letting fly. That was the usual senior officer agenda, so why should Peter suddenly begin subscribing to the terms of the Geneva Convention in his old age?

He had, as usual, appropriated my chair. An immutable law of nature; the man behind the desk was the man in charge. Peter, who only regarded chief constables in the light of a necessary, if faintly irritating administrative adjunct to the CID, was definitely the man in charge.

'I'm sorry about the Rachel Foster thing,' I said, getting my blow in first.

'Rachel Foster?' He looked genuinely puzzled for an instant; then he looked down his nose. 'Don't worry about her, Robert: too much wind in her knickers, silly cow!'

'I thought she'd made a complaint?'

'If she has she's made it in Notts, and nobody's told me.'

Sunday evening: three officers from the Nottingham office of the Crime Squad had arrived to collect her, one a woman. A male and one female escort for Rachel, and a third officer to drive her car. A thoughtful gesture, I would have thought, but entirely unappreciated by the recipient at the time.

'They took her back in custody,' I reminded him. 'She wasn't pleased.'

'Pooh!' He waved one hand dismissively. 'You've not seen today's *Chronicle*, then?'

'No.' It was my turn to look puzzled. No connection, so far as I was aware, between Sunday's small-town police complaint and tales in the tabloid press. Patrick was a purely local phenomenon, or so I would have thought. Too young, too inexperienced for the national stage – or at least so I hoped, yet awhile.

'Well, Frankie and his troops have got a lot more to worry about than a stroppy childminder this morning, believe me.'

Struggling to accommodate his bulk within my office chair he finally managed to pull a crumpled, roughly folded copy of the newspaper from the pocket of his disgracefully creased and rumpled suit. Somebody, well out of his hearing, had once described Peter Fairfield's sartorial style as Jumble Sale, combined with an individualistic touch of designer crud.

'Take a look at this.'

The current copy of the *News Chronicle*, I gathered, but from the ragged state of the pages it already looked as though it had led a long and stressful existence on the local tip.

'YOUR BABY AT RISK!'

'Deadly Food Scam Baffles Cops.'

'National Crime Squad detectives based at Nottingham are today hunting a vicious blackmailer who has poisoned baby food in a number of Midland's stores. Following the introduction of a deadly poison into jars of its own-brand baby food products, Cary's Supermarkets, a privately-owned chain of shops based in the city, has twice secretly removed and replaced all stocks from its shelves.

The company, with branches throughout the East Midlands and North, is facing demands for a half-million-pound payoff from a ruthless criminal whose activities may have placed your child at risk. Senior management, however, fearful of Cary's reputation, has so far refused to allow detectives to publicise details of the enquiry. It has, once again, been left to your campaigning *Chronicle* to publicise details of this appalling threat to the safety of YOUR child.'

Turning my attention from a slightly muzzy photograph of a grim-faced, heavily overcoated, obviously angry man, I glanced across at Peter. Celebrations were apparently in progress; he was wearing his big, bucolic grin.

'Crime Squad detectives, fearing panic, have struggled to keep details of their investigation under wraps. Yesterday, faced with revelations by a member of the public innocently caught up in the enquiry, the head of the investigation, Detective Superintendent Frank Purcell, refused either to admit or deny the failure of a major police sting operation to trap the offender over the past few days.'

'WHY THE WHITEWASH? Full Story Page 5.'

'Which innocent member of the public,' I enquired, 'seems to have been caught up in Faithless Frankie's web?'

Picking up on the nickname, but failing to note the distinct note of irony in my voice, Peter looked pleased. 'Feller they arrested in Newark,' he said succinctly. 'Another late arrival at the cash point; another false arrest.'

I winced.

Oblivious to my feelings, he continued. 'Have you seen,' he asked, his face expressionless, 'the photograph of Frank on the front page?'

Yes, thanks, I could hardly have avoided it, and I'd already seen the caption, too. No need whatsoever to rub it in.

'He looks,' said my superior officer crudely, 'as though he's had a porcupine stuck up his arse.'

Unfortunate, but you don't always get the gentler, self-effacing type of officer in the senior ranks of the CID, and once Peter made an enemy he was obviously the sort to want to cherish him for life. I started to flip my way through the paper to page five.

'Don't worry about the gory detail,' he said impatiently. 'Most of it's speculative, anyway. I can dish the dirt on a lot more than that.'

I raised my eyebrows interrogatively; there was obviously more to come.

'I want you to pack your suitcase, Robert, you're coming with me. Look on it as a holiday in your old stamping-ground, it will probably do you good!' He leaned back smugly in my steel and leather office chair, ignoring the ominous, almost tortured creak of metal against metal at the joint.

'I'm still not with you, sir.'

'It's Nottingham that's got the police complaint, never mind Rachel ruddy Foster, old son. Neglect of duty, inadequate investigation, and the feller that Frankie's merry men nicked on Sunday is suing for false arrest.

'We're doing the enquiry, OK? The Police Complaints Authority has appointed me the senior officer in charge, and I have appointed you as my nominated deputy.' He paused for a moment to let this sink in.

It was the tone of voice rather than the words that did it, combined with the wolfish grin. And there are people who complain about the cosy, mutually protective canteen culture said to exist in the British police.

Some holiday, and, having suffered a dose of Angela's full and frank opinion of me and my temporary return to my native city, I doubted whether the experience would do me any good.

Almost dusk, and I stared out of a crumbling first floor bay window of the Sunrise Hotel. A view, as the under-manager had said, of the park. The city Arboretum to be exact, but only if I craned my head wrenchingly to one side, peering sharply to the right at the same time, and stood pressed up against the glass.

Not that I particularly wanted to view the Arboretum, anyway, especially in late October when it was getting dark. I already knew that beyond the railings, the trees would be dripping, the leaves would be sodden underfoot, and the dank, soured duck pond near the entrance would, absolutely unsurprisingly, be wet. Still, the man said I'd got a view, and I thought I might as well make a liar of him if I could. Something else to complain about, after being dumped in a faintly disreputable area of Nottingham in a very, very average commercial hotel.

Detective Chief Superintendent Fairfield had ended up in the room opposite, the less-than-proud possessor of the other bay. No Arboretum for him; a slightly better room, but an almost uninterrupted view of a long wall on the other side of the road relieved by a glimpse of the side entrance to the High School, instead.

We'd been lodged fairly close to the Central police station and our newly allocated office, I had to admit. Nevertheless, the major advantage of the situation appeared to be our proximity to the Forest Road area of the city, its pavements patrolled by squadrons of ever-hopeful whores. Whoever booked this place either hated Fairfield specifically, or, as a junior plod, our anonymous benefactor was indulging himself in a touch of anti-Complaints and Discipline fun.

Eventually, I picked up my briefcase and switched on the

light. Considerate as ever, Peter had supplied me with a copy of the complaint and a set of the witness statements relating to the Cary's case. Not, I thought, handed over purely for my own amusement; I'd been appointed the official bagman and dogsbody for Fairfield. This, I shrewdly suspected, would probably entail me doing much of the legwork, or even the lion's share of the whole messy job.

I hated the very idea of being involved in the investigation of a complaint. I'm at one with the libertarian enemy here: if the buggers want to complain, the investigation shouldn't be left to a fellow cop. It satisfies nobody, and the 'supervision' by the Police Complaints Authority amounts to little more than a paper sift followed by the swift application of a rubber stamp, eighty percent of the time. Unless, of course, there's political capital to be made out of screwing some hapless, preferably junior, gendarme.

Sure, disciplinary enquiries are full and presumably fair – most of the time. But they tie down an inordinate number of senior officers of superintendent rank who would be better employed in a hands-on role overlooking the activities of their subordinates in the first place.

Besides, every Force has a small C & D department whose members are largely engaged in shuffling mounds of paper at an incredible rate of knots. They can't possibly deal with the volume of complaints themselves, so the operational superintendents get lumbered with jobs they can only regard in the light of unpleasant chores. It's not often you find a Peter Fairfield full of enthusiasm for the task, and busily planning the Special Persecutor's revenge. Bill Clinton wouldn't have got away with a chaste goodnight kiss on the doorstep, if he'd been dealing with Pete.

Idly, I wondered how Fairfield had managed to get the job in the first place; coincidence, or what? And, more importantly from my point of view, what would happen if he went too far and his activities resulted in a counter complaint on the part of Faithless Frank?

Robert Graham, I decided, ought to pack his parachute,

and on the merest tinge of green in the light above the exit to this particular aircraft, he was definitely going to bail out.

I spent an hour on the case papers and the resume of Maurice Cary's complaint. The Chairman of Cary's Supermarkets (1958) Ltd., had certainly pitched it hot and strong. According to the two sides of closely-typed pink complaint form, he and Frank Purcell had never hit it off, right from the start.

Not unnaturally, the Crime Squad superintendent had resented the family's attempts to keep their problems to themselves. He gave them his cold, considered opinion of private detective agencies right from the start, and demanded to know what they were playing at by fooling around with amateurs when a potential poisoner was putting the public at risk. Pompous; an unimaginative stuffed-shirt, according to old man Cary. Personally, I was prepared to warm to the man, whatever Peter Fairfield thought about him. In my opinion the company and its directors were playing dangerous games, and Frank, whatever his failings, was absolutely right.

He had, perhaps, gone a bit too far: he'd begun operations by taking the private eye apart. According to Cary, he'd sent a couple of men around to see the owner of the detecting outfit, Simon Gell. They'd milked him of every scrap of information he possessed, criticised his methods, distributed an almighty bollocking on behalf of Faithless Frank and departed. Again, according to Cary, they'd got in touch with the banks and building societies themselves, and used Gell's methods on a larger scale. This hadn't pleased the Cary family: Gell was a cousin or something, once removed.

I glanced through a list of executives belonging to the supermarkets and an associated wholesale firm. It was a family-orientated show all right. Maurice Cary was the chairman, and Richard Cary the MD. Bernard and Tony Cary were also on the Board while Bernard doubled as the Company Secretary.

According to the Nottinghamshire officer who'd taken the complaint, a wife and a daughter were also busy collecting their directors' fees, and an assortment of more distant relatives were scattered about running the wholesale side of the business, and managing shops.

Unnecessary information; nothing to do with the complaint. Then I had second thoughts; somebody, somewhere was on our side. Whoever had taken the initial complaint was telling us gently; don't trust any of the management, they're more than likely to form part of the Cary clan.

Never mind the word *Limited* after the company title; Maurice Cary, I gathered, had lost £52,000 to date, and Maurice Cary was pretty mad. Policemen in general, he declared, were a gang of complete incompetents who'd never survive in the commercial world, while Superintendent Frank Purcell was an arrogant, negligent fool.

The inadequacies of the investigation, he claimed, were compounded by the leaks to the newspapers that had led to the exposure of his company's problems by the press and severe damage to the Cary reputation.

Negligence, an inadequate investigation, and breach of confidence: I could see the problem. Cary was being slapped right in the pocket book, just where it hurt. But he hadn't played straight with his customers in the first place. My sympathy was strictly limited; they were the ones on the receiving end of the food contamination, if things turned sour.

I checked the names of the potential witnesses and followed up with a quick listing of things to be done before I turned to the second complainant. Harold Andrews, 43 years, Insurance Agent, of Elston near Newark, had spent six hours and twenty minutes under arrest; three hours five minutes, poor fellow, actually in the cells.

He had, during the course of his detention, led a fairly exciting life. Firstly, he'd been arrested at a cash machine at Newark, accused of being a blackmailer and dragged off to durance vile in Nottingham a bare hour before Sunday lunch. Then he'd been deposited in a cold, faintly smelly cell for something over an hour, prior to being abused by an elderly vulgarian who'd indulged in threatening and oppressive behaviour for another hour and a half.

Then he'd been taken home; his house searched in the presence of his wife and kids, prior to being returned to Nottingham and shouted at some more, before suffering a further stint in the cells. His release, when it came, had not been accompanied by an apology. He hadn't called a solicitor because he'd been frightened, and his persecutors had been deliberately vague about his rights.

Despite the circumstances of the arrest, it wasn't so much the oiks on the ground that he wanted to pursue, apparently. He simply wanted the blood and guts of the man in charge, the elderly, fat, abusive vulgarian, according to the information lovingly recorded on the sheet. By the time I'd finished skipping through his advance publicity, I was almost looking forward to our meeting with Frank.

It was dark by the time I'd finished, and bored, I went across to Peter Fairfield to see if he had any plans for going out. I'd already inspected the dining facilities in the Sunrise, a bleak room in the basement with far too many squared-off pillars, nooks and crannies, dusty sombreros on walls and bullfight posters hiding cracks in the roughened plasterwork for my particular taste.

I knocked on his door and received some sort of unintelligible grunt in reply, and entered. Peter being his usual sociable self I decided.

He was sprawled across the bed, jacket off, tie half-undone, with his briefcase beside him and his carefully assembled and indexed file divided up and scattered across the floor like so much wastepaper. Read it and dump it, his usual untidy style. I took one look at the mess he was making, and spared a sympathetic thought for his secretary immediately prior to realising that in her absence the potential dogsbody might well turn out to be me.

'Finished reading it, sir?' Said, I have to admit, a touch too brightly.

Grunt.

'Thought you might fancy a bite to eat?'

Slowly, deliberately, he finished the page he was reading and filed it with the rest of the documents on the floor. The space between bed and wardrobe was beginning to look as though he was protecting the carpet against the moment a painter and decorator was likely to arrive.

'Sorry, didn't I tell you? Going out.'

'That's what I thought, so—'

'Don't eat downstairs, Bob, not if you value your life. Personally, I'm having dinner with an old friend.'

'Oh.' Long embarrassed pause, 'I'll, er, see you later then.'

'I might be late.' He was already engaged with another sheet. The classic Fairfield brush-off: his version, as I understood it, of *Shut the door as you go out.* So I did, very quietly, and I refrained, unlike the more sensitive among us, from raising a single finger in salute once I'd safely reached the other side.

'Bastard,' I saved that one for the pavement in front of the hotel.

'Not me, I hope,' a familiar face was grinning at me from the wound down window of a car, engine running, wipers sweeping busily against the rain. It was only then that I realised that I'd been angry enough to make my grand exit without collecting a rainproof coat.

'Colin! What the hell are you doing here?'

'Waiting for you?' Colin Templeton suggested calmly. 'Saving a colleague from shrinking his suit in the rain?'

'For crying out loud, I'm not supposed to be talking to you, I'm helping Fairfield investigate your complaint!'

'You look pretty stupid,' he offered, 'standing there like that.' He swung round and opened the front passenger door. 'What the eye doesn't see, the heart doesn't grieve over. In any case, this one's an exclusive – it isn't mine, it's poor old Frank's complaint.'

I wasn't entirely convinced, and I took a careful look around before getting in anyway. I didn't want to break the rules, nor was I deliberately setting out to bugger up the disciplinary system. I was simply following a basic instinct: a good policeman never gets wet.

Chapter Six

'There's nothing like a good steak,' said Colin.

'There's nothing like keeping well out of the way!' I looked around the newly refurbished bar of the Traveller's Rest. A bit early: a mere half a dozen tables occupied by midweek commuters, probably still on the way home. Up on Mapperly Plains, well out of town and largely unfrequented by early-drinking cops. A wise choice of venue if you were intent on bending a few disciplinary rules.

I wasn't altogether happy with the newly faked olde worlde décor though, including the gilt slogans and quotations painted on the beams, not in a 1920s pub. Nor was I totally enamoured of the BMW-On-Hire-Purchase set which composed at least part of the clientele, but the food was very good. And, to be absolutely fair, Colin Templeton seemed determined to pay.

'I am,' I said after the second round, 'entitled to a subsistence allowance, you know.'

'You can put the claim in anyway, can't you?' He grinned at me, changed his mind at the last moment when he saw my face and added, 'Come on, Bob, lighten up a bit, it was a joke.'

'Yeah.' I waited for the next move, in the meantime cutting, forking and disposing of another mouthful of steak. 'Pity about the ban on T-bones,' I said. 'I could have fancied one of them.'

'Oh,' the grin was back, 'you are prepared to do something a bit illegal, then? I thought for a minute you'd turned religious on me, or something.'

'Illegal?'

'Meeting me.'

'That's not illegal, just a bit unethical for the moment, mate.'

'And do you care?'

'About as much as you,' I glanced briefly, significantly, around the poorly populated, out-of-town room. I was having second thoughts about the fixtures and fittings; the oak tables, the assortment of ladderback chairs, the settles, brass, china and pictures, as well as the quarry-tiled floor by the bar. Reproduction rather than fake, perhaps, and it had obviously cost a bomb. However I looked at it, the new décor had to be an improvement on the out-at-elbows, slightly depressing middle class watering hole I remembered from days of yore.

'I'm not in trouble, Bob. I just wanted to put you wise on one or two points, that's all.'

'That's what I thought.' We looked across at one another with complete mutual understanding, if ever the wheel came off or somebody blew the whistle on our little tête à tête, that was a pretty good line.

'Your girlfriend, for a start.'

What girlfriend? For a moment I thought that an extra-large piece of steak was going down the wrong way.

'All part of Sunday's little disaster; Rachel Foster,' he said.

'Oh, her.'

'You got any other girlfriends in mind?' He looked at me doubtfully.

'No.'

'That's all right, then.' He still wore the look of a man who thought he might have scored a point. Wrong, but I knew coppers, if I protested both he and the rest of the local rumourmongers would be pretty well convinced. 'What do you think?'

'Respectable school-teaching type; very indignant, especially when your mob turned up to lift her. Said she was going to make a complaint.'

'She might be a schoolteacher, but she hasn't got a proper job; she's a whatyoumaycallit?'

'A supply teacher? Goes in to cover illnesses and so on? So what?'

'No consistent source of income; maybe she's short of cash.'

'Anything else?'

'This complaint of hers, it never surfaced once we let her go.'

'And?'

Colin Templeton shrugged, 'That lot at Retton, I suppose they did go round and thoroughly search the scene?'

'Absolutely, but I can't guarantee that nothing had been taken before they arrived.'

'That detective constable of yours is a prat!'

'Could be,' Patrick had been bollocked up hill and down dale for his failings, but no need to give the details of my purely domestic disputes to outsiders. Eddathorpe family business, strictly private bollocking, full stop.

'If that's all you've got against Rachel Foster, you're making bricks without straw, old pal.'

'I'm not making anything; I'm not ultimately responsible for the running of this enquiry, either; it's all down to Faithless Frank.'

'Ah.' Angie had been right, Colin was out to look after Colin, and now he'd changed his tune. Successes were down to Colin, while trials and tribulations were now going to be foisted on Frank. A spot of Colin's version of the nitty-gritty was obviously on its way.

'I'm not out to screw him to the deck, you understand?'

'But you've your way to make, and if there's any mud flying, you don't want any of it sticking to you?'

'That's putting it a bit brutally, Bob.'

I waited: Faithless Frank, from what I'd heard of him, had it coming, no doubt. But Colin couldn't have it both ways at once, either. He couldn't play the good, solid subordinate and do a sneaky imitation of Deep Throat, both at the same time.

'There were problems with this enquiry, Bob, right from the start.'

'Yes?'

'You can be sorry for Frank, in a way. Maurice Cary, for example, he isn't the easiest of men.'

'Hmm?'

'It's everything for the family with him. Right from the start he was out to support Richard, his son. Richard grabbed hold of the letters as soon as they came. He threatened the managers with instant dismissal if they didn't keep everything to do with the poisoned food story under wraps, and he was responsible for going to this distant cousin or something, Simon Gell.'

'The private investigator?'

'Yes. Gell apparently tried to run this as a sting operation; he liaised with one or two of the banks, but he'd no real idea of the resources he'd need to try to grab chummy in the act.

'By the time Frank came on the scene, the blackmailer had established a sound routine, he was pretty well top dog. Poor old Frank has been lashing out with overtime money hand over fist ever since.'

'But we're not sitting here just so you can tell me that?'

'It's a bit difficult, Bob,' he looked at me with something approaching genuine unease. 'Firstly, old man Cary is convinced it's not an inside job, and Frank started off on the wrong foot with him, he was all for a bit of peace and quiet.'

'So you're telling me that all the time he's allowed himself to be dictated to by his complainant, and the tail has been wagging the dog?'

'Yeah, to some extent. Nobody's pushed any of the family members much for a start, nor any of the other employees and executives come to that.'

'One expensive, exclusive line of enquiry, all the time?'

'Pretty much.'

'And you've gone along with this?'

'Not entirely, but I've been a DCI for precisely seven months.'

I looked at him sharply, and he returned the glance with a

semi-embarrassed grin. 'It's all very well,' he said, 'playing Jack the Lad, but we all change over time. It's nothing like the old days anymore. I've got a wife to support and an ex-wife to pay off. I'm buying her share of the house, and I'm the wrong side of forty, so I've got the future to think of, mate.'

'Yeah.' I dropped my gaze, and buried my face in my glass. Not heroic, but who was I to criticise when I'd made plenty of compromises of my own in recent years?

'I suppose,' I said carefully, 'that there's bound to be something else?'

He nodded, 'This isn't pretty either, but it's got to be done. Nothing direct, you understand, but there are those among us who wouldn't mind at all if your boss put the skids under Frank.'

Somehow the wine began to taste a trifle sour. He was right about one thing, it was nothing whatsoever like the old days any more. 'Go on.'

'Frank Purcell should never have been appointed, right? Everything was done in a rush, and the North Central Area of the Crime Squad was never supposed to exist.

'They started out with a three-area plan under the new regime, East, West and North. At the last minute, either the politicians got cold feet, or the Chief Officers' Association screamed, so they introduced a fourth, North Central or North Midlands, call it what you like, with its Headquarters here in Notts. There's supposed to be an Assistant Chief Constable rank standing behind us, and a Detective Chief Superintendent in operational charge.'

'And so?'

'The Chief Super is in place, but they still haven't appointed the ACC. The guy we've got – Charlie Renshaw, our Detective Chief – is on the shortlist for ACC, and Faithless Frank has dropped so many clangers that he's queering Charlie's pitch.'

'Politics. I'm surprised at you,' I said with disgust.

'Look,' he replied, a note of self-justification creeping into his voice, 'it's more than that. Frank was a disaster, right from the start. Staff-wise, enquiry-wise, every bloody wise. I don't want to bore you with all the gory details, but he's a bloody menace, that man.

'Nobody wants him busted; no big scandal, OK? A discreet enquiry, followed by a nice cheese and wine party, and a slightly premature retirement: what's wrong with that?'

Nothing, apart from the fact that Colin would have despised himself for saying it, not so long ago.

'What about last Sunday's disaster, then?' I said, evading the question. 'Is that now down to him, too?'

'Our arrest or your arrest?' Ho, ho, ruddy ho, Colin; a touch of resentment was creeping in.

'Yours will do.'

'I admit I was running the field operation, but Frank was running the whole show, and he insisted on doing the interview himself, once he thought we'd scored.'

'And he blew you out?' I might as well know the whole of the story, I'd committed myself by this time, and I wanted to know exactly how much of this evening's show was down to Colin Templeton's revenge.

'No-o,' he admitted reluctantly, 'the man who made the snatch was the arresting syndicate's DI, and he was bound to take part in the interview. But I was in immediate operational control, so naturally . . .' he let his voice trail away.

'So naturally, you expected to sit down with the arresting officer once he'd got the prisoner back to Nottingham, and do your stuff?'

'Damn glad I didn't,' he admitted, 'now.' Still uneasy, however, and again he grinned. 'The Newark feller, Andrews, had fifty quid, and his very own banker's card, that's all. Frank still tried to put him through the mincer despite the lack of evidence, and that's why the poor bugger's started to scream false arrest.'

'Yeah,' thoughtfully, I shoved the remains of my meal to one side, and finished my drink. I didn't think I'd bother with a dessert. I had, I realised, been set up as the bearer of the news. I was being used as Colin's link with the investigating officer; the unofficial channel through which he could plead that none of the leaks were anything to do with him.

'OK,' I said, making my bid for the rest. 'It's all very interesting, no doubt. But what do you expect me to do, Colin? I'm not in charge of this enquiry, I'm just a DCI, like you. Even if I wanted to, I'm in no position to ditch a superintendent, either with a scandal or without.'

'We-ll,' again the hesitation, 'most of this is background, I was just filling you in. Frank's, er, problems have gone a bit deeper than this one over the past few months. We thought, maybe, that your boss might like to broaden his enquiry a bit. Cover all the aspects, so to speak?'

'And do what?'

'Look at one or two area office files, maybe? You know, a nod's as good as a wink to a blind hoss!' He injected a false note of levity into his voice, prior to shoving his own empty plate to one side and briefly dropping his eyes down to the cloth.

So that was it, Colin was merely the mouthpiece, however willing; somewhere in the background lurked Colin's ambitious boss. Then the messenger looked up and stared hopefully at the other reluctant messenger, and all I wanted to do was walk away.

Eventually the waitress arrived and made the usual polite enquiry about the quality of the meal as she cleared the plates, while I stared glumly at the gilded offering on the beam above the bar, '*Poor and content*,' suggested the slogan, '*is rich enough*.'

'Will there be anything further, gentlemen?'

'Yes please,' I said flatly, 'If it's not too much trouble, I'd prefer two separate accounts.'

Chapter Seven

Maurice Cary sat at the head of the highly polished, oval boardroom table flanked by two of his sons, and with a severely dressed, earnest brunette in her late twenties whom I took to be his secretary, seated below Richard to his right.

We, his apparent antagonists, occupied the other end of the table. Peter Fairfield, bloody-minded as usual, one seat off-centre, not that the table was overlarge and there wasn't much of a gap.

Cary was short for a man, sharp-featured with iron-grey hair and slim, immaculately manicured hands placed neatly on the table before him. He kept very still, apart from his eyes, which moved from side to side to encompass both of us whenever he spoke. Courteous, smooth-voiced, he created an atmosphere of contained energy, tension, a man to watch.

His male companions were built on a larger scale, although something of a family resemblance was there. Richard was around five foot seven or eight, thirty-odd, his hair receding, his features already blurring and with the hint of a double chin. His younger brother Bernard, an inch taller, somewhat slimmer, stared consideringly at each of us in turn, occasionally smoothing the invisible creases in the waistcoat of his three-piece suit. Alert, intelligent, a not altogether prepossessing lot, I decided. But then again, I wasn't in business, I wasn't rich and I wasn't currently being hammered both by a blackmailer and the vultures of an entirely unsympathetic press.

'I received a note this morning,' said Maurice Cary quietly, 'through the post.' He tapped the manila folder in front of him, opened it, and produced a sheaf of photocopied papers and passed them around. His sons each took a copy and passed the remainder, together with the plastic-encased original, on to us.

'You're indebted to Linda,' he announced, 'for the preservation of the original. A touch of smart thinking there.' Linda, the brunette, otherwise unintroduced, brushed back her short, trendily styled hair making her earrings bounce, and looked smug. For the first time, I took note of her high cheekbones; the bold, not unhandsome features and the expensive cut of her dark two-piece. Not perhaps a secretary, after all. Poised, athletic, lightly built, thin-lipped, there was distinct resemblance to Cary senior, the old man.

The message, assembled from a mixture of newspaper headlines and lower case, was short and sweet, *'BY INVOLVING THE POLICE, however INCOMPETENT, YOU HAVE made a grave MISTAKE. MORE, much MORE TO FOLLOW believe me.'*

Fairfield read the note and sighed, 'I'd like to keep the original together with its envelope, please. I'll pass them on.'

'To whom?' Cary's voice sharpened.

'The investigating officers, of course.'

'I'm sorry, Chief Superintendent, I naturally thought that you . . .'

'I think, Mr Cary, that we'd better get this matter quite clear from the start. The Crime Squad is still dealing with the criminal enquiry, and it's a matter for their area commander as to whether the officers currently involved continue to deal with the case. My colleague and I are here as independent investigators to deal with your police complaint.'

'Good God! You mean I've still got to deal with that overbearing idiot?' Richard Cary spoke for the first time.

'It rather depends on which overbearing idiot you mean.' Fairfield's voice was quiet, but it too had acquired an edge: feud or not, when you scratch a copper the rest of the fraternity have this inclination to bleed. I experienced a small sense of relief; whatever his personal feelings towards Frank Purcell, Peter sounded as though he might be prepared to referee an impartial game.

Maurice Cary reached out a restraining hand, stopping short of touching his son. 'We had rather hoped, Chief Superintendent,' he said smoothly, 'that we could begin this enquiry again with a clean slate.'

'I appreciate your feelings,' Peter, given the opportunity, could be equally smooth, 'but that's hardly likely, anyway. Our criminal has already moved on, and we're in no position to rewrite the script.' He tapped the documents in front of him and smiled gently.

'What exactly are you here for, then?' It was Bernard's turn to speak up, whatever their management qualities, the father's urbanity had not been inherited by either son.

'To introduce ourselves, to discuss your concerns, and, if necessary, to arrange to take statements.' Never short of an answer, Peter, he spoke briskly, and neither of the brothers were likely to beat him in a game of conversational bat and ball.

'In other words to give us the run around and see if we're likely to back down, or get fed up with the whole idea.'

I looked up from the notes I was taking and practised my look of injured innocence, while Peter tried out his expression of gentle reproof. 'Not at all,' he said, his eyes on the senior member of the consortium. Maurice Cary inclined his head. Subtle, which is more than anybody could say for either of his sons, he obviously thought that he knew rules of the constabulary game. He was unaware, however, that Fairfield was engaged in a totally different event.

'Perhaps, Richard,' he said softly, 'you had better explain to Chief Superintendent Fairfield the nature of our concerns.' A man who never raised his voice, the slight hesitation prior to the delivery of the last word of the sentence said it all.

'We, that is the board,' said Richard Cary, 'feel that this farce has gone on long enough. I admit that in the first place I made a mistake. I thought this offender was some sort of local crank and that we could handle him ourselves. I used a private enquiry agency in an attempt to sort this out. A relative, somebody I could trust.'

He paused momentarily, and glanced at his father before continuing. 'It was only after I had recognised the scale of the potential problem that we decided collectively to call in the police. By that time, despite his best efforts, Simon and his organisation had got practically nowhere, the blackmailer had demonstrated that he could deliver on his threats, and he'd milked us of several thousand pounds.'

'And,' snapped Bernard vindictively, 'he's had a lot more since.'

'Simon?' said Fairfield interrogatively. I knew he'd read the file and knew the answer already, idle and provocative remarks were being ignored.

'My cousin, Simon Gell.' Richard scarcely acknowledged his brother's interference; he was keeping his eyes on the main event. 'He advised me that the police were the only people with sufficient clout to bring this one to a successful conclusion, and,' a note of bitterness entered into his voice, 'he convinced me that they were discreet.'

'But experience has shown us how wrong he was!' Bernard Cary's voice rose. 'First, your man has to be restrained from shouting and raving at every employee and ex-employee in sight. After that he simply persuades the building societies and banks to keep an eye on their computers for twenty-four hours a day, and then he involves every plod in five counties in a game of chase-my-tail.'

'I would have thought,' murmured Peter Fairfield, 'that getting the banks to cooperate to that extent was a fairly substantial achievement in itself.'

'We do not dispute the extent of the effort,' Maurice Cary chipped in, 'we feel, however, that it has been misdirected to a great extent. And, more importantly, we are still losing substantial sums of money, and now the company is being subjected to widespread criticism in the press.'

'Forgive me,' said Fairfield wickedly, 'but from what I hear, you seem to want to make an omelette without the hens even laying, let alone allowing the cook to crack any eggs. Firstly, you object to a basic line of enquiry, then you go on to criticise Superintendent Purcell for deploying the very resources your relative's firm were unable to call down themselves.'

For a moment the young woman, who had hitherto kept her eyes firmly on her notes, looked up, eyed Fairfield covertly from under her lids, and gave him an appraising stare. Whatever the rest of the family thought, I was certain that she'd put his carefully cultivated bumpkin image entirely out of her mind. She remained silent, but by the expression on her face, the lady was definitely not his friend.

'It was the way it was done,' snapped Richard Cary. 'Of course he was supposed to make enquiries among employees, but there was no need to blunder about like a bull at a gate. That's why I had it stopped.'

'Indeed? *You* had it *stopped*?' Fairfield's voice held a mixture of sarcasm and ice. In the silence that followed I kept my head down and sought to catch up with my own documentation of the events. There was no doubt about it, with ammunition like this at his disposal, nobody, least of all Frank Purcell, would be able to claim that Peter Fairfield hadn't given his old enemy a fair crack of the investigative whip.

'Tell me,' he continued, apparently oblivious to the atmosphere he'd created, 'did you object simply to the way that junior employees were being questioned, or did your resentment centre around his officers speaking to senior executives and members of the board?'

'I expected him,' snarled Richard Cary, 'to go about his job with a modicum of tact.'

Fairfield said nothing; he simply waited with an air of expectation until the rest of the answer came.

'Look,' the man leaned forward. 'Maybe I was exaggerating a few moments ago. I didn't stop anybody doing anything at all. I merely pointed out that firstly, we have a business to run, and that neither we nor he could afford to go around antagonising everyone in sight.'

'And secondly?'

'I suggested, merely suggested, mind you, that the whole affair was sensitive and that he ought to operate strictly on a need-to-know basis.'

'And what happened then?'

'He seemed to lose interest in questioning members of the company at all. Concentrate on the cash machines; all the eggs in one basket, that became his style.'

'I see.'

I didn't: I was damned if I'd have done it. Downright bloody-mindedness? Fear of the consequences? A fit of pique? And now the Cary family apparently wanted it both ends on: at their instigation, a senior officer had apparently backed away from a vital part of his enquiry, leaving himself open to charges of incompetence and wilful neglect.

The morning ground on while Fairfield prised out his nuggets from the slag. Purcell was overbearing, rude: did that amount to a complaint of incivility, yes or no? Purcell was incompetent: a complaint of neglect of duty, eh? The enquiry was supposed to be a secret, and now they had the hounds of the press baying at the door: did that involve other disciplinary offences – corrupt practices, or a breach of confidentiality, or what?

The more I listened, the more I wrote, the less I liked what was going on. Peter Fairfield wasn't exactly ecstatic, either. The Carys might be victims, but they came over as a grudging, petty, ungrateful lot. The youngsters, especially, were more than eager to pass their problems, together with whatever blame was going, to somebody else. Cary senior remained largely silent, not so much the chief complainant, I thought, as the judge of the family performance and the principal referee. The girl, Linda, kept her dark head well down, and apart from the occasional enigmatic glance at Cary senior, she concentrated solely on her notes.

We were there for well over two hours before I got around to making appointments to take statements. Colin Templeton was mentioned only in passing, common courtesy was at a premium and coffee wasn't served.

Once outside in the visitors' car park, Peter stretched, stared balefully back at the two-storey 1960s administration building and warehouse and passed his judgement before climbing stiffly into the front passenger seat of our car, 'Know the old adage, Bob?'

'What's that?'

'Clogs to clogs in three generations, and the quicker the better so far as I am concerned!' It was, I gathered, the Fairfield valedictory curse. 'And what's more I'm spitting feathers. Not so much as a carafe of water from those mean bastards,' he said.

We both stared out over the weed-infested window box of Fairfield's first floor office in Central police station, and watched the messenger climb the ramp into the car park of the Crime Squad offices backing on to Trinity Square.

Central, built for the old Nottingham City force in the thirties, had some minor claims to architectural distinction; at least it was clad in stone. The Squad, however, temporarily at least, occupied the ninth and tenth floors of a late 1960s block, the back of which could be clearly seen from what was laughingly described as Fairfield's office suite.

'What a dump,' said Peter witheringly.

'Them or us?'

I looked around his office, the shrivelled weeds in the window box on the ledge outside, the dust on the furniture, and a less than pristine strip of carpet on the floor in front of his desk. The message was clear enough: *welcome, chaps, this is to show you how much we appreciate colleagues who come into our area to investigate police complaints!*

'Them, of course.'

It figured. Untidy by nature, almost oblivious to the inadequacies of his own personal appearance, he hadn't even noticed that somebody around here had been dropping far from subtle hints. The Crime Squad might not be very popular, but they were damn nearly Top of the Pops in comparison with us.

'We could,' I said tentatively, 'have taken the package across ourselves.'

'No,' he shook his head. 'I'm certainly not going across there, not yet. Why should we go rushing around at their beck and call? Their chief superintendent passed on the message via your extremely loyal pal, and I've got the drift.

'He wants to get rid of Frankie, and at the same time he wants to become an ACC. Well, I'm not yet ready to widen this enquiry just to oblige him, or even to serve disciplinary notices on Faithless Frank. Let both the buggers stew for a bit, say I!'

By this time the young DC from Central, clutching the security-sealed original of the blackmailer's latest threat, had reached the top of the ramp. He crossed the car park, punched a code into the electronic lock, and disappeared inside the building, eliciting a grunt of, 'Good. Nice to have a willing gofer,' as Peter slumped into the seat behind his desk.

Or even two: I was becoming more convinced by the minute that the second, and rather less important gofer, was probably me. After coming back to the hotel after midnight by taxi on the previous evening, flushed and smelling of expensive booze, he'd greeted my slightly censored resume of my meeting with Colin with little more than a cynical grin.

'Sorry your illusions have been shattered,' he'd muttered. 'So much for your dear old mate.' Then, prior to the door closing behind him he added indistinctly, 'One thing I will tell you, Robert. It's not wise to piss on people when you're on the way up, 'cos they're equally likely to return the compliment when you meet 'em again when you're on the way down.'

As an exit line, it had been neither particularly cryptic, or entirely original. Police cliché number forty-seven, in fact. I'd not had a particularly good evening, however, and in the course of it I'd acquired a tendency to brood. Had he, I wondered, been taking a poke at Colin and his careerist tendencies, or equally, once I'd passed on the information, was he having a go at me?

Peter Fairfield leaned forward, his hands linked loosely in front of him and resting on his desk.

'You reckon I'm out to get him, don't you?'

'Get who, boss?'

'Don't you play the bloody smart arse with me, Chief Inspector; Frank Purcell, of course.'

'You're not? I know the background, though.'

'You and every other copper within a hundred miles, I suppose. Funny, inn it, how fate takes a few unexpected whirls? Who'd have thought that one bright day I'd ever have the black on Faithless Frank?'

'Personally, in his position, I'd have screamed like hell to the Federation if you'd been appointed to investigate me.'

Peter beamed, 'That's better, for a minute there, I thought you were becoming some sort of creeping Judas like your bloody mate. Anyway, if Frank wants to bellyache, it's the Superintendents Association he goes to, right?'

'Right.' It didn't answer my unspoken question, though.

'OK, Robert; this is how it goes. Frank is in no position to go howling to anybody about that old story about Thea and me. Anyway, it'd make him look totally daft; it was twenty-odd years ago after all. Likewise, I'm not barmy, I wouldn't dream of playing all that dirty myself at this late stage.'

'Glad to hear it, sir.' But I'd spoken too soon.

'If it's gotta be done,' he said vengefully, 'it'll be much more fun doing it fair and square.' Then, seeing my expression, he added a rider. 'It's a duty as well as a pleasure, Bob; there are a few professional bits and pieces in the background, things you wouldn't know.'

'I do know.' I left the rest unspoken, a touch of the tacky here, nevertheless.

He looked up, mildly surprised, 'Old coppers, huh? It isn't wise to cross 'em; they're just like ancient elephants, they never forget.'

'Or forgive?'

He bared his teeth, 'Leave that one to the clowns in the Social Services, son.'

The grey phone on his desk rang twice before he picked it up.

'Fairfield; yeah, he's here. Yeah.'

He listened for almost a minute to the tinny babbling at the other end. 'Want to tell him yourself? OK, I'll pass it on, OK.' He waited a few more seconds, 'Nasty,' he said, and then, somewhat reluctantly, I thought, 'Thanks.'

He replaced the receiver, and paused for a moment. 'That was Templeton,' he said. 'They've got the note.'

'Yes?'

'They've also heard from old man Cary, he's a bit upset. Four people in hospital here in Nottingham, and they've had to clear the chilled meats off their shelves in every single store. They think that some bastard has been injecting washing soda into their packaged sausages with a hypodermic syringe.'

Chapter Eight

His offices were situated on the second floor of what had once been an elegant eighteenth century town house on Angel Row, overlooking Nottingham's Slab Square. The lower floors were still occupied by a venerable provincial club, the sort that attracts the well-heeled middle aged, but there was little that was elegant, or even slightly venerable, about Simon Gell.

Pseudo-trendy, yes, with his rosewood veneer office, his four-button suit, screaming red and yellow silk tie and over-pointed black lace-up shoes. It was also possible, at first sight, to believe that he was wearing a real steel and gold Rolex watch on his left wrist. Until, that is, you took a closer look at the hesitant progress of the second hand around the dial. Still, it made a statement about him: an apparently much-travelled man. Hong Kong at a guess, the equivalent of about twenty-five quid on Nathan Road.

Aged about thirty-five, with dark-brown bouffant hair, the family's beady brown eyes and a well-rehearsed twist to his narrow lips. We were unlikely to fall in love with one another, right from the start.

'Personally,' he told Peter Fairfield almost as soon as we were settled, and once his secretary was safely on the other side of the door, 'I do not altogether care for cops.'

'You surprise me,' said my cuddly chief superintendent calmly. 'I thought that private investigators spent their time creeping around CID men for any bits and pieces they might pick up.'

Gell glared at him from under half-lowered eyelids, 'Hardball, huh?'

'Hardball, softball, any game you like. But I'm still surprised at your attitude, Mr Gell. After all, it's your uncle's complaint.'

'Ah,' he swung forward dangerously in his creaking swivel chair. 'That's where you're wrong, it's Cousin Richard and to some extent cousin Bernard who're kicking up the fuss. Unless they come up with some good excuses, Papa is quite likely to confiscate their keys to the executive lavatory, kick their arses and send 'em for a stint as trolley-boys and shelf stackers down on the shop floor.'

'Are you telling me that this complaint against Superintendent Purcell is a sham?'

'Perish the thought! Waddaya call him, now, Frankie? He's the sham; he sent a couple of his bully boys around to see me at the beginning of the enquiry, then when that didn't satisfy him he came round himself. He spent half an hour throwing his weight about, shouting his mouth off and telling me how I should have left it to the real professionals right from the start.

'After that he milks me for all he can get, sneaks off to all the banks and building societies where chummy opened an account, and bugger me, he follows exactly the same plan, only on a bigger scale.'

'So?'

'Copycat tactics, and it took him no further. Other than that he's sat on his hands, and left the Templeton guy to do all the work. Such as it is.'

'Is this a separate complaint of neglect?'

'Not at all, I don't even know why you've bothered seeing me. Head down, mouth shut, that's me. I just do what I get paid to do, and afterwards I cash the cheque.'

'And what exactly do you get paid to do in your uncle's firm?'

'I'm an independent security contractor, not as you so charmingly put it, a scrubby private eye. All the security, OK?'

He watched Fairfield's face for a few seconds; then he shrugged. 'Uniformed guards, mostly, at all fourteen stores. I also run a team of operatives to cut down on shop theft, internal leakages and minor fraud.'

'So Cary's forms the major part of your business?' Fairfield unfazed, apparently unimpressed.

'The bread and butter, sure. Around sixty, sixty-five percent, but I do have other contracts and individual clients as well.'

'And how many people do you employ?'

'A couple of dozen regulars.' He paused again for a few moments to let the statistic sink in, 'With a number of part-timers, and a few more casuals on and off.'

'These others, part-time; freelances, or what?'

'About half are part-timers, mostly uniformed guards. As for the rest,' he shrugged, 'they're basically as and when.'

'And how reliable are they, these *as and when?*'

'They do the job, I pay 'em, and then they go away. One or two of them are pensioners, ex-police.'

'People you don't much like?'

'They have their place, naturally. But I thought I'd tell you where I stood.'

'This newspaper article,' said Fairfield slowly. 'You've read the piece about Cary's in the *Chronicle*, of course?'

Gell released his breath slowly in a long drawn-out hiss, 'I'm way ahead of you brother; so that's your game!'

'I'm not quite with you?' Fairfield, still playing it straight.

'Find yourself a big can of whitewash, and blame any leaks and back-handers on the employees of the unreliable security outfit, yes?

'You've got the perfect excuse for dropping the corruption allegation and the breach of confidence. You can say that Cary's should have come to the cops in the first place, and you can blame all Purcell's current troubles on some anonymous ex-plod with itchy palms and a big mouth for spilling the beans.'

'That,' said Fairfield his mouth shutting like a trap, 'is not the case, and even if it were, you don't seem to care very much, either way.'

'You're perfectly right, I don't. Maurice is not exactly my favourite uncle, geddit? And as for Richard and Bernard and the lovely Linda, well . . .'

'The lovely Linda?' I said, surprised.

'Surely you've met her?' He waited for me to nod, 'And you mean you didn't know? Now isn't that absolutely typical of the old man! The boys are boys, so they count, but daughters are only girls, so they're just part of the furniture, or Maurice Cary's mousy little PA.'

'She's a bit on the severe side,' I admitted, 'but that's a bit unfair, surely? She's pretty enough.'

'Bright, too.' He relaxed suddenly, 'but she's a lesser relation in his scheme of things, just like me. A few shares, of course, and a nominal seat on the Board, but Maurice is out to found a dynasty of rich male grocers, if he can. Sorry if you fancy her, but there are no vacancies for fortune-hunting toy-boys from the CID, and besides . . .'

'Thanks,' I cut in sweetly, 'I'll bear that in mind.'

Peter Fairfield checked me over; he had never seen me in quite that light before, the fortune-hunting smoothie from the one-donkey town. He placed one diplomatic hand in front of his mouth, and coughed.

'I take it,' said Gell, reverting to the subject in hand, 'that you two are only looking into the moans and groans?'

'The complaints.'

'Yeah, well lucky you. I didn't envy Purcell, you know, however big a prat he is. The bank and building society accounts had been set up for months, existing people mostly, fitted out with a bogus new address. Whoever did this is *very* smart indeed, it's almost textbook stuff.'

'Which particular textbook had you got in mind?'

He nodded in the general direction of a well-stocked bookcase beside him. 'Oh, come on now, Superintendent, take your pick. I'm one jump ahead of you, I'm pretty sure the thought must have already occurred.'

Fairfield ignored the invitation. 'Quite apart from the chip on your shoulder, do you really think it was an inside job?'

Gell appeared to consider the question. 'Maybe, but there are plenty of people to chose from,' he shrugged.

'Some of them quite senior,' agreed Fairfield smoothly. 'People who didn't immediately think to call in the police, and people who might have hinted to you, ever so slightly, that it might not be a good idea to tread too heavily on their toes?'

Bored, I occupied a stool at the bar of the Vernon Arms on the corner of Forest Road, well into my second pint, and by now it was twenty-five past six. Fairfield was nearly an hour late, and pending his arrival, the available entertainment was on a strictly limited scale.

Three middle aged and one elderly man sat at a table behind me, three suits plus one orange shirt, suede boots and a pair of expensive, yellowish cords. Loud voiced in their eagerness to get their stories across, and all discussing the shortcomings of the traffic police.

I have to admit that I'm inclined to tell the occasional anti-flattop saga myself. But *sotto voce* and in carefully selected company, of course. And anyway, I've got something approaching a right; they, after all, are equally inclined to unburden themselves on the subject of late-night encounters with tired and over-emotional Jacks. Inter-departmental rivalry it's called, and anyway, if you can't take a joke you shouldn't have joined.

I do not go in for a lot of barroom entertainment, myself, and these four overgrown schoolboys wanted everybody to hear. Yellow Cords – tall and gangling, with slightly protruding teeth and a stubble of auburn beard – set them off with the story of his own victory over the wicked, breathalyser-bearing coppers. He had, he claimed achieved first prize in his own particular contest, and the uniformed fascist had been made to look a fool. Something he'd bravely taken pleasure in pointing out.

The geriatric chipped in with a tale of terror and persecution, which had almost resulted in the loss of his licence after he'd reversed across a junction on a bend.

'I fixed 'em, though,' he crowed. 'I took another driving test and passed it, the week before I went to court. The magistrates didn't dare ban me after that!'

The barman, busily stacking glasses with totally unnecessary vigour, turned and leaned confidentially across the bar, 'You can always get 'em bagged an' blown when they leave,' he offered. 'Use the phone in the next room.'

'How did you know?'

'Well, it could be me secret barman's radar, an' then again, squire, it could be the expression on your face. One way or another, I can always tell a cop.'

'It's all right,' I said cheerfully. 'With a bit of luck, they'll have probably all been burgled by the time they get home.'

'I'll drink to that!'

Naturally, his was a small drop of short, and I drank up and ordered another pint.

Fairfield didn't arrive until a few minutes before seven o'clock. By this time I was beginning to recall the majority of the unpleasant side effects of living out of a suitcase, miles away from home. For one thing I was hungry, and for another three pints of bitter and an over-watered whiskey sloshing around in an empty stomach were not doing me a lot of good. Nor had Peter spent the happiest of afternoons.

'That man!' he muttered resentfully as soon as we sat down, and gulped his drink.

'Frank Purcell?'

'No, Charlie Renshaw, his ruddy boss. Did you know,' he asked a touch resentfully, 'that they've retained the chief superintendent title as a Crime Squad rank?'

'No.'

'Ever since that bloody report from Sheehey,' he snarled. 'No consistency any more. On the one hand they're supposed to have abolished us, and now the Crime Squad have turned cocky and called the newer higher-grade Supers by their old name.'

There had been confusion, ever since the Sheehey Report in 1994. Deputy chiefs and chief superintendents were supposed to have been kicked into touch, and designated-deputies with the rank of ACC and so-called higher-grade superintendents had been introduced instead. God alone knows what this grand reform had been designed to achieve.

Some Forces had followed the new rules, but others had not. It made life complicated and it marginally increased the potential for Mickey-taking and unintended slights, but I couldn't for the life of me see what Fairfield was on about. If people wanted to promote their own sense of self-importance it was OK by me; a major source of resentment it was not.

'Is Purcell a detective superintendent, or a lower grade detective superintendent, then?' I asked innocently.

'Don't you bloody start!' He took a second, reviving pull at his pint and took a rolled up local newspaper from his pocket. 'Have you seen this?'

The front page of the local paper, naturally, and a blow-by-blow account of the sausage poisoning, the current state of the victims (comfortable) and the removal of the packaged fresh and chilled meat from all Cary's supermarket shelves.

'They aren't being as nasty about it as the Nationals,' I said.

Fairfield nodded, 'Local newspaper, local firm, but something's going to have to be done about this lot, pretty damn quick. Would your wife shop there now?'

'I hope not, no.'

'Exactly, and thousands of other people will feel exactly the same.'

'This, er, Detective Chief Superintendent Renshaw, sir; what's he going to do?'

'Well, he's dumped Frank Purcell, for a start. He's off the case, and your pal Templeton has been placed in immediate charge. And Charlie Renshaw has taken overall responsibility, himself.'

'Bit unusual, isn't it?'

'Not a lot of alternative. I suspect that he'd probably like to pass the buck, but he can't, not if he wants to be the Crime Squad blue-eyed-boy as well as the new ACC.

'That's not all he's doing either, he's got a list of cases a mile long he wants me to look at. Reinvestigate this; reinvestigate that, he went on for hours about Purcell. The man's obsessed, and he's throwing Faithless Frankie to the wolves.'

'But—' I said.

'OK, OK, they've only been going since last April,' he admitted, 'so there aren't all that many cases to follow up, all right? It's the sheer bloody hypocrisy of the thing that irritates me.'

'You're feeling a touch of sympathy for Superintendent Purcell?'

'Don't you turn smart on me, Robert. I just don't like being used as anybody's cats-paw, that's all.'

I could sympathise; I hadn't been terribly keen on being used as the messenger boy by somebody I'd thought of as an old friend, either. Some of this new, high-powered management stuff was definitely getting on my nerves. I almost felt it coming, the bitter little speech about integrity, loyalty and getting on with the job.

'Fancy another of those?' He indicated the dregs of my drink.

'Not just now.'

'No stamina, eh?' Then he looked at my face. 'You all right?'

'Fine, fine: it's just that I've been here a while, that's all.'

'Hungry, huh? The restaurant here's not bad, we can always have a bottle or two with the food, I suppose.' Beer, whiskey and now the prospect of more than one bottle of wine. I shuddered as he struggled to his feet. 'Oh, I almost forgot,' he muttered, 'and it's on your patch, an' all. Remember that Foster woman, the one you arrested?'

Totally inaccurate, vaguely insulting, but I let that one slide. 'Rachel Foster, she's complaining, I suppose?'

'Not there to complain, old son. She went back to her auntie's at Eddathorpe when she was released from custody the other night, and now she's gone missing from home.'

Chapter Nine

The cabin cruiser, a courtesy title if ever there was, lay on the soft sand well above the watermark in Ansell's Creek. Clinker built and painted in flaking blue and white, to my cowardly, unseamanlike eye it looked more like one of those proverbial coffin ships than something in which anybody but a madman would seriously want to go to sea.

Props had been placed on either side of the hull to secure it in a more or less upright position, and a crudely made arrangement of planks and rail led up to the deck. The proud possessor of *The North Star*, a scattering of paint pots, scrubbing brushes, raw timber, buckets and sealed tin cans around him, was leaning against an Austin Cambridge saloon of indeterminate age when I arrived. He had a police escort, I noticed. An obvious connoisseur of crumbling antiques, he was being kept well away from the immediate scene of the crime.

Apart from a grunted, 'Good morning,' I ignored him for the time being. People who find bodies attract immediate police suspicions, so deploying a spot of what passes for the psychological approach in this primitive neck of the woods, I let him stew.

The fifty yards of track leading from the road between the pine trees to the Creek had already been sealed off, and I'd had to pick my way through a succession of tree roots, assorted rubbish and the confining bands of blue and white tape before I reached the boat. Five distant wooden chalet bungalows poked their shabby roofs above the line of the sandstone bluff at one side of the creek. Apart from the usual gang of voracious gulls, a vandalised public lavatory and four or five other semi-abandoned boats beside the concrete slip, they completed the total attractions available to the casual visitor. To anybody unfortunate enough to claim permanent residence too, come to that.

Once aboard *The North Star* I found the victim lying on her back, legs twisted awkwardly, fully dressed apart from her shoes, partially under the canopy in the well of the craft. Her face was bloody, her tights ripped, her skirt rucked up almost to the waist. She had odd bits of twig, sandy earth and pine needles adhering to her clothing, back and front. There was, I noted, something which looked like a touch of yellowish vomit around her lips.

Saturday morning: welcome back to Eddathorpe, Robert. The perfect beginning to the perfect weekend at home.

It was quiet under the protective cover of the tarpaulin that somebody had improvised beyond the edge of the fixed canopy and aft over the open cockpit of the boat. Apart, that is, from the steady drip, drip, drip of rain on canvas, and the murmuring of Professor Andrew Lawrence, the Home Office Pathologist, busy taking samples, and muttering unintelligibly into his dictaphone now and again.

'Know her, do you?' he eventually asked.

'Rachel Foster,' I replied. 'Reported missing from home earlier this week, and before that one of my lads had arrested her at Retton last weekend.'

'Anything exciting?'

'An unauthorised withdrawal,' I was being cautious, 'from a building society cash machine, that's all.'

Lawrence sighed, bent his thin, almost cadaverous body, and returned to the task in hand. 'Good, good,' he murmured absently, making it obvious how little he cared anyway. 'It isn't obvious how she died; only superficial wounding, here.' He moved his hands gently over the skull for a few moments and shook his head. No fractures found.

The whole enquiry, I decided, had been enough of a

witches' brew already prior to this. I couldn't see anything good about the latest development at all.

'Concealed here, killed somewhere else?' I said. It wasn't so much a question, more like something to say. Our Home Office Pathologist was pretty uncommunicative, even at the best of times.

'One shoe in the woods, the second on the beach, so very probably, yes.'

'She's from Nottingham,' I persisted, 'but she's been staying locally with her aunt.'

'Not any more she's not.' Unusual for Lawrence; unpleasant, even. But maybe pathologists are human; perhaps they too can be rattled, after all.

'Her aunt,' I continued, babbling, never ever intending to get blasé in the presence of violent death, 'keeps a small hotel. None too savoury, or so I'm told.'

'I have never,' said Lawrence distinctly, 'ever found it necessary to stay in Eddathorpe overnight.'

That will teach me to make idle conversation with professional ghouls. I promptly shut up.

Seconds stretched into minutes before he looked up, 'Any immediate questions, Mr Graham?' he finally asked.

'Provisional cause of death, weapon used, confirmation that she wasn't killed here, and, er, some idea of when she died?' I can be like that, too.

'Cause of death? Something in the nature of a guess at the moment, you understand? And as for the weapon, she's been struck repeatedly, probably with a plain old-fashioned human fist.' He stretched and sucked his lower lip, as if undecided whether he was going to share the rest of his news at such an early stage. 'How about ingestion of stomach contents and vagal shock?'

'Then it's not necessarily murder?' I could already hear the drawling voice of some smart-arse defence barrister playing it down for all he was worth. Judge sympathetic, jury in tears. Forget the corpse and its friends and family: charge reduced to manslaughter. Practically an accident, me Lud, tut, tut! Two hundred hours community service, and don't do it again.

Still, do not worry too much about potential excuses at this early stage. Dragged, dishevelled bodies with facial injuries do not often hide themselves in beached and crumbling maritime death traps of their own accord.

'She was certainly violently, but not necessarily fatally, assaulted,' said Lawrence. 'As a working hypothesis, it is also likely that she then tried to be sick. The vomit,' he added with entirely unnecessary relish, 'may have been ingested into her lungs, and she then either choked to death, or died of shock.'

'You mentioned vagal shock, what exactly does it mean?'

'An involuntary spasm of the vagus; the tenth pair of cranial nerves which have branches to the heart, lungs and viscera. It's the sort of thing,' he added helpfully, 'which sometimes happens to drunks.'

'And . . .' I started.

'I have probably speculated more than enough already,' he interrupted with his usual thin, humourless stretching of the lips. 'There is, as you will no doubt have observed, a very faint taint of stale alcohol about her mouth. As for the rest—' he shrugged.

'And the time of death?' I reiterated.

'Oh, around thirty-six to forty-eight hours.'

I stared at him dumbly; the usual pathologist's run-around. I waited for him to relent.

'The blood has fully settled into the dependent parts of the body; lividity is fixed. Rigor mortis is completely resolved, the limbs are flaccid, the temperature is that of the surrounding deck, but the body shows no obvious signs of swelling at this stage. We have both seen such scenarios before, Chief Inspector. Now, as an experienced layman, you tell me.'

'She's been dead more than thirty hours,' I admitted miserably, 'and less than three days.'

'So,' he sounded like a man who took no pleasure in his triumph over the lesser breeds, 'in the absence of a more thorough examination in laboratory conditions, if I say thirty-six to forty-eight hours, with a bias towards the lower estimate, I am doing the best I can for you, am I not?'

Andrew Lawrence. Somebody, I thought a trifle bitterly, whose sentences terminated only through shortness of breath.

'Thursday.' I even did my best to sound grateful, 'Sometime between ten in the morning and ten at night?'

'More likely Thursday afternoon or evening,' he said; he was even trying to be helpful. 'Perhaps.'

There was a rumble of voices outside and George Caunt, the borough detective sergeant, poked his thick grey thatch under the flapping canvas. 'Mr Fairfield's here.'

'Does he, er, want . . .' I waved one all-encompassing hand at the cramped and sordid scene.

'Apparently not.' George hesitated. 'He says he doesn't keep dogs for the sheer pleasure of doing all the barking himself. He simply wants a word.'

Lawrence choked back a comment, changed his mind, and turned it into a request for the Forensic Liaison Officer, instead. I pushed my way up and out through a shower of raindrops from the slightly smelly tarp and negotiated the crudely nailed-together planks.

'Trouble with him,' said George as we wove our way between the blue and white tapes, 'he thinks everybody is as keen on gunk, bodies an' bits of intestine as he is.'

'He also thinks that all investigating officers are gun-shy at heart.'

'It's not something people ought to relish doing for a living,' said George briefly, 'if they've got any sense.'

'Pathology or police work?'

'That as well.'

Fairfield was waiting, slightly defiantly I thought, feet planted firmly apart on the solid tarmac of the lane, well beyond the gate and track to the beach.

He looked disapprovingly at the waiting hearse, the tight little groups of policemen and the line of vehicles parked by the side of the road, and sniffed. 'Too many cooks,' he said.

'It always happens, the world and his ruddy wife always come to watch.'

'I called out a search team,' I said, stung, 'just in case.'

'In case of what?'

'In case we had to search for a weapon, for one thing.'

'And we don't?'

'Somebody apparently used his fists.'

'In that case, Bob, I don't want to tell you your own business, but why don't you send at least some of these rubber-necks home?'

'I still,' I said flatly, 'intend to search the pines and the area of the beach.'

'And take tyre impressions from the side of the track?'

'Yes.'

'It's probably a waste of time.' He sounded gloomy this morning. He stared at the ruts in the churned-up mud leading to the tangle of underbrush and trees. 'You've probably got a cast of thousands. It looks like a regular shagger's alley around here.'

'It's Rachel Foster, sir.'

'George told me; at least you know now why she didn't make a complaint.'

Unbelievably callous, and having viewed the body I just wasn't in the mood. 'In that case,' I snapped, 'you'd better get a team from another division to do the job. We're all suspects here.'

'Feeling touchy, are we? Doesn't do to let these things get on top of you, Bob.' All at once he was playing the munificent, totally understanding boss. My hackles rose.

'I wonder, sergeant,' he turned to George, 'if you'd like to take a bit of a walk. Organise something, perhaps.'

'Yes, sir.' George, excluded, irritated, turned away. That's another thing about Peter, he can offend for Europe when he likes.

'Problem?' I asked.

'We-ll,' he drew the word out slowly, if I hadn't known him better I would have thought that a touch of embarrassment was creeping in. 'You realise, of course, that you can't be in two places at once?'

Very, very faintly, the glimmerings of a silver lining began to appear. It didn't do, however, to let any trace of overt enthusiasm show.

'You, er, want to leave this one with me?'

'Exactly, Bob. You're the man on the spot. Your area, your enquiry: slightly inconvenient for me, of course.'

Fairfield, the selfless martyr. Like hell.

'There are,' he admitted, 'one or two political aspects to this police complaint business which I hadn't, er, fully considered right at the start.' Tell me about it, Peter, not to mention the internecine war.

'The Cary's complaint? My involvement with Colin Templeton, for example?'

'Exactly, I've been thinking, it's not that I don't totally trust you, of course . . .'

'But it might be a bit too much to swallow, on the one hand you and Frank Purcell hate one another, and on the other Colin and me are mates?'

'I wouldn't have put it that way myself.' I was prepared to bet he wouldn't. 'But a legitimate opportunity has arisen for you to step back, and as there may be some sort of connection between these, ah, events, you do have a valuable insight into what might have been going on.' Too many buzzwords, I decided, too many hours on Working Parties once you get to higher rank.

'You don't think this might be a coincidence, then? So far as Rachel Foster is concerned?'

He shrugged, then, forever an each-way punter, he shook his head.

'The Nottingham enquiry,' I said. 'Who's taking over from me?'

'Chris Bowyer, the Chief Inspector from Complaints.' He spoke casually, but he couldn't quite meet my eye. He knew perfectly well that we'd had previous dealings; not exactly bosom pals, me and good old Chris.

The rain hadn't stopped, but for me, personally, the sun came out. Fairfield might be watching me for signs of annoyance or discomfort, but I was examining things from an entirely different point of view.

Wendy Pointer wept; the tears trickling down her fleshy, raw-looking cheeks while her shoulders shook as she took in great, uncoordinated gulps of air. We were sorry for her, all three of us. Embarrassed too as we watched this huge, tough-looking sixty-year-old woman giving up to such uncontrollable grief. Only an aunt, as she repeatedly informed us between body-convulsing sobs, but Rachel was all she'd got. Or had, to be precise. Dead husband, dead niece, and neither chick nor child of her own. Her way of putting it, not mine.

George was balanced uneasily on the edge of a chintzy armchair in her private sitting room at the back of the Britannia Hotel, leaning forward, trying to interest her in a cup of hot, sweet tea. Her own quarters were comfortable enough, but it wasn't the most salubrious crash-out in town.

Three floors and a basement of cream-painted Victorian family house on crumbling Clarence Parade, with railings around the area steps, and a drunken green-and-gold sign proclaiming full board at £165 a week. There were, although the sign failed to publicise the fact, other, off-season terms. Unemployed seasonal workers on benefit were something of a speciality at this time of year. We had already accumulated a list of five, which, with two elderly couples on an out of season break, comprised the entire guest list of her Chamber of Commerce listed, but entirely unstarred, hotel.

I'd set out to ask Wendy some questions, but, having broken the news, I'd somehow lost heart for the task. I felt a bit like Bluebeard, Doctor Crippen and the Black Panther all rolled into one.

Sylvia Doyle, plump, pretty and as smart as paint in her uniform, joined the sobbing woman on the sofa, and placed her left arm tentatively round the older woman's shoulders. Plump or not, she looked like a tug beside a battleship in comparison with the bereaved. The tears continued to roll.

'Why don't you take the cup from Sergeant Caunt?' she asked helplessly. 'Take a sip. Or maybe there's a friend or relative you'd like us to bring around?'

Mute, bloated, slobbering, mouth slack and with saliva mixing with the tears at the corners of her mouth, the woman shook her head.

'Who's your GP, Mrs Pointer?' I asked. Worrying, the extent of the grief, her size, and the colour of her face. Unless she calmed down soon, a heart attack could well be on the way.

Again there was no coherent reply, but gradually the heaving sobs became sniffles, and eventually, not without a degree of dignity, she removed the comforting arm from around her shoulders. 'Don't want a doctor. You are going to get the bastard who did this, aren't you?' she said.

'Yes.'

George gave me a long, disapproving look. Stupid bugger, he was saying, you ought to be on the way to the funny farm for saying things like that. All very well for him, anything less than a straight answer, and I was pretty certain she'd be off again. No comfort in diplomatic evasions and carefully calculated weasel words at a time like this.

'Can we talk about Rachel?' I asked, judging that the initial storm was dying down.

'All these years. She's been with me ever since she was six, and now it's ended up like this.' She gulped.

'Her parents are dead?' Get in quick; give her something else to think about before she starts again.

'Roxanne, that was me sister, she died.' Roxanne and Wendy Foster, quite a combination, there. She waited while I thought that one through, then she added vindictively, 'Dunno about *him!*'

'Any idea where her father might be? I appreciate that you brought her up, but we'd like to trace next of kin.'

She stared at me indignantly through heavy-lidded, cow-like eyes, 'Think I wouldn't have gone after him if I'd 'a known? Child maintenance and such? Mr no-name, that was him.'

'I'm sorry, love, so effectively there's only you?'

'S' right.'

'So you brought her up, and you sent her to University. You were pretty close?'

'Until she went off to college, b-but everybody has to grow up, and there was nothing much for her here. It was when she came back that she got a flat and moved out.'

'To Nottingham?'

'No, she got a full-time job in Birmingham – Handsworth – for her first year. She hated it, but jobs weren't easy, and last year she ended up doing supply teaching in Nottingham. She could just about make ends meet.'

'What about boyfriends?'

She hesitated, 'When she lived here, you mean? She had one or two.'

'Anybody special; anybody still hanging around?'

'Not so far as I know.'

'Names?'

'One was called Alan, Alan Peters, he lives up by the golf course. There was a Roy something-or-other, as well. But they fizzled out when she moved away.'

'Anybody current?'

Again, she hesitated. 'Not here. Not so far as I know.'

'And in Nottingham?'

'She never said.'

'How often did she come over?'

'About once a month.'

'Just for the day?'

'The weekend, usually.'

'And last weekend?'

'Your lot knew about that,' she gave me a hostile look. 'Nonsense, complete rubbish was that. Coppers coming around here on a Sunday afternoon, yattering about bank cards an' such. *Did I know Rachel Foster?* Of course I bloody well did! And it didn't even stop there, did it? They even had to have a look at her room.'

'So you don't think she was involved in anything; you believe it was all a mistake?'

'Course it was.' The tears, never far away, over-spilled again. 'She's dead, she's dead! I don't know how you could say such things.'

'Last Sunday,' said George, 'did Rachel phone before she came?'

'She never came,' replied Mrs Pointer spiritedly, 'thanks to you.'

'OK,' George's back was broad. 'Let me put it another way, did you expect her, did she phone in advance?'

'Yes, and by the time your friends got around to seeing me I was worried sick. I thought she must have broken down or been in a smash, or something.'

'And she was coming over for the day?'

'That's right, and I've been along this road before. Goodall asked me, if that was his name. A right cocky article an' all. Definitely God's gift.'

Sylvia Doyle, forgetful of the occasion, smiled, immediately recollected herself, and sat up very straight indeed.

'So,' persisted George, 'having been interviewed by the police in Nottingham, she returned on the Monday, instead?'

'Yes.'

'By car?'

'We've already been over all that, her Mini's still here. It's parked on the service road round the back.'

'So when she left here on Thursday morning, she was on foot?'

'Nobody called for her here, not so far as I know.'

'So she stayed here Monday and Tuesday and Wednesday nights. She wasn't working in Nottingham, right in the middle of term time. Why?'

'Why not? This was her home, she knew that, whenever she liked.'

'Look, I'm not trying to upset you, love.' George was doing

his best, 'but she was a fairly regular weekend visitor, but not over-frequent, OK? Didn't her arrival on a Monday strike you as strange?'

'You lot had spoiled her Sunday, and she wasn't working this week.'

'That's what she told you?'

'Yes.'

'And she'd decided to stay in Eddathorpe for the whole time?'

Again the pause, the same uncertain expression flickering across her reddened, bloated face. More puzzled than evasive, I decided. 'I don't exactly know. She said she wanted to be around for a couple of days. She never said anything about leaving, not even on Wednesday night. Thursday she was out by nine, but she never said anything about not coming back. I rep-reported her,' her voice broke and she snuffled, 'when she stayed out overnight.'

'Did she tell you why she was staying so long?'

'No, but she might have been waiting for a letter, I think.'

'What sort of letter?'

'How should I know? She turned up here late on Monday afternoon, and almost the first thing she did was ask me if the second post had been. It hadn't, but she was looking for something on Tuesday morning, and again on Wednesday.'

'And is that when she received it, whatever it was?'

'I suppose so; I was busy in the kitchen doing the breakfasts with Lizzie when she came in. She gave me my letters, and she kept her own.'

'Who's Lizzie?'

She looked at George almost proudly, 'She's me permanent staff.' It figured; this was autumn, getting on for winter, and this was not the Ritz.

'But you'd no idea what her letter contained?'

'What's this about?'

I was not inclined to enlighten her, so she answered the question anyway. 'No.'

By this time the same unpleasant thought had obviously

occurred to George. We exchanged a single, malevolent, anti-Patrick glance before he took up the trail. 'So she was expecting mail here, wasn't that unusual?' he said.

'She gets bits and pieces from time to time, insurance and her RAC membership and stuff.'

'But this time she was expecting a letter or a package on a particular day?' By this time we were more than interested, a big black cloud was beginning to form.

'I suppose.'

'We'd like,' I said, 'to have a look at her room.'

'It's going to be necessary to bag up her stuff for the time being, and take it away. Just in case.' Tactful George, slightly anxious, and disinclined to be overly truthful, vaguely explained.

She failed to take it up. 'Your man looked on Sunday, but of course her clothes are in there now. It's too much for me, mister, I couldn't face it, but you can go up if you like.'

'We'd, er, like somebody with us while we look. This Lizzie, for example . . .'

'OK.'

Gratefully, we left Wendy Pointer, subdued but no longer weeping, to the counselling skills of Sylvia Doyle. Tea, our young policewoman was claiming hopefully as we left the room, was apparently still the thing. Personally, I was more than doubtful, in my opinion its restorative powers fall something short of a palliative for violent death.

Chapter Ten

'What's his name?' I hissed to the uniform man through one side of my mouth.

'Wayne Armstrong, boss,' murmured the PC semi-audibly, closing the interview room door behind him, 'and he's thoroughly pissed off about it, so I don't recommend any jokes.'

'John Wayne?'

'Exactly, he reckons it's a sixties blight, only one step up from Cheyenne.'

'Has he said anything else?'

'Married man lives just this side of Lincoln. He's a carpenter by trade, and that's why he bought the boat. He says he could have fixed it up a treat, given time.'

'Could have?'

'He also says that his missis wouldn't fancy going on it now, given that it's the place where some poor tottie croaked.'

'A prostitute?' My voice sharpened, and George immediately brightened up. 'Who told him that?'

The PC went on to the defensive straight away. 'Not me, boss. Nobody, so far as I know.'

'OK, thanks for looking after him, it's time we had a word.'

As soon as we walked in it became obvious that Wayne Armstrong was not a happy man. Mid thirties, designer stubble, old green T-shirt; zip-up golf jacket, trainers, and paint stained jeans. A man frustrated in his desire for a quiet working day on his boat.

'Sorry to keep you waiting, Mr Armstrong,' I said.

'Not as sorry as me.' He eyed the assembly of plastic cups on the table in front of him. 'I've got tea coming out me ears.'

'I'll try not to keep you long.'

'I don't suppose I'll be doing much more on that boat, anyway. Not till I've had a word with the wife.'

'How much did you pay for it?' Well, you have to start somewhere, lead your way in.

'Six hundred notes.'

'I'd have thought it was cheap at half the price,' said George.

'Ah, that's where you'd be wrong. It's basically sound, is that. A few weeks work and she'll be as good as new. See the car, did you? Nearly three hundred hours work on that, restored her myself and now she's a little gem.'

I should have been warned, an anorak rather than golf jacket man, I decided. A few more untimely words on my part and this could turn into a long and boring lecture on the joys of DIY.

'Bit late in the season, isn't it, for coming down now?'

'Getting on a bit,' he admitted agreeably, 'but I've got a lot of work on back home, I have to come down when I can.'

'When did you last come down to the boat?'

'Beginning of the month.'

'So why did you come down today?'

'Why not?' He shrugged, 'Not a bad morning until the rain started. We're not going to get many more of these before winter sets in, I should think.'

'No other reason? Sure you didn't pay a visit earlier this week?'

He looked down at the scattering of empty cups for a moment, and then slowly he raised his head. 'Don't be so bloody daft!'

'That's a no, I take it,' said George.

'Listen, you, if you've got a question to ask me, ask it straight and I'll answer. I've read about murder enquiries, I'm not a mug, and you've got a job to do. But if you ask me shitty questions like that, mate, you'll get shite replies.'

'Fair enough,' I stepped in quickly. 'So you know that we have to cover all the angles, er, Wayne.'

He looked at me sharply, 'Mister Armstrong will do.'

'OK, but before we get down to this morning's events, can you give me some idea of your movements earlier in the week?'

'From when?'

'Wednesday onwards, say?'

'Wednesday and Thursday I was at North Hykham, doing a job.'

'A job?'

'Rebuilding an old conservatory, the owner was with me all day.'

'And in the evening?'

'I went home to the wife and kids.'

'And,' asked George, 'they can all confirm this, of course?'

'You bet. And don't you go upsetting my customer, either. She's an old biddy, and she's been going on about cowboys and crooks in the building trade something rotten.'

'Got to go back, have you?'

'Half a day, next week.'

'What did you do on Friday?'

'Replaced a floor in a loft that some jackass of a DIY'er had buggered up.'

'And again, I suppose the owner was there?'

'Yep, well his wife was, all day. Y'know, mister, I don't know what I ought to feel about all this.'

'All what?'

'Being practically accused of murder,' he said.

'Nobody's accusing you of anything, Mr Armstrong, we're just eliminating you as a remote possibility, that's all.'

'Oh, yeah?'

'Why did you say she was a prostitute?' asked George.

'Just a guess. Bit of a slag, maybe, just the sort to get strangled. Short skirt.'

'Know many prostitutes, do you?'

'No, and as I told you at the start, you can watch it, mate!'

'Her skirt was just rucked-up where she'd been dragged. For your information,' snapped George.

'OK, right.' He'd jumped to conclusions, he hadn't had too close a look, and now he was a trifle ashamed. 'Sorry,' he said.

It wasn't much of an interview, as interviews went. He's decided to have a day, or perhaps a morning repairing his boat. He's arrived at Ansell's Creek a few minutes before half-past eight. He's unloaded his gear, recovered his gangplank from where it was lying beside the concrete apron and slip, put it in position and climbed aboard.

No, he hadn't taken much of a look; the bird was definitely dead, wasn't she? Made him feel really, really sick at the time. He'd been up and out of there like a rabbit meeting a fox. Next thing he knew, he was up the path to those chalet things and banging on doors. And did we know there were only two of them inhabited permanently out of five? Shameful, with all these people homeless, mate. Anyway, one had been the home of an old retired couple with a telephone, and they'd let him phone the police. Bit of a shabby old place, if you asked him. Not that they'd been all that keen on letting him in at first. Scary, they'd told him about people driving cars, flashing lights, slamming doors at all hours of the day and night up and down that track . . .

Or, as George said later, 'Just like a little dripping tap, wasn't he? A bloody fine suspect he turned out to be!'

We had the usual form of organised chaos in the rest of the nick. An Incident Room was being set up on the first floor, and Paula, in her capacity as IT-Person-in-Chief, had bagged the Office Manager's job prior to any other potential candidate drawing breath.

Computer-trundlers, desk-toters, stationery providers and the usual gaggle of BT technicians quailed under her expert eye. If you wanted a murder room organising Detective Inspector Paula Spriggs, née Baily, was definitely, to re-coin Armstrong's phraseology, your bird. Not that I would ever have dared use the expression to her face. Pretty, boldly made-up, aggressively blonde and with a derisive sense of humour, she would have soon said something anti-chauvinist and probably ego-wounding back.

'My, my,' she said, eyeing the two matching suitcases we'd recovered from the Britannia Hotel, 'designer luggage, whatever next?'

'There's some very nice schmutter inside,' answered George, 'care to give it the once-over for price?'

Laid out on a cartridge-paper covered bench, Rachel Foster's clothes didn't look excessive in terms of quantity, a little more than you would have expected for a long weekend, in fact. The quality was something else.

Paula flipped through a small pile of gossamer bras and briefs, 'Silk next to the skin,' she murmured, then, pointing to a blue two-piece suit, 'that's wild silk too, and what's more, it looks as though it's never been worn.' She pointed to the price labels inside the collar and skirt. Jessops of Nottingham, not exactly a budget store. With just a hint of envy, Paula listed the Alexon jacket and skirt, two designer dresses, and the two hundred pound Burberry mac. The shoes we'd brought, she pointed out quickly, were also new, the soles scarcely scratched. Even the four pairs of packaged tights, according to the ticket, were £5.75 a pair.

'Not bad,' said Paula, 'for a second-year teacher with an uncertain part-time job.'

'That's not all,' I muttered, taking a crumpled, plastic-enclosed A4 envelope out of my briefcase, and placing it on the bench. 'It's probably time to kill Pat!'

'I don't object in principle,' admitted Paula smoothly, 'but what exactly has he done?'

'Care to look at the postmark?' I suggested.

'Eddathorpe sorted,' interposed George, spoiling it all. 'Franked at 8 p.m. on the Sunday night, and addressed to her in her own writing at the Britannia Hotel.'

'Got there on Wednesday morning, or so we're told.'

'Personally,' said Paula unsubtly, 'I'd get him to go round

to the sorting office and complain about the slowness of the local post.'

'Think,' said George. 'She uses a card in the Retton machine and collects the cash. She bungs both in a self-addressed envelope, hares off round the corner and posts it, and leaves Pat Goodall with egg all over his stupid face.'

'Recover any more cash cards?'

'No.'

'Or an excessive amount of cash?'

'No again.'

She glanced at the envelope, at the pile of expensive clothes. 'It's all very circumstantial.'

'In the olden days,' said George vengefully, 'they used to hang people on less circumstantial evidence than that.'

'But not usually the Bow Street Runner,' warned Paula. 'Besides, don't you think you'd better check that there *is* a postbox around the corner first?'

'Prepared to bet?' asked George, with the bit firmly between his teeth. Nevertheless he picked up the phone.

I left them to it and wandered off in search of a clipboard. More than time to sort myself out, the enquiry teams were gathering, even Dorothea Spinks at Aylfleet wasn't arguing about manpower this time, she'd sent me a sergeant and six. Manpower, rotas, focus of enquiries . . . I began to jot them all down, what to include, what to exclude – the preliminary outlines of all the policy stuff. It would all go into the computer eventually, and it could all be checked. Any inadequacies, failures, or holes in my system and Fairfield, or even Her Majesty's Inspector of Constabulary could track me down and bollock me, later on.

It was only after the initial briefing that I caught up with George. Mealtime in the canteen, and the uniformed search teams were in, gossiping as usual and scoffing immense quantities of chips. So too were some of the CID crews, most of whom were on weekend overtime with no subsistence allowance, and therefore, following immemorial custom, making the most of a free meal.

'How's it going?' I asked George.

'Settling down, now we've kicked a few little backsides. Some of these buggers think it's party time, once they're away from home.'

I nodded, it's amazing how many CID men working on a murder want to do all their enquiries in a pub.

'And the postbox?'

'Speak of the devil,' said George.

I followed his gaze across the room to where Pat Goodall, accompanied by a partner, had just joined the canteen queue. I couldn't quite put my finger on it, but he didn't altogether look his cocky, totally arrogant self. What's more, his arrival hadn't gone unnoticed by the rest of the assembled throng, a certain amount of muttering and shuffling broke out before the denouement came.

'Postman Pat, Postman Pat,
Postman Pat is a pretty big prat . . .'

they sang it through, then, with a peculiar and not entirely kindly emphasis,

'Oh, Patrick is a very unha-ppy man!'

No need to ask, there was definitely, I gathered, a postbox close to the scene of the Goodall disaster. You just can't keep any secrets around here.

'Rachel's aunt got us mixed up,' he said, 'I'm Roy.'

'Roy Peters?'

'That's right, I was her boyfriend all right, but Alan came after me. Alan Cobden, he's still around, I think. I see him occasionally in town.'

'Know where he lives?'

'Nope,' he shrugged.

Mid-to-late twenties, so far as I could judge, with a check sports coat, wool tie and a brown V-necked jumper that almost matched. Twenty-five, rising fifty by the way he dressed. He'd probably been studying the *Young Fogey's Handbook* somewhere along the line.

'Good of you to come,' I murmured.

The full, almost girlish lips curled upwards and he brushed a stray lock of mousy brown hair out of his eyes. 'So I'm not going to need a solicitor for the time being, eh?'

'What makes you say that, Roy?' Christian names already, and three cheers for the bogus amiability of the CID.

'I teach at the local Comp.'

I looked at him blankly, no lights whatsoever came on. Personally, I didn't care where he taught or what he did. Whatever had that got to do with the price of fish?

The soft smile widened into a derisive grin. 'Such a short memory, chief inspector, oh dear! It's only three or four years since you were after one of my colleagues for murder. He almost got the chop.'

'The Alice Draper murder? I remember now.' I remembered all right. Innocent schoolmaster gets engaged to good-time party girl. One or two minor repercussions as I recalled it, he'd been one of six suspects, but that potential victim of police oppression had a very self-important, very loud-mouthed dad.

'Then again,' the voice was almost coquettish, 'maybe I should.'

George looked up from his notes, but he held his peace.

'You came here voluntarily, right?'

'Oh, yes.'

'And nobody told you that you were under arrest?'

'No.'

'This officer,' I pointed to George, 'is taking notes for a witness statement, he isn't recording your conversation on tape, and you can leave here anytime you like.'

'Oh well then, perhaps I should take the risk.'

Rachel Foster's ex-boyfriend? This was almost surreal. The

bugger appeared to be playing camp, and by the expression of suppressed amusement on his face, George was getting the message too. I thought of the obvious question, but for the moment at least, I was too much of a coward to ask.

'You don't appear to be taking this altogether seriously, Mr Peters,' I said.

'Oh, but I am. It's a shock all right, believe me.' Do not pursue this line of enquiry, Robert. It takes all sorts, he's probably a very worthy citizen, and anyway, live and let live. Soothe yourself with a cliché. It's something you do not particularly want to know.

'How long have you known Rachel Foster?'

'Seven, maybe eight years. My family moved to Eddathorpe, and that's when I met her – at school.'

'The school where you now teach?'

'That's right, we met while we were both in the lower sixth. It was a bit of a strain, I can tell you, we moved house at exactly the wrong time for me, I had to work like hell.'

He seemed to have a talent for irrelevancies, time to move on.

'But you went out together, nevertheless?'

He shrugged. 'One of those boy and girl things, that's all.'

'And afterwards?'

'She went off to Birmingham University, I went off to Leeds. Once I got my degree I came back here. I was lucky I suppose, getting a local job. She ended up teaching in some foul inner city dump.'

'No trouble, no falling outs then?'

'Not at all,' he gave me a disingenuous, almost seraphic smile. 'You *must* be clutching at straws. I used to see her at the jazz club now and again, just to say hello. She went around with Alan while she was at University, on and off. But to be honest, I don't really see him as a fiend in human shape, either, if that's what you want.'

I couldn't work it out exactly, but this one was beginning to get on my nerves. 'I'd like you,' I reiterated snappishly, 'to adjust your attitude, that's what I want.'

'OK,' he stared at me calmly, retaining a hint of that smooth, superior smile, almost as if he knew something and I did not. 'People live and people die, it's happened and there's nothing any of us can do. It's not that I'm unsympathetic towards her, and all that.'

Did he know what sort of impression he was creating? It wasn't something I'd have fancied doing if I'd have been a civvy, sorry, a member of the public, being questioned by the police. An odd attitude, certainly, but he was hardly nervous, and, according to him, he'd not been close to the girl for years. A boy and girl relationship followed by a casual conversation now and again whenever they happened to meet, and that was all.

'When did you last see her?'

He paused, giving it some thought. 'I don't know really, in the summer sometime, two or three months ago.'

'In the school holidays?'

'I think so. She was over here for a few days seeing her aunt; that's right, yes.'

'Ever made any enquiries about her, Roy?'

'Whenever I've seen her, sure. *How are you? What are you up to these days?* That sort of thing.'

'You misunderstand me; have you ever enquired about her to her friends?'

'Not that I remember, no.'

'Or to her aunt, for example?'

'Oh, I get it, you've got me down as some sort of obsessive. Well, I'm not.'

'And you didn't?'

'Didn't what?'

'Ever make enquiries with her aunt?'

'No, I didn't. And as far as I remember her at all, auntie isn't exactly the social enquiries type.'

'Bit of a snob, are you?' Time to get under his skin.

'Sorry as I am for the lady,' he said coolly, 'she is hardly my type. Auntie is as rough as a badger's arse.'

A self-sufficient, possibly armoured personality. This man used words to defend himself, to keep people away. Tough in his own way, maybe, or was he merely playing at it? Only pseudo-tough?

I took a very deep breath and changed the subject. 'And precisely how do you see this Alan Cobden, Roy?'

'Just another bloke, that's all. He was a year below us, so I didn't know him well. Just somebody we both knew vaguely at school.'

'And you don't know where he lives?' George, getting bored, apparently, had decided to chip in.

'Sorry, no.'

'But you see him occasionally around town?'

'Correct.'

'Anywhere special?'

'Ah, you want to *see* him, do you? Now I know what you mean.'

'And?' There are times when George, fingers twitching for a suitable throat, nevertheless deploys the patience of Job.

'Try Cary's supermarket. He's the new manager,' he said.

Chapter Eleven

'Not on your life,' said Angie. 'Definitely the big N-O!'

'I thought I'd run it past you,' I said weakly. 'It's pretty insubstantial at present, anyway. Just a half-formed idea.'

'Half-baked more like. We come to Eddathorpe, and solve our domestic problems. We buy a house, we get settled and we put down roots. Everything else is behind us, right?

'Then all you want to do is go back to the big city to work all the hours God sends, probably leaving me and Laura alone for sixteen hours out of the twenty-four, just for the sake of one more step in rank.'

'It's not exactly on the cards at the moment,' I protested. 'This guy Charlie Renshaw on the Crime Squad wants to be the new ACC. Frank Purcell won't succeed him as the operational boss, because he's probably on his way to an early bath. If all that happens, there'll be a superintendent post coming up, and I might consider applying for it, that's all.'

'Not much wonder your mate Colin has been using you,' sniffed Angie. 'I bet he's already thought of that.'

'I doubt it, he's not even been a chief inspector all that long.'

'Long enough to get the taste,' she muttered obscurely. 'I don't know what gets into you lot. Power mad, you're all the same.'

'Look, it hasn't even happened yet. No need to jump down

my throat, is there? I just want to know how you feel about it, that's all.'

'Well, now you know.'

'I didn't think you were all that passionately fond of Eddathorpe, anyway.'

'There's nothing wrong with Eddathorpe,' said Angie firmly. 'Sand, sea, pleasant life-style, pleasant location. Just the place for Laura to grow up.'

'It's a one-horse town at the edge of the world,' I protested, 'and some of the natives—'

'Can be safely ignored.'

'Especially,' I said, descending to cheap sarcasm, 'the ones who go rushing around committing murders from time to time.'

'And what about Nottingham?' Angela's voice acquired that warning, razor-like edge. 'Paradise on earth, is it? Some of the worst crime statistics in the country; Broxtowe, Canning Circus, Hyson Green?'

'No fear of police redundancies,' I offered. I always go that bit too far.

'That's more or less my point,' she even laughed. 'Pressure, pressure, pressure; you were hardly ever at home. So let's forget about it, huh?'

'Yes,' I said.

For the moment, anyway, I thought.

'This ex-boyfriend, you know, the supermarket geek,' said Colin Templeton a trifle sourly, 'I wouldn't mind a little chat with him.'

'Join the queue,' I replied.

'You haven't interviewed him yourself, yet?'

'Gone to the Lake District for the weekend. Climbing Dove Crag.'

'Establishing some sort of alibi?' He still sounded miffed.

'Hardly, Alan Cobden was at work until four o'clock on Friday afternoon, it's a seven-day-a-week outfit, and it was just his weekend off.'

'When does he get back?'

'Tomorrow.'

He was back at work in Eddathorpe tomorrow, but I was hoping to catch him at home by that night. I was indulging in a little grey lie to ensure that Colin, selfish and sod-'em-all Colin, didn't steal a march.

The CID car drew to a halt in front of Hampden House, and the driver parked neatly behind a brown Mercedes, nearside to the kerb.

'Here we are, All Saint's Street for them as likes it, boss.' The Crime Squad sergeant behind the wheel obviously didn't, and I could see what he meant.

Barely two hundred yards from the previous week's Nottingham hotel, Rachel Foster's former abode was yet another massive, double-fronted, run-down Victorian house. Even less paint, no gate and a battered, half-open door, Hampden House had been imposing once. Now, converted into flats, it presented a ragged, unclipped hedge and half a dozen different sets of violently conflicting curtains to the unswept street.

'Sew that lot together, and you could get the Zimbabwe flag or something,' suggested George.

'Careful with remarks like that around here; it sounds racist,' said the Crime Squad man, and grinned.

George, offended, with no ready reply handy, grunted and got out.

'Hey, it was only a joke,' said the driver placatingly, 'it's just that there's lots of blacks and Asians in this neck of the woods.'

'We know.'

A serious sense of humour failure, here. Sunday morning, nine o'clock, and for George and me on long-distance enquiries, it had been a six a.m. start. It must be the weekend working, I decided, that had suddenly made him sound particularly curmudgeonly and old.

The landlord, a small, pale-skinned Indian in his fifties, was waiting for us inside.

'Chowdray,' he said formally, shaking hands all round. 'I'm sorry for your trouble, gentlemen, I truly am.'

The phraseology was almost Irish, the accent could have originated in an English public school and he was treating us with something approaching cautious sympathy, as though we were the bereaved.

George, caught on the hop for some reason, muttered an embarrassed, 'Thanks!'

'You wish to search her flat?' said Mr Chowdray. 'I understand you have the permission of the poor young lady's relatives, yes?'

George, ever ready, handed him a scribbled note, 'This is from her aunt,' he explained. 'She gave us permission to look, but it's your property, Mr Chowdray, so, more importantly, do we have yours?'

'Of course, of course! But so far as I am concerned, I visit these premises very seldom, you understand?' He turned, key in hand, to lead the way upstairs.

'Don't you collect the rents?' Colin Templeton addressed his slight, grey-suited back.

'Miss Foster paid by bank standing order, as a matter of fact. My better tenants do the same.'

'And the rest?'

'My nephew does it,' the landlord sounded pained. 'He collects from my other houses too. He is also responsible for seeing to repairs, and for the cleaning and maintenance of the stairways, hall and common areas of the house.' He sounded a bit like a council official paying a flying visit in order to establish a fair rent.

The nephew, I could see, did a surprisingly good job. The tiles in the entrance hall shone, the numbered pigeonholes for letters gleamed, the stair carpet was clean, and all the lights worked on the landing, stairs and in the hall. All something of a miracle for the area and property type. No vandalism, no casual thefts of fittings. Mr Chowdray's nephew, I surmised, had a persuasive personality. Either that or he was very, very big.

Rachel Foster's flat wasn't all that bad as these places went;

a living room-kitchen, and a good-sized bedroom with a fitted plastic box for a shower, and something resembling a big cupboard tiled, and transformed into a loo. Whatever she'd earned, I suspected a good proportion of it had been devoted to her rent.

Good quality curtains, I noted, matching the loose covers on her two armchairs and bed-settee. Two old, but highly polished dining chairs on either side of a drop leaf table which, from the white marks on one side, had been used as an ironing board at some stage of the game. The carpet, the bookcase, a small pine table with drawers, a few pictures and an elderly sideboard completed the living-room furniture, apart from an elaborate CD stack and a very shiny free-standing TV.

The kitchen area, however cramped the available space, contained a brand new microwave as well as a dinky electric stove, an impressive array of crockery and glassware, an expensive set of steel saucepans, colanders, and three sizes of frying pan.

George looked critical. 'Those pans must have set her back something like a hundred and twenty, hundred and thirty quid.'

Colin fiddled with a couple of microwave dials. 'And this one's the all-singing, all-dancing version. You could probably get Radio Moscow on here.'

'Is all this hers, Mr Chowdray?' I asked.

'The basic furniture is not. The dining table, chairs, carpet and the sideboard are all mine. So is the wardrobe, and the carpet and the bed next door. She has covered my armchairs and the bed settee. I have an inventory, if you wish to see exactly what is what.' Chowdray stood by the door as he spoke, his hands carefully folded in front of him, the epitome of a man who was not going to touch anything, or get in the way of the police.

'You wish me to obtain the list?' His left hand was already reaching for his jacket pocket and his mobile phone.

'No thanks; is her rent up to date?'

'Since the summer, yes. She was, as I say, on direct debit

for the past few months. There was some difficulty prior to that, around last Christmas, when she first came.'

'She came here partway through the school year?' I was mildly surprised, her aunt had spoken as if she'd moved directly to Nottingham after a single year in the Handsworth job.

'That is correct; she told me that she had worked in Birmingham at first. I believe she had been unemployed, but she preferred – what is the expression? Supply teaching in this city, the children in her previous school did not wish to learn.'

'Did you have many conversations with her?'

Chowdray shrugged, 'We spoke from time to time. There were, as I say, some early financial difficulties. I did not leave these to my nephew, a professional person deserves to be treated with some degree of respect.'

The unknown nephew, whatever his domestic virtues, was beginning to sound more and more like a local version of The Enforcer to me.

'You sound, Mr Chowdray, as though you are a patient man.'

He smiled gently, 'You think that I took a small risk? Perhaps, but she was not in my judgement an exponent of the moonlight flit.' Colin turned away quickly, and the Crime Squad sergeant choked.

'Well,' said Colin, 'I suppose we'd better take a look around. Although,' he added a trifle maliciously, 'I'm sure we didn't leave any stones unturned the last time my officers searched.'

'Ah,' said Chowdray slowly, 'you are the man who roused my nephew last Sunday night?'

'No,' Templeton treated the landlord to a thin, smooth smile, 'but Dave here, and one of our young ladies did.' He indicated his detective sergeant. 'And he tells me that they went through this place like a dose of salts. Of course,' he added, 'Rachel was a suspect, not a victim at the time.'

Crime Squad David looked smug, Chowdray looked him over for an instant, a slight, almost unnoticeable tension in his facial muscles, his stare just a trifle over-polite. Not an altogether favourable verdict if I read the situation correctly, whatever reports the landlord's nephew had passed.

This time there were four of us to search, and two, however methodical they appeared, were obviously going through the motions just to satisfy the oiks from the sticks. Dauntless Dave in particular, smiling, using over-elaborate gestures, taking out and overturning drawers with the air of a stage magician, started getting on my nerves. Colin, with the occasional sly glances at me out of the corners of his eyes, took pleasure in his game. It hadn't been all that much of a friendship, I decided, after all.

'Nothing,' said his stroppy detective sergeant with satisfaction, after something over an hour.

'Anything else we can do?' Colin, I had to admit, was good at concealing his delight.

'No thanks,' I gave him my wide-eyed innocent look. 'Our own teams will have started the house-to-house enquiries here, by now.'

'What?' Betrayed by a bumpkin, he was saying, and very much kept in the dark. His voice lost its note of self-satisfaction; it even rose a notch.

'Helped,' I added easily, 'by the lads and lasses from Central and Canning Circus CID. I asked their sub-divisional commanders yesterday, and very cooperative they were.'

I looked from Colin to his subordinate and back. Crab apple time at a guess, although George, and possibly the landlord, looked marginally pleased.

'I understood,' said Colin stiffly, 'that this was going to be a joint event with us, not a divisional thing.'

'But of course, I'll pass on anything that may be of use to your enquiry, and I hope you'll do the same. After all,' I said disingenuously, 'that's why I wanted a Crime Squad presence here today.

'If we'd found anything to do with, er,' I glanced at the fascinated Mr Chowdray, 'your problem, we could have shared the information right from the start.'

'Excuse me,' the landlord chimed in, 'I hear from my

nephew that you were looking for bank cards and documents last week?'

'Yes!' I wasn't entirely sure whether that was a reply or a snarl from the egregious Dave.

'You know your own business best, of course, but some people hide things in the freezer compartment of the fridge.'

'You saw me look,' snapped the Crime Squad sergeant dismissively, 'and so did your nephew, come to that. I've tried the ruddy fridge, thank you. Twice, now.'

'Ye-es,' the landlord's voice remained diffident, he even managed a weak, conciliatory smile. He was not, however, feeling either weak or conciliatory by this time, of that I was pretty sure. 'But some of the frozen food packets are still supposedly sealed. Hadn't you better make sure and look inside?'

'If they're still sealed—' started the cocky, Crime Squad Jack-the-Lad, but George, seizing his opportunity, was already on his way.

Fridge door open, cover of the freezer compartment down: one small packet of frozen chips, open, one ditto packet of six lamb grills. The unused steaklets were in a transparent cover, and so was the bargain packet of eight pork chops. That only left the pepperoni pizza and the complete turkey dinner, and it was typical of George that he managed to leave the best until last.

No score on the Big Chicago Blaster, and as he slid the blade of his pocket-knife along the pasted cardboard cover of the dinner, his Crime Squad colleague was already taking a big self-satisfied breath.

'Well, well,' said George modestly, as he plucked a cash card as well as a sellotaped savings account card from the top of the sealed inner package. It was still Sunday morning, but he no longer had the grumps. True happiness, according to George, has something to do with being able to screw the occasional hated rival from time to time.

I stared interrogatively at Mr Chowdray, who was still maintaining his attitude of diffident, studied calm. Then I smiled at him encouragingly; it was, after all, his turn to add a touch of spice to the script.

'I am such a terrific fan of all your English detective stories,' he said.

Chapter Twelve

'Another ruddy flat, and four flights of stairs to go with it,' whined George.

'These are better than All Saint's Street,' I consoled him, 'you must admit.'

Alan Cobden occupied an apartment in a smartish block of Eddathorpe seafront flats. Something of a whiz-kid grocer, a manager at twenty-five or twenty-six, and obviously earning a bob or two. Shame about George, though, he had good reason for a bit of a moan. It had been a long day, a boring return drive and almost inevitably, there was an 'Out of Order' notice on the lift.

'I'd want much better service,' muttered George somewhat breathlessly, 'if I was paying a fortune in rent for a pad like this.'

'What is the rent?' I asked, reaching the top of the stairs, and deliberately breathing slowly and evenly through my nose. To tell the truth, I was feeling slightly fragile myself, but, short of a heart attack, it doesn't do to let your subordinates know too much at times like these.

'Lease really, it works out at around six hundred a month.'

'In Eddathorpe? Bloody hell, I can do better than that buying a full-scale house.'

'You get services,' explained George.

'Like free exercise instead of a lift?'

George, for reasons known best to himself, failed to respond.

He walked over to the front door of Cobden's apartment and stabbed brutally at the buzzer instead. There was no immediate reply, but faintly, inside the flat, we could hear the steady rise and fall of voices from the TV.

He tried again, 'Just a minute!' The television was turned off and Alan Cobden came to the door.

'Yes?' A short, muscular figure, his shirt half-unbuttoned, peered out warily through a six inch, chain-guarded gap.

'Sorry to disturb you, Mr Cobden, police.'

'Are you? Well, if you are, I'd like to see your warrant cards, first.' Not exactly the trustful type, but who could blame him late on a Sunday evening, with two over-large strangers at his door.

We went through the usual ritual. 'Can we come in?'

'Supermarket burglary, is it? I'm not the first on the key-holders' list, you know. The assistant manager's supposed to be called out first.'

'Er, no, it's not a burglary, we'd like to talk to you about something else.'

If anything, the look of nervous suspicion deepened. He undid the chain on the door, nevertheless. 'Samantha!' he called over his shoulder, 'it's the police!'

There were sounds of hurried movements, someone banging cushions as we went through to the living room, and once we saw Samantha we could guess why. We had, thoughtless as we were, disturbed a very intimate evening at home.

Samantha, a bottled-blonde all right, but pretty enough in her way, with vivid, slightly smudged make up and a nice line in perfume, a short silk dressing gown inadequately covering her nicely crossed legs. A couple of years younger than the boyfriend, perhaps, and a very cheering sight to the tired, work-worn male, especially George. And what's more, sergeants are paid overtime for this sort of thing, while I am not.

Introductions were effected, I don't know how he does it, but she immediately smiled brilliantly at my detective sergeant. It has to be something to do with his deceptively fatherly manner, not to mention the glint of something downright immoral in his eye. To stand a chance myself, she'd have had to have seen Casanova puffing and panting his way up the stairs.

'Would you like a drink?' She waved a hand in the direction of a well-stocked ormolu table practically groaning with bottles and glasses on the far side of the room.

'Yes please.'

'No thank you.' Personally, I had thoughts of upsetting her boyfriend any moment, now. Therefore I was doing the tactful; my, '*Not while I'm on duty, thank you, madam,*' bit.

'Well, a coffee would be nice,' I compromised firmly to George's disgust. I am told that it's a skill lying at the very heart of diplomacy, but it didn't mollify a weary George. It did, however, get her out of the room while we sorted out the lie of the land.

'What's all this about?'

'Rachel Foster, Mr Cobden. You haven't heard?'

'Heard what?'

'We're investigating the circumstances of her death.' A touch over-formal, perhaps, a hint of pomposity even, nevertheless, for purposes of my own, it was straight John Bull.

'What!' Mouth ajar, eyes open wide, and a very good impression of somebody who had not been expecting that. Our initial problem, however, was he acting, or was it spontaneous and true?

'Oh, my God! When? How?'

OK so far, apparently, but you never know.

'I understand she was an old girlfriend of yours?'

'Eh?' He hesitated. 'Who told you that?' Another pause. 'Yes.'

George rumbled into gear, 'We appreciate that this might be a trifle embarrassing for you,' he gestured towards the kitchen door. 'Would you like to do this somewhere else?'

Cobden lifted his head, 'At the cop shop, for example? Is that why you told me like that, is that the game?'

'Game?'

'Look, this is terrible, I hardly know what I'm saying. Just let me gather my thoughts. I've only just got back, anyway, ask Sam; I've been away climbing all weekend.'

'Alone?'

'No, no, with friends.' He looked at me sharply, it was hard to tell, but he might have marginally relaxed. 'It's all right, you know, talking in front of Sam. It was all a long time ago.'

'What was?'

'Going out with Rachel, of course. Look, what are you doing, are you trying to trip me up?'

'We came here looking for your help, Mr Cobden. Why on earth would you think a thing like that?'

'I assume her death is suspicious, that's why you're here?'

'You're right, but aren't you making one or two other assumptions, too?'

'Such as? Oh, oh.' The penny appeared to drop. 'Of course, she's living in Nottingham, right? Well, in that case . . . I haven't been anywhere near Nottingham, all weekend.'

'Not a lot of mountains in the Midlands,' grunted George.

'Do you go there a lot?'

'Well, yes, occasionally. Well, as a matter of fact, quite a lot. The head offices of my company are on a Nottingham Trading Estate.'

'Cary's Supermarkets,' I said.

'Yes, yes – you mean you've been asking after me at work?'

'We understood you'd gone away for a couple of days.'

'Oh, well, that's bloody charming, that is! Imagine the gossip! Now they'll all think that the manager's being sought by the police.'

'You do,' said George gently, 'have this tendency, don't you, to think the very worst?'

'I've got,' said Cobden stiffly, 'something of a position to keep up.'

George gave the merest flicker of a lascivious glance at the kitchen door. Fortunately for my peace of mind, Cobden didn't get the joke, 'OK,' he added, misunderstanding, 'She's a checkout supervisor. Samantha works with me.'

'When did you last see Rachel Foster?'

'I've never been to see her in Nottingham, if that's what you mean.'

'Here in Eddathorpe, then?'

'I saw her in the shop about a month ago, just to say hello.'

'She came to see you?'

He stared at George with something like contempt. 'She was buying groceries. People do.'

I stepped in quickly; it only took a single remark like that for George to start one of his feuds. 'A weekend, then?'

He paused to consider, 'No-o, I don't think it was. Longer than a month, maybe. Right at the end of the school holidays, perhaps. Yeah, she was getting a few things for her aunt.'

'I would have thought she'd have gone to the cash and carry,' muttered George a trifle sullenly. 'Especially as auntie keeps a hotel.'

'Cary's,' said Alan Cobden proudly, 'has lines as cheap, if not cheaper, than anything you'll find around here.'

'But—' started George.

'Rachel,' I interposed smartly, 'was assaulted locally, near Eddathorpe, not where she usually lived.' Right now, questions regarding retail-pricing policies were hardly part of my script.

'Raped?'

I simply stared. Slowly, he reddened. 'Sorry, that wasn't the right thing to say, was it? Sorry, no.'

The kitchen door opened hesitantly, and George gallantly sprang to his feet to assist. Samantha rewarded him with a big, inviting smile, edged around him and deposited a silver plated tray containing a coffee-pot and an assortment of china on a tile-top table beside my chair.

Her boyfriend wore the look of a man who'd been saved by the bell. 'You remember Rachel Foster, don't you, Sam? Apparently, she's dead.'

'I know, I was listening. Fittings in these modern flats.' She nodded over one shoulder before sitting down on the sofa beside him. 'Those kitchen doors . . .'

I watched Cobden carefully; he seemed to be taking her knowledge in his stride, although there was something about his general attitude which I didn't quite like. Not one word of sorrow yet, hardly anything in his demeanour that I could honestly put down to genuine regrets. And as for the question about the rape . . .

'I am genuinely sorry,' he said, as if he was reading my mind. 'You mustn't think I'm callous, you know. I just can't take it in, really, and it seems silly, saying how sorry you are about something like this to the police.'

'Why not?'

'Well,' he hesitated, 'I feel embarrassed if you must know. It's something you're expected to say, isn't it? Almost as if you're going to be suspected of something, if you don't, and then it sounds contrived if you do.'

'As bad burnt as scalded,' said George with a degree of relish he reserved for those occasions when he wanted to make a dig.

'That's daft,' Samantha poured the coffee, looked across at him and gave the ghost of a smile. 'He's never good at emotions,' she said, turning to me. 'Sticks his big feet in all over the place, to tell the truth. And it's nothing to do with me, if that's what you're thinking. I'm sure we're both very sorry for whatever's happened, but him and Rachel haven't been an item for yonks.'

'How long?' I was still concentrating on Alan Cobden, assessing him and talking to him across his female support.

He cleared his throat, 'Must be a couple of years.'

'And you've hardly seen her since?'

'Look,' he leaned forward to get a proper view. 'I don't know what you've been told, but Rachel and I went our separate ways. It was difficult enough when she was at University; we could only see each other on the odd weekend. Then she started blowing hot and cold, it wasn't all that serious in the first place, and then it just fizzled out.

'Anyway, people change, they don't go on forever, and they don't always want the same things.' Samantha stiffened slightly, taking it personally, I thought. Someday he'd change towards her. She hadn't at all liked that.

'In what way?'

'Look, I don't see what . . .'

'I'd just like to know a bit about her, it might help.'

'Oh, sure.' Once again, he relaxed. 'Rachel.' He stared at the ceiling, then at his partner before returning to us. 'Rachel was quiet. Very committed at school, always wanted to be top of the class. Get an education, girl, and then you can get on. That was her aunt.'

'And you didn't approve?'

'I never said that. Besides, there are different ways of getting on, you don't have to drive yourself blind, reading and slogging away at books every night.' His gaze shifted again, he looked complacently around the newly furnished room.

'And you thought like this, even before she went away?'

'No-o,' once again he was hesitant, 'not exactly. But I stayed here in Eddathorpe, apart from my training, and I had my own way to make. Besides, she soon had different friends, different values; to tell the truth it was she who dropped me in the end.'

'These friends?'

'I don't know. Other girls, mostly, I think. She was in Birmingham, and I was either in Nottingham doing my bit as a management trainee, or here.' He studied Samantha in all her silk-clad glory, and for the first time he genuinely smiled. 'We were intellectually and materialistically incompatible, I think.'

George stirred, 'Quite a mouthful, is that.'

'Well, that was Rachel. I was a money-grubber by this time; she'd got ideals, or so she said.'

'Politics, for example?'

'After a fashion; women's rights.'

'Oh.' George's interest dropped to zero with an almost audible thud. Even Samantha, whose interest in feminism probably lurked somewhere near the back of the queue, looked mildly surprised. All too obviously her young Lothario was the chauvinistic type.

'How was she off for cash?'

'Recently? Dunno really, not the sort of thing you ask. When she left college she was in debt. Pretty strapped for cash, and it probably hadn't changed much, knowing her. I know she'd left her proper job in Birmingham, and she was working as a sort of temp for Notts.'

'Supply teaching?'

He wasn't interested, 'Yeah.'

'Any other current boyfriends in or around Eddathorpe?'

'I don't think so; I wouldn't really know.'

'You didn't talk about very much when you met her,' muttered George.

'Look, you came to ask me whether I was still seeing her, right? I told you that there was nothing doing, it was over long ago. Yes, I saw her, and yes we passed the time of day. I'm sorry she's dead, it's a waste of a life, but that is definitely your lot.'

'You've not,' persisted George a trifle cruelly, 'even asked us how she died.'

'OK, then, you seem to be determined to tell me, pal.'

George scowled, there were at least two other people in the room who suspected by this time that he was anything but.

'She was beaten to death.' There are times when detective sergeants gild the lily a trifle, and George Caunt had something of a reputation for trying it on. Upsetting their equilibrium, he called it, but much as I liked him, I sometimes felt he enjoyed being a bad bastard on the quiet.

'Christ!' said Alan Cobden, and Samantha gasped and put one hand over her mouth.

'Sorry, love.' Momentarily, George switched his attention to the young woman on the settee.

'I should bloody well think so, and now if you've finished . . .'

'After she'd been hammer-assaulted,' amended George hastily, 'she was dumped somewhere out by Ansell's Creek. Know it, do you?'

'Yes.'

'A popular spot for courting couples, or so I've heard.'

'I wouldn't know about that.'

'You know it, but you've never been there?'

'Yes, all right if you must know, I have, but it was a long time ago.'

'With Rachel?'

'Yes.'

'But not recently?'

'OK, if you're trying to embarrass me in front of Samantha, you're succeeding. Anyway, here it is, good and straight. I haven't been anywhere near the Creek for something like a couple of years. I don't enjoy getting cramp anymore in the back seats of cars, and if I want sex I can enjoy it in the comfort of my own home.'

'Did you take your car?'

'What?'

'On this climbing weekend,' I explained.

'No, I went with a couple of mates. Shared the petrol with one of 'em, OK?'

'So your car's down below in the garage, untouched?'

'Underground car park, yes.'

'Mind if somebody takes a look at it?'

'I don't suppose it would matter if I did.'

'Have you cleaned it recently?' Impossible George.

'No, I haven't, and if that means what I think it means, you can go and get stuffed.'

'Sergeant Caunt,' I said primly, directing winged daggers in his direction, nevertheless, 'is just doing his job.'

'So were the Gestapo, and the SS.'

'I wish you'd stop getting so upset,' said Samantha unexpectedly. 'I've been reading about it, it's just a touch of the good cop, bad cop routine.' It wasn't altogether true, but I had to concede that it wasn't bad for a beginner, all the same. What with her tongue, her legs and a new and exciting top-of-the-dressing-gown gap, she'd easily succeeded in demolishing George, who took refuge in a quick rummage in his document case, and by reaching for his pen.

'I'll just need to complete a descriptive form,' he said a touch too brightly, 'and I'll take some details, if you don't mind, about all your movements between Thursday morning and Saturday lunch.'

'Well?' I said to George, once we were outside, leaving two half-empty coffee cups behind us. 'Is he a runner, or not?'

He shrugged, 'Lots of people to see, lots of checking involved, if we're going to alibi him up.'

'Yes, I know, but how do you feel?' I persisted.

'Not entirely comfortable, I suppose. Just a tad uneasy about his attitude,' he said.

Chapter Thirteen

Unlike the Boardroom, the scene of our initial confrontation, Cary's general offices were open plan, with a screened off reception area guarding Maurice Cary's oak-doored holy of holies at the far end of a long, glass-walled room. From the moment we left the lift and entered the carefully arranged open-plan working area, we became the cynosure of approximately thirty, largely feminine, possibly hostile, pairs of eyes.

Even the departmental managers had a mere yard-and-a-half of extra space to define their status, and only a strip of corded carpet to call their own. Personally, I would have hated working there. Maurice Cary, who must have approved the original plans, and who skulked in his own private office nevertheless, obviously thought that there were limits to Liberty, Equality and Fraternity, from his personal point of view. He remained firmly out of sight behind thick closed doors.

Linda Cary, half hidden by the reception screen, watched us advance. An expression of unconditional welcome was not her style.

'Good morning,' she said flatly as we came into range, 'and what can I do for you?' Her eyes travelled from me to George and back, and having decided that he was a subordinate and therefore unworthy of any exercises in charm, she did her considerable best to look severe.

'Good morning, Miss Cary, this is Detective Sergeant Caunt, we'd like to see your father, please.'

'He's in a meeting, you should have telephoned first.' Battle was joined.

'I did, at about ten minutes to nine.' Before she'd arrived, obviously, but I left that unsaid.

'He's engaged in business of considerable importance this morning. It's quite possible he forgot.'

George stirred; apparently not his type. Twenty-six or twenty-seven at a guess, the female version of the grey business suit with somewhat eighties-style padded shoulders, the family's beady brown eyes, less make-up today, and taller than I had expected now that she was standing up.

'He was going to do some further enquiries on our behalf, perhaps one of your brothers . . .'

'Both Mr Richard Cary and Mr Bernard Cary are in the meeting, too.' Mister this and mister that, it was her way of putting the proles in their place. 'The police seem to be quite unable to prevent the ruin of our business, so we are left with no option but to try to look after ourselves.' The voice, Nottingham, overlaid with her version of a posh accent, was harsh and chill.

People in hospital, shelves stripped of chilled meats, futile police observations, a bad press and money, not to mention customers, haemorrhaging away. Murder enquiry or not, I could see why requests from the forces of law and order were not seen as a top priority from the Cary point of view.

'Could you—'

'Perhaps.' A lengthy pause, 'But only if you tell me what it's about.' No trace of the little mouse I'd met in company with her family the other day; a touch the dictatorial, given the opportunity, playing up to the roughie-toughie business image. Knowing the background, I received the distinct impression that she was probably striving to impress Dad.

'Rachel Foster,' I started, but once again, she was in there like a knife.

'We examined our personnel records for you, she was never employed by us.'

This time I was determined to get a word in edgeways, 'I broke the news to your father earlier on; she's dead.'

'Oh.'

'Found at a place called Ansell's Creek near Eddathorpe. Murdered,' said George.

For once, there was a very satisfactory silence all round.

'I'm very sorry,' she said finally. Just like her father, it was a very cursory expression of regret. 'Are you able to say . . .'

'Somebody hit her too hard.' It was, I suppose, given his previous efforts, George's version of tact.

'I can see why you're here; it *is* something of a coincidence,' she said. 'Nevertheless, she's not in our records, even as a casual member of staff, and I really don't see how we can help.'

'What I wanted,' I said cunningly, 'were the personnel records of all your Eddathorpe and Aylfleet staff.'

Nice one, Robert: time to cloud the waters of the investigative pond a bit. I was not about part with my very own nitty-gritty, and expose Alan Cobden to the skills of the likes of Simon Gell.

'Managers and supervisors, or would you prefer a list of checkout girls, too?' She sounded almost amused.

'Everybody, please.' That should do more than cloud the waters, it ought to turn them positively opaque.

'Male *and* female?' Putting coppers in their place, was she? Or conducting an exercise in the politically correct?

No skin off my nose, anyway. 'Yes.'

'How very thorough,' for the first time she smiled. 'Do you want a copy of Superintendent Templeton's list of ex-employees, too?'

'Chief Inspector,' I muttered, 'and no, he's already supplied me with a copy, thanks.'

'Oh, he's still only a chief inspector? I thought he'd taken over, now we've managed to get rid of that awful man.'

It was one of those definitive moments. The members of the Cary family, from captain to cabin girl, I decided, were never likely to be numbered among my warmest friends.

* * *

'We're supposed to be backing off a bit,' said Colin Templeton, 'didn't you know?'

'And are you, sir?'

He looked at George thoughtfully, deciding how far he could trust the lesser breeds, and then he winked elaborately and grinned. 'In a pig's eye, but we've got to box a bit clever, now.' He took a long, satisfying pull at his pint, and tapped imperiously on the bar, 'Three more, Eric!' Once again we were back in the Vernon Arms.

Eric, deadpan, and not entirely enamoured of Colin, I gathered, pulled the second round of pints, and this time we left the bar and sat down in the far corner of the room. Plenty of spare seats, steady but unspectacular, the Monday lunchtime trade.

'What's happening?' I asked.

'Three more meetings with the Carys. Lots of screams of rage. They up the ante every time I see them, more and more precautions, more and more expense. They certainly don't like the police anymore, and they've filled their stores with contract security staff. More uniforms than customers over the past few days. Their insurers are going crazy, what they really want is the SAS.'

'And?'

'Another spate of nice little earners for our villain, if you must know, and he's started timing the deliveries from the ruddy machines. If he doesn't get his cash quickly, he recovers his card and buggers off.'

'Saves money, anyway.'

'Not any more. We've had to back down on the cash machine delays. Old man Cary is going frantic, one more balls-up or another batch of poisonings, and he reckons that somebody could wind up dead.'

'Somebody did.'

'Yeah, OK, your Rachel Foster, but it's still a bit coincidental at this stage, how can we be sure?'

'Remember the savings account? I've got an appointment with her bank manager at two o'clock this afternoon.'

'You've obtained an order to inspect?'

'Not exactly, no.' I allowed myself a slow, smug smile. 'We've come to this, er, informal arrangement with the bank. No court order until we require yer actual signed witness statement, pal.'

Colin, wise in the cautious, not to say uncooperative ways of banks, looked impressed. 'Christ! You've done well: you know her balance, yet?'

George, a good Catholic, who deployed all the other blasphemies as and when he wanted to express his feelings, looked down his nose.

'It's quite a nice little nest egg,' I admitted, 'especially for somebody who was recently in debt. And guess what? All deposits in the last three months, and most of them in blocks of five, or multiples of five hundred pounds.'

'It looks like game, set and match to us,' said George.

'It would be, Sergeant,' murmured Colin Templeton with what I took to be dawning dislike, 'if only you could find out who killed the girl.'

'The Nottinghamshire lads are calling it our Government in Exile,' said Roger Prentice, the Aylfleet detective sergeant, with a grin. 'And what with Fairfield and Bowyer's little effort downstairs, rumours of a takeover bid are beginning to spread.'

I looked around the second set of accommodation we'd appropriated at Nottingham Central Police Station within the past week. A big airy room on the second floor, two computer terminals, a typist, a few scattered chairs and desks, a bulletin board, and plenty of room for our enquiry team of six. As an incident room outpost it was fine.

'Seriously?' I said.

'No!' The grin remained firmly in place, 'It's just their little joke. They've been pretty good on the whole, they've got officers pairing up with ours for the house to house enquiries over the next couple of days.'

'How's it going then?'

'We're covering the ground, but there's nothing special so far. All Saint's Street, Tennyson Street, Portland Road. It's mostly bed-sit land, as you know, and it isn't easy to find people at home. I reckon we should have it wound up nicely by tomorrow or perhaps Wednesday night.'

'What about the Cary ex-employee stuff?'

'Division of labour, boss. The Crime Squad is doing the Notts and Derby part of that, it fits in with their supermarket poisoning side.'

'What a bloody awful mess,' I muttered disgruntled. 'How can anybody be expected to control an enquiry like this when it's all bits and bobs.'

'Never mind, boss,' said George smartly, 'we all know it's Bob's.'

Silly, but just for the look of the thing, both detective sergeants gave that one a couple of swift yuk, yuks.

'Mind you,' said Roger, the smile fading, 'that's not entirely true.'

'What do you mean?'

'Detective Chief Inspector Bowyer paid me a visit a couple of hours ago.'

'Oh, yes?' My hackles immediately rose. I'd once done a murder enquiry with Chris Bowyer, prior to us both being promoted, and we'd had this long, acrimonious battle before I'd sorted out why, on my own patch, and doing my own enquiry, I was the one in charge. Christopher Bowyer, in my humble opinion, was a selfish, arrogant sod.

'He, er, wanted some of my men to take statements for him for his police complaints. Said that my lads were officers from our force, and therefore he was in charge.'

'Did he now.' I couldn't help it, I can never take my own best advice, and I tend to speak before I think. 'I hope you told him to get off his fat, lazy arse and do some work himself.'

They both thought that was funny, but Roger laid three spread fingers over his upper arm, and ruefully shook his head. 'I'm not a detective chief inspector, sir, I have to deploy some tact.'

'OK, what did you say?'

'That I'd have to clear it with Detective Chief Superintendent Fairfield, first.'

'And Fairfield said . . . ?'

'Nothing, boss. Mr Bowyer left before I could pick up the phone.'

Nice one, Roger; Christopher, as well as being a bully, was rumoured to have the backbone of a jellied eel. I gave it a few moments' thought; me in Eddathorpe mostly, and Christopher in company with Peter Fairfield, buggering about with his complaints enquiry in Notts. He could easily return to Roger's enquiry team and try it on again. If I went complaining to Fairfield I'd sound like a whinger, if I spoke to Bowyer, it might be making a mountain out of a molehill. It was probably an isolated incident best left in the past.

Still, forewarned is forearmed, and all that junk . . .

I took a piece of paper and scribbled a simple two-line message, signed it and sealed it up. Addressing the envelope in my best copperplate, I handed it over to Roger Prentice.

'From me to DCI Bowyer, but only to be handed over if he comes up here again invading my space.'

Roger took the note, deadpan, and filed it securely away. 'Now then,' I said, 'back to Rachel Foster. How many Nottinghamshire schools did she visit, how many has she taught in, how many friends and contacts has she made during the past year?'

'Boss?' said George, a trifle hesitantly, once we were safely back in the car.

'Yes, George?'

'I've got a question to ask, so long as it's not a top secret, senior officer sort of thing.'

'You'd ask it anyway,' I said.

'What did you put in that note?'

'You're right, it's a secret.'

'Aw, I won't tell a soul, come on.'

'*Dear Christopher,*' I quoted. '*Thank you for your interest, but this is my enquiry and these are my people, now kindly fuck off.*'

He was only silent for a moment.

'Have you ever had any of your poetry published?' he asked.

Chapter Fourteen

Early morning on the deserted beach, and the autumn air was bright and chill. The tide was way out, apparently doing its best to tempt pedestrians to stroll over to the Dutch or Belgian coast. It was my favourite time of day.

Joe was in one of his crazy moods: gambolling, racing, dashing around me in ever decreasing circles prior to bolting away to the water's edge, and then halting, a distant dot, before he actually came into contact with the stuff. Ungroomed, he appeared to have swollen by fifty percent of his normal size. By this time of year he was frequently a gross, tangled roly-poly dog, peering at the world through a tangle of unkempt eyebrows, whiskers and his Russian-dictator's moustache.

Nobody else wanted to brave the cutting wind and the wet sands, so I let him run, wondering whether I should let my rocketing tangle of fur and excess teeth remain unclipped for a few more days. A clipped Lakeland would equal a cold terrier, but I wasn't about to be seen in public with a mollycoddled old ladies' pet with a dinky little blanket buckled over his back.

If I left him much longer, however, winter would set in before he'd had much chance to start to grow a new protective coat. He was happy as he was, but right now he was beginning to look like a moth-eaten hearthrug travelling at thirty miles an hour.

Inquest this afternoon: a quick burst of medical evidence in the presence of a scattering of reporters, the idly morbid and the unemployed who tend to assemble on these occasions, then an adjournment *sine die*. A date to be fixed; I started to feel depressed. Three days into the enquiry, the first, vital seventy-two hours and I hadn't got a clue. Not only that, we hadn't got a unified team; we'd acquired some sort of inter-force, multi-tasked version of match-and-mix.

We had, for a start, an independent Crime Squad enquiry, closely followed by the separate Fairfield-Bowyer police complaint. This in turn was becoming entangled in my homegrown murder investigation, and if that wasn't bad enough, I had to send one of my teams across force boundaries, and temporarily engage the services of the Nottinghamshire police.

Nobody, apart from Eddathorpe and probably Nottingham Central CID, had compatible goals, and even they weren't exactly committed to the cause, they were simply helping out. Colin and his Crime Squad might be pursuing ex-Cary employees, they might well feed their results into our computer, but in pursuit of his own ends I had the feeling that old-mate Colin would have no compunction in screwing me any time he liked. Add Christopher bloody Bowyer, the distances involved, the usual inter-force and inter-departmental rivalries and stir, and you had a complete investigative mess. Dimly, I was almost beginning to sympathise with somebody-or-other's demand for an integrated National CID.

The people who passed for suspects weren't doing me a lot of good; Roy Peters was almost a non-runner from the start. How could anyone build a story of unbridled passion, murder and blackmail out of a long-dead boy and girl romance? No evidence whatsoever linking him to the victim, and as for Cary's, it was just a place where they both used to take a trolley to shop.

Cobden was somewhat better, I had to admit. In fact he was practically all I'd got. A boyfriend who wasn't quite so ex, a man who oh-so-coincidentally worked for the blackmail victims, with expensive consumerist tendencies for a man of his salary and age.

The supermarket version of a whiz-kid; but he wasn't exactly a potential chairman of ICI. Not on a salary of seventeen and a half thousand a year. Not a lot if you were paying out something in the region of six hundred a month for accommodation before you start . . . But then there was Sam, Samantha Hobbs, they were an item, and she was almost certainly chipping in from her thirteen and a half K as a supervisor. Count two salaries, then.

The lifestyle wasn't all that excessive . . . I drifted back to Rachel, no connection with Cary's apart from Cobden. My semi-employed schoolteacher had been nicked next to a cash machine, nevertheless; she was now very dead and she'd turned out to have hidden wealth.

Supposing, just supposing that either Richard or Bernard were in play? Milking their domineering old man? But there was no known connection with Rachel. Anyway, why should they? They were in the driving seats of a very prosperous firm. I thought about them, together with their Crime Squad witness statements; maybe I hadn't ought to take them for granted. Maybe I ought to see them, or have them seen by my very own murder team . . .

I was saving the best till last: not that I had any evidence, not an iota of reasonable suspicion, come to that. Pure prejudice, I just did not like the Cary poor relation, Simon Gell. After all, he was jealous of his rich relations, he lived in Nottingham, so he could have a connection with Rachel and maybe he wanted half a million pounds. Pathetic: couldn't detect a piss-up in a brewery, Chief Inspector, wading through unfounded speculations like that.

Maybe we were nowhere near a legitimate suspect. Hadn't even set eyes on anybody who was anything to do with anything, yet. After all, we were still looking for disgruntled ex-employees, or perhaps, sipping tea in some school staffroom, an ex-lover of Rachel, an academic master criminal lurked. I kept on walking, and thinking up excuses for a permanently undetected crime.

Thank God that real policemen don't have to rely on the workings of a superior intellect, because I'd just run out. Personally, when push comes to shove, I'm a big believer in lots of witness statements, thorough crosschecking and a giant investigative sausage machine that just keeps grinding on.

Joe was still enjoying himself, and I had just passed yet another of those yellow and black notices that are meant to discourage dog-owners from exercising their little darlings on the town beach. Between May and September, that is. Half-past October didn't count, but I thought I'd travelled far enough, and duty called.

I turned, shouted and whistled, and for once the tatters of his dog training classes inclined him to respond. Abandoning the edges of the cold German Ocean, he came racing back, jumped all over me and left tasteful patterns of wet sand all over the lower half of my business suit. He barked happily, and full and frank expressions of opinion were exchanged between us before he realised that discretion was the better part.

He ran off again, making for the belt of concrete below the sea wall and the steps leading to the roadway almost opposite my house. I wasn't too worried; experience had taught me that the one thing he wasn't going to do was to rush away and play in the traffic. He has too much respect for his own wicked neck. Too late, however, I noticed a male, middle-aged, neatly besuited figure on the concrete apron at the bottom of the steps.

'Hey, Joe, Joe!'

Absolutely no reaction at all. A dog with a single idea, it was sandy-paws time and let's bounce! He's a very discriminating dog; he seldom falls in love with a scruffy anorak and a torn pair of jeans. Always wants to play with people in their Sunday best, does Joe. Messing about with somebody in a morning suit en route to a wedding would be his idea of bliss.

Hurrying forward, well knowing that I would be too late, I saw the drama unfold. Firstly, a quick circle of the victim, a couple of joyful barks. The man bent down, one encouraging hand held out. At least he wasn't afraid of dogs. Joe, having established the basics, backed off. The would-be dog lover straightened and awaited developments; they were not long in coming. With one happy bound, Joe established a new friendship by making one of his famous vertical leaps and spreading wet sand and affection all over the stranger's chest.

'You're a fine little feller, aren't you?' The man must be mad.

Having judged the distance and the impossibility of arriving in time, I hadn't broken into a run. There's nothing more humiliating than turning up at the heel of the hunt, red-faced, panting and unable even to apologise through shortness of breath. This way I could at least try to conciliate the victim, and have enough air left to swear at Joe.

'I'm sor—' I started.

'No harm done.' Nothing permanent, I noticed, but it was, by the looks of things, a very expensive suit. Not, together with the shiny Gucci-looking shoes, the attire in which I would have chosen to visit the beach. Big, beefy, hard-faced and in his late fifties, this fellow had all the hallmarks of a senior cop.

'Grand little animal.' He bent down to cement relations with an equally eager Joe on the old principle of love-me, love-my-dog, I suppose. 'Pleased to meet you. Your wife said you'd probably be down here, Bob; I'm Frank.'

•

Significant, that. Not Detective Superintendent Purcell, not throwing his weight about, either, plain old Frank. In other words, somebody who wanted something. Early morning too, and seeking out a foreign-force DCI some eighty miles away from home. Revelations or even an exchange of favours was in the air, or perhaps I was looking at an angry, dispirited man putting the boot in, seeking a measure of revenge?

'Surprised to see me, eh?'

'It's a bit unexpected,' I admitted, 'sir.'

'I've told you laddie, it's Frank. There won't be a lot more bowing and scraping anyway, on either side. Once this mess is cleared up, I'm getting out.'

I stared at him interrogatively and waited. This did not sound very much like the thick-skinned monster I had been led to expect, and he appeared to read my mind.

'It's not what I expected, either. Not what I wanted when I took the job,' he said. 'But the CID's too full of buzzwords, too full of ambitious wankers these days. I thought I'd do a year or two back in the old department, go out on a high, but things aren't all they're cracked up to be any more.

'Oh, I'm not planning on lying down and letting the bastards trample all over me, if that's what you're thinking.' He looked me boldly in the eye; 'I'd go out and shoot myself if I didn't think I could outsmart a gang of second-rate chancers like that.'

'Like what?'

'Well,' he looked at me slyly, 'what about Charlie Renshaw, for a start?'

'I don't know the man.'

'Lucky you. But I thought he'd as good as promised to mark your card for services rendered, once he manages to get rid of me and reaches Assistant Chief Constable, eh?'

Nothing, I was pleased to think, had ever been stated quite so clearly as that. Besides, I'd always flattered myself that I'd got a conscience of sorts.

'That's news to me, er, Frank.'

'We-ll,' he wasn't convinced, 'don't go relying too much on any of their promises, that's all. Especially anything channelled through that mate of yours, good old Colin, Bob.'

In the light of recent events I wasn't planning to do anything of the sort, but I wasn't about to commit myself to somebody with the reputation of Faithless Frank. 'Oh, yes?'

'Something more subtle, perhaps? Help 'em out with screwing me, and then you'll very likely get on?'

'That's hardly likely, Frank. I'm no longer involved in the Cary complaint; I'm doing a murder enquiry, now. You're obviously talking to the wrong man.'

'I ought to be talking to Bowyer, you mean? Think I don't know about him, either, the newly-elected shit of the year? No thanks! Besides, I thought you ought to know that Renshaw isn't the only one on the shortlist for ACC.'

A few drops of carefully distilled malice sharpened his voice. I waited for what was coming next.

'I bet your old friend Templeton hasn't said a word about Clive Jones.'

I tried not to show it, but he'd triumphed at last. So Faithless

Frankie Purcell knew all about Angie's ex-lover, the man I'd hammered immediately prior to being sent into exile on the East Coast. I scowled at the man who was rapidly transforming himself into my new *bête noire*. Here was another born trouble-maker, Faithless Frank Purcell, a man with an obvious talent for looking under stones.

'Hey!' equally obviously he could read my face. 'Jones isn't my business, and he isn't my fault. I'm not here to stir you up. This is just a word to the wise.'

'And that's what you came all this way to tell me?' I asked.

'In part. I'm right though, aren't I? Templeton never let on to you that your old mate Jones was on the short list.'

He stopped, leaned on the rails set into the fancy concrete wall of the esplanade and stared out to sea. 'You've got an enviable little billet here.'

'Does that come under the heading of free advice?'

'Sorry?' he paused, stared blankly at me for a moment, and then he grinned. 'Stay here and box within your own weight, you mean?' The grin turned into a laugh, but it had a bit of an edge. 'Somebody else been giving you advice, have they? I wish I'd done the same, relaxed, and kept myself to myself, long ago.

'No, I've no idea what you're capable of, Bob. I don't know you. I'm not here to give you advice and you can do what you like, for me. I'll tell you one thing, though; you're probably better off staying where you are. Middle managers have a comfy lifestyle in comparison to some, they can let the internal politics and all the shit flow off 'em like water off the old duck's arse.'

'You reckon?'

'Sure. Take Richard Cary for example: director of a fair-sized outfit, you'd think he had it made. But he's got his dad and his brother on his back, and that's only the icing on the cake.'

'What else?'

'An estranged wife for a start. Heather, a lady with expensive tastes, or so they tell me, who didn't take kindly to his outbursts of temper. Then again he may have had good reason, she'd got that cousin of his sniffing around her, Simon Gell.'

'What exactly are you saying, Frank?'

'Hinting, maybe. Only exploring one or two of the possibilities, old son. Perm any two from four, if you like. Gell hasn't got any money, and her who doesn't stay indoors very much, likes throwing cash around. Supposing, just supposing, now . . .'

'Point taken, but what about my murder victim in that case. Where does Rachel Foster fit in?'

'Oddly enough, she doesn't. Not so far as I know, but there's one other little scrap of information that your mate Colin hasn't got, or he'd have been out with a search team trespassing on your territory by the beginning of the week.'

'And telling me nothing about it?'

'Absolutely bloody nowt, not until after he'd made the arrest and taken all the credit for himself.'

Full of bile was Frank, and itching to do the opposition down. So anxious to do the devious before he went, that he didn't even care about letting a complete stranger see what made him tick.

'Go on.'

'This Rachel Foster, she was dumped, wasn't she? Didn't die where she was found, in whatsitsname, Ansell's Creek?'

'She could have died anywhere, she'd obviously been moved, her shoes were found lying around on the way to the boat. She was assaulted, and she died from ingested stomach contents and vagal shock, apparently, following a series of blows.'

'Been drinking?'

'Smelled of it, but not a lot.'

'Richard Cary can be violent,' he said musingly, 'or so I've heard, and he's got a weekend cottage about four miles from your scene. There you go, laddie,' he gave me a final vulpine grin. 'That's the rest of it, Frank's revenge on the whole boiling lot of 'em. And as I say, you can still perm any two from four!'

He was still chuckling when we parted. Another day, another dollar, Charlie Renshaw and Colin Templeton, two more added to the list of men whose little plans he'd screwed. Thoughtfully, I crossed the road and walked Joe home.

Chapter Fifteen

Judge Ralph Brand treated me to a sample of his gently curving smile. 'Yes, Mr Graham?' he said.

Deceptive, that courteous, almost timid look. Known far and wide in police circles as The Smiling Assassin, but only behind his back. Judge Ralph had something of a reputation as a hanging judge. Which was odd, considering the fact that they'd abolished the death penalty when he was still a pup, over thirty years ago.

He sat at the head of the conference-size table in his chambers, wigless, but still in his robes, peering at me over his half-moon spectacles, and doing his impression of rosy, round-faced Pickwick. An inappropriate comparison, though. Pickwick, I remembered, had little reason to love either lawyers or the law.

Here we go. I took a first deep breath. 'My application this morning, your Honour, is for a warrant under the provisions of the first schedule of the Police and Criminal Evidence Act, 1984, to search premises in connection with a serious arrestable offence.'

'And the offence in question is . . . ?'

'Murder, your Honour.'

'Ah,' the smile curved smoothly upwards. 'I must concede, Mr Graham, that you can't get very much more serious than that.'

I smiled back hopefully. I always liked, if at all possible, to stay on the right side of the judicial joke.

'Also,' I said, piling it on, 'I have good cause to believe that my murder enquiries are connected to serious offences of corporate blackmail committed against the Cary Supermarket chain. I am sure you are already aware, your Honour, of the widespread press publicity regarding threats to poison Cary products, followed by the placing of contaminated items in the chill cabinets of Nottingham shops.

'This has resulted in serious personal injury to four members of the public, the Company has had to clear its chilled foods from all its branches, and this again has been followed by considerable loss of confidence among customers.'

'Very well, you have at least *two* serious arrestable offences. Can you now convince me that all the conditions necessary for the issue of a warrant apply in this case?'

Yeah, well, it's not often you get the opportunity of skating on very thin ice with a purple judge . . .

'I have here, your Honour, a report from Professor Lawrence, the Home Office Pathologist, covering the circumstances of the death of Rachel Foster, the murder victim.

'I also have statements taken in connection with the various occasions in which money has been extorted from the Cary company as a result of unlawful demands made upon it with menaces, contrary to Section 23 of the Theft Act, 1968.

'Rachel Foster was arrested by one of my officers at a local cash point where money had been removed from the bank machine. Unfortunately, we allege that she had time to place the cash in an envelope and post it prior to her detention.'

I paused for breath, not to mention a swift review of the moment where I had, perhaps, been marginally economical with the facts. Did I really have that much confidence in my speculations regarding Rachel and the post? I pushed conscience to one side: yes I ruddy well did, and Ralph was going to get the benefit of my very best shot.

'Subsequently, after her death, we found that despite the fact she had substantial debts at one point, over the past few months she had repaid them, and at the time of her death she had £11,263.70 in a bank account. These copy statements, by the way, relate to a relatively new account, unknown to her usual bankers. This was all despite the fact that she had only irregular employment as a supply teacher in the Nottingham area during the current year.

'She was found dead in a semi-derelict boat at Ansell's Creek near Eddathorpe in this county. You will see, however, that she was certainly killed elsewhere. The property I wish to search is approximately three and a half miles from the place where she was discovered. Richard Cary, the owner, and a director of the Complainant Company, uses it for a weekend retreat. He has one conviction for violence, assault occasioning actual bodily harm on his estranged wife, Heather, and there is an order in force forbidding him to approach within two hundred yards of her current home. I have here the necessary documentary . . .'

'I'm sure you have, Mr Graham, I'm absolutely sure that you have.' He flapped at me impatiently with one immaculately manicured hand. 'But let me, if you will allow me, put your very persuasive rhetoric to one side for the moment and concentrate on the facts.'

He looked distastefully at my carefully bulked-up file and placed it, unopened, beside his blotter. I'd been counting on him getting bogged down, at least for a few minutes, on one murder, several cases of severe stomach upsets and lots of abstracted cash. Instead, things were taking an immediate turn for the worse.

'Yes, your Honour.'

'Bearing in mind that I am not in my dotage yet?'

'No, your Honour.'

'And, as we are in private, might I remind you that, er, bullshit does not invariably baffle brains, despite what they say in the lower echelons of the CID?'

'Thank you, your Honour.'

'Right, now we have cleared up our little misunderstanding, I'd be grateful if you'd stop gabbling and tell me what you want.'

'I think that the second set of conditions under the schedule to the Act have been satisfied, that giving him seven days to comply with an order would result in the evidence being disposed of, and that an immediate search under warrant would therefore be justified.'

'From what I've heard so far, Chief Inspector, I am prepared only to congratulate you on your unbridled optimism. What are your reasonable grounds for believing that Mr Cary is involved in either the murder, or the unwarranted demands with menaces, at all?'

'Well,' I said, hope rapidly flying out of the Chambers' windows, 'the blackmail offences may well be an inside job. Foster was obviously involved, Cary has a holiday home close to the murder scene, and there is considerable friction between individuals within the family business.

'I also have good reason to believe that he is under considerable financial pressure as well as having a conviction for violence which involved a woman.'

'And what about the material for which you wish to search?'

'Human blood, traces of vomit or tissue from Miss Foster, and the possibility of finding bank documents, cash or other private papers in connection with the blackmail offences.'

'All right,' his whole attitude was still benign, 'what do you do, Mr Graham, if you have reasonable suspicion that a person has committed a criminal offence?'

Dimly, I could see that the axe was about to fall. 'Arrest him,' I said.

'Very good. Now, correct me if I'm wrong, but once you've arrested a suspect for a serious arrestable offence, Section 18 of the Police And Criminal Evidence Act confers upon you a very extensive power to enter and search premises, does it not?'

'Yes, your Honour.'

'So you would therefore have all the power and majesty of Parliament behind you, without recourse to somebody as insignificant as me?' No longer Pickwick, he appeared to be making a bid for the part of Uriah Heep.

'But, your Honour knows that . . .'

'If you haven't got sufficient reason to arrest the man, not hard evidence, mind you, just reasonable suspicion, why on earth do you think I'm going to grant a warrant under the tightly defined provisions of this Act, to infringe his liberties and search his house?'

'But, your Honour . . .'

'Please go away, Mr Graham. Find me a genuine connection between this man Cary and your victim, and I'd be quite delighted to do what you ask.' He straightened his face and looked serious, almost sad. 'I suspect,' he added, 'that once you have found this connection, that you will arrest him and search his premises without any further assistance from my humble self.'

'Yes, your Honour.' I gathered up my useless file and prepared to depart.

'Good morning, your Honour.'

'Extraordinary, quite extraordinary,' he said.

The inquest consisted mainly of the medical evidence from Professor Lawrence, followed by an adjournment to a date to be fixed. I hadn't had much heart for another legalistic junket, not after my bruising experiences with Judge Brand. Funny how you can go off courts and lawyers and legal procedures within a matter of hours.

Afterwards, Andrew Lawrence, George and myself fore-gathered politely on the town hall steps, all of us overcoated in the face of another bitter Eddathorpe wind. There wasn't much to say. Lawrence's preliminary findings had been quite correct. His early assessment about the blow or blows, the victim's attempt to vomit and the ingestion of her stomach contents had been absolutely right. The only extra factor had been the alcohol, and at an estimated eighty millilitres per litre of blood there hadn't been a vast amount of that. We weren't, after all, looking at Rachel Foster's fitness to drive a car.

We were not a convivial party, and there was nothing outstanding to provide the content of a good professional chat. Lawrence, as usual, was stiff and distant, he simply found it difficult to socialise with the CID. George and I were just being formal-friendly, hoping for an early escape. We hadn't got anything against him, and, to tell the hypocritical truth, it was always in our own interests to stay on his right side with a spot of cautious buttering-up. I think he felt exactly the same.

We exchanged a few courtesies, said a word or two about the Coroner, his questions and the current state of play. Lawrence, swinging his briefcase, semi-consciously impatient to be gone, was already backing away when Simon Gell, accompanied by a smaller, plumper man in a raincoat came puffing up.

'It was supposed to start at two-thirty,' he said. 'Never expected to see you hanging around outside, I thought we were late.'

'Too late,' said George. 'We were on at two o'clock.'

'Damn!'

'You didn't miss much.'

'I was supposed to phone Maurice with the verdict.' He looked and sounded aggrieved, staring at all three of us as if his failure was somehow connected with a joint conspiracy directed against him. Andrew Lawrence, unintroduced, smiled vaguely, nodded, and took the opportunity to clear off. Personally, I was pleased to save myself a journey to Nottingham. It might be an opportune moment to have another chat with Mr Gell.

'There wasn't a verdict,' I explained, 'just the medical evidence from Professor Lawrence, there. Then they adjourned the inquest *sine die*.'

He glanced uncertainly from his tubby middle-aged companion to Lawrence who had immediately seized his opportunity; he had little to gaze upon but the pathologist's retreating back. The smaller, older man was obviously an employee, and I could see that Gell was dying to ask what one of my few phrases in Latin meant. He was reluctant to lose face, however, especially in the presence of one of his lowly-paid plebes.

'I wonder,' he said, almost diffidently, 'whether I could have a word?'

'Of course.' Generosity, after all, is my middle name. 'Why

don't you come and have a coffee with me, back at the nick? You could bring your friend.'

'Ron?' He looked more than doubtful. 'Look, I'm on a yellow line. I can park in your car park, can't I, and he can make his own way there?' Ronald, the inferior, was being dumped. Not entitled to share in conference secrets, then. 'You know your way, don't you, Ron? You could meet me there in about three-quarters of an hour.'

I nodded while George and I exchanged a significant glance. Three-quarters of an hour, and only for coffee? Perhaps.

'I'm a couple of hundred yards away, I don't suppose you want a lift?'

We shook our heads and turned away. I even gave Ron a smile and an amiable, backhanded wave. He was so obviously expendable, poor bugger, that I hoped he'd spend his time profitably in the nearest pub. Wherever he went, he was almost certainly going to have a more entertaining time than Simon Gell.

We stepped out briskly. 'The bleating of the goat attracteth the tiger,' murmured George.

'Something like that,' I agreed. 'Or maybe in this case, it's the other way round.'

'You're a bloody con man,' he said, and scowled.

'You came to the police station of your own accord, Simon, it was you who wanted a word.'

'And it was you who seized the opportunity to entrap me into coming here under false pretences.'

I sipped my coffee and sighed. Simon – we have this nasty habit of calling suspects by their first names – left his coffee untouched on my desk. George, asbestos-throated, rattled his empty cup and saucer over by the office window and treated our latest victim to his sharky smile.

'You aren't under arrest,' I explained, 'and you're just as free now as you were the moment you stepped in. I want you to understand that.' You can feel quite ashamed of yourself on these occasions, they're more of a well-worn cliché than a cunning ploy.

'And if I so much as twitch you'll lock me up as soon as look at me, won't you? D'you think I don't know that those are just weasel words?'

'Have I cautioned you?'

'No.'

'Am I recording what you're saying on tape?'

He looked around the room suspiciously. 'Not openly, not so far as I know.'

'Well, then,' I said.

'I'll tell you what,' said Simon Gell finally. 'I'll talk to you, if you'll talk to me.'

'Okay.'

George stirred, 'Within the constraints imposed on us by the nature of the enquiry, of course.'

'That's very good,' he said to me. 'I didn't see your lips move, and I didn't even notice when you pulled his strings just now.'

It was George's turn to scowl. He opened his mouth to make a withering reply, but at the last moment, well knowing that we wanted something, he restrained himself and held his peace.

'I don't see why we should fall out over this,' I said smoothly. 'There's just one or two things I'd like to clear up.'

'Me too.'

I ignored that, but I'd got a pretty good idea, apart from the question of the inquest, why he was visiting Eddathorpe, the seaside at the end of the world. I also knew, having stirred up the subject of personnel records with the lovely Linda, what his questions were likely to be.

'Tell me,' I said, 'exactly how long have you been working for the Carys?'

'It depends what you mean by work. I was a management trainee at one time, but it didn't work out.'

I raised my eyebrows and waited for him to volunteer some more.

'Oh, come on, Mr Graham, you've met them, you must

know how it is. Private company, the overwhelming majority of the shares divided six ways, and nobody except the old man, his wife and his brood are ever going to get a look-in there. Everybody else is dust under their chariot wheels. I can tell you that.'

'A six-way split?' I asked.

'Effectively, yes. The old man with the lion's share, sixty percent, the boys each have ten, Mrs Cary and Linda hold five percent apiece, no room for outsiders and that's it.'

'That,' said George, 'only came to ninety percent when I was at school.'

'There's Tony, you won't have met him; he's the youngest son. Second year at University now, I think.'

'Non-dissident, I take it? Satisfied with his ten percent?'

'Unlikely to poison Papa's food-stocks, you mean? You've got a cheek of your own, asking questions like that.'

'Because blood is thicker than water, after all?' George turned towards the table and replaced his empty cup.

'Something like that. Besides, I've got a living to earn, Sergeant. I left them to their own family devices seven or eight years ago, but I've had a contract with the Company for security for the past four. What makes you think I'd ever want to rock the boat?'

'What about your, er, girlfriend, Richard Cary's wife?'

He stared at me, apparently dumbfounded. Then, 'The little bitch!'

'Heather Cary?'

'Linda, you know very well who I mean.'

'I think you may be jumping to false conclusions,' I said.

'Never mind the whitewash, she's the only one of 'em you've seen and spoken to over the last couple of days.'

So much for family unity, but I wasn't there to protest anybody's innocence about anything, so I let that one ride.

'Please yourself, Simon. Is it true?'

'It wouldn't be Richard who told you,' he muttered, 'he's got too much to lose in the way of face.'

'Have you,' said George with intent to offend, 'been having it away with Richard Cary's wife?'

'Why ask me something that you obviously already know?'

'We wanted you to confirm it in your own fair words.'

Simon Gell levitated from his seat as if pulled by invisible cords.

'Whoa, George!'

'Sorry, Simon, but you aren't the only one who can make a smart-arse crack.' George sounded almost satisfied, the man who had done his bit.

Gell bared his teeth; nevertheless he relaxed and sank back into his place, 'Got to you, did I? Reckon it's only coppers who can bully people, do you, and steal all the best lines?'

'All right, that's enough, if we can clear up one or two problems here and now, Simon, you could say we're likely to be on the same side.'

'That's fine by me, so long as you keep your monkey quiet, that's all.'

George said nothing, but he gave him a look, which implied an immediate desire for a set of over-tightened handcuffs, followed by a long, bleak night in the cells.

'No offence, I just meant that I'm talking to the organ grinder right now, OK?'

'In that case, you can talk to me about your relationship with Richard's wife.'

'He's not *that* bothered about her,' said Gell. 'They've separated, anyway. Heather is over and done with, she's last year's model so far as he's concerned.'

'Apart from the loss of face?'

'Family business is family business, he got that from his dad. As for the rest, he's got other fish to fry.'

'Other women?'

'Sure.'

'Pays maintenance to Heather, does he?' George was trying again.

Simon Gell signalled an uneasy truce by answering the question, 'Sure, and he's still paying the mortgage on the family house until they sell it up, but he's living in an apartment now. You might as well know, she's still a director of the Company too, although she never attends. She gets directors' fees because she qualifies for the Board with two of Richard's shares.'

'But his sister and his mother have got five percent each. Richard Cary, the last of the big spenders, eh?'

'Directors' fees, housekeeping money,' Gell shrugged. 'Call it what you like, it served Richard's purpose at the time.'

'Is he broke?'

'On his salary? Plus the directors' fees, plus a list of expenses as long as your arm? I should worry if I was him!'

'What about you, Simon,' I asked, 'how much did you earn last year?'

'Around thirty-five thou . . .' he pulled himself up short. 'You devious bastard,' he said.

'Sorry?'

'Somebody really has been filling you up with poison, haven't they? Heather and her legend of shop till you drop? Is that it, the story of the plastic lady, eh? How can I afford to entertain such an expensive woman? It had to be a Cary, telling stories like that.'

'You mean it wasn't true?'

He looked at me with such an air of exasperation that I had to believe it was unforced. 'Of course it was true at the time. It was one of the few ways she had of getting her own back, spending his cash. He was a serial screwer; she was left at home. And just for your information, mate, it isn't always your slummy yobbos who go around beating up their wives.'

'Hence his conviction for assault and the restraining order, eh?'

'You have been busy,' he said in mock admiration. 'And now I get your drift. Simon hates his cousin; Simon beds his cousin's injured wife. She's a bit of a gold-digger and he's a bit of a mug, so he starts to blackmail his relations to finance the affair, and poisons the meat in the chill-cabinets in the family firm.'

'You've forgotten something,' said George. 'As the security

adviser, he then gets the job of tracking down the offender, too.'

'And where does Rachel Foster come in?' Totally unfazed by the accusation, he turned in his seat and stared ironically at George.

'Funny, that's just what I was going to ask you.'

'Sorry, can't help.' Suddenly, unexpectedly, instead of being offended, he laughed. 'But I'm sure you'll think of something in due course. Mind you, if you're thinking of Richard, you might ask him where he spent last weekend.'

'Go on,' I said, sounding bored, 'where did he spend last weekend?'

'Haven't you heard about the little cottage locally; roses round the door?'

'Yes,' said George happily, chipping in, 'we have. Pity you weren't at the inquest, though.'

Gell rose to the bait, 'Why's that?'

'If you had, you'd know that Richard Cary's weekend visits are neither here nor there. Rachel Foster was definitely dead by midnight Thursday night.'

'Oh, well then,' he didn't appear to be in the least disconcerted. 'Is it my turn now?'

'Turn?'

'To ask the questions. You've taken Cary's local personnel files, right?'

'Correct,' I nodded my head.

'And you're only really interested in the management, aren't you? The rest is just a smokescreen, OK?'

There was no point in being silly; he was obviously brighter than the average bear, 'OK.'

'Right then, one word, one question: Eddathorpe? What do you say?'

I stared at him woodenly.

'Aylfleet, then?'

I just couldn't resist it, never give a sucker an even break. 'I couldn't possibly comment on that,' I replied.

Chapter Sixteen

'I suppose,' said Superintendent Edward Baring, wearing his grim, early-morning face, 'that it was one of those things that seemed funny at the time?'

The Eddathorpe divisional commander leaned back in his chair and regarded me calmly across the width of his luxurious, leather-covered desk. Eddathorpe had been an independent Borough police force once, some fifty years before, and Teddy, the heir to the dear, dead past, had appropriated the office, the bookcase, the desk, the inkstand, and all the assorted fittings as well as the uncompromising attitudes associated with the long-dead chief constable's power.

'Sir?'

'Don't give me that, you know perfectly well what I mean.' He treated me to a fixed stare from his pale, slightly protrudent grey eyes, and compressed his thin, bloodless lips into a trap. Not, I gathered, an entirely happy man.

'Something to do with Aylfleet,' I asked cautiously, awaiting developments. 'Simon Gell?'

'Something to do with Aylfleet,' agreed Teddy not without irony, 'and a row involving a man called Reed. You've heard of him, I suppose?'

'Cary's manager in Aylfleet,' I said.

'The head of Cary's security turned up at his store first thing this morning, and started going through everything like a plague of locusts. Then he wanted sight of this Reed character's personal bank and building society accounts as well. He claimed he wanted to see if the manager was involved in any kind of scam.'

'Did he get them?' It was only of academic interest, and it probably wasn't the right thing to say.

'Mr Reed,' said Teddy, with icy restraint, 'called the police. He wanted Simon Gell and his accomplice thrown out of his store. He claimed that Gell was an independent contractor, not an employee of the company, and if his proper employers wanted to ask him any questions or see any documents, they could send an executive to see him themselves.'

'What happened?'

'Gell and his colleague left, eventually. Not before he'd told the Aylfleet uniform lads that the whole thing was entirely your fault. He claims that you've misled him, and he's on his way back to Eddathorpe right now.' He brushed one hand over the greying, scanty hair covering his narrow skull, awaiting, semi-patiently for my latest excuse. Narrow-skulled, narrow-minded, puritanical, that was Teddy. Despite a fundamental difference in temperament between us, however, we usually got on. My trials and tribulations, especially my occasional spats with Dorothea Spinks, the Aylfleet divisional commander, added interest and excitement to his somewhat mundane seaside life.

'Not misled him, exactly,' I said. 'I was preserving confidentiality; I allowed him to jump to the wrong conclusion, that's all.'

'All you've achieved is to set him on the rampage, he reckons he's now going to interview the managers of both the local stores.'

'Good luck!'

'Superintendent Spinks,' said Teddy with a hint of self-satisfaction, 'doesn't see things in quite that light. She says that her uniformed staff have got better things to do.'

'Sorry, boss.'

'You don't have to apologise to me. Talk to Miss Spinks, that's where you've got to make your peace.'

'Yes, sir.' I turned to leave.

'And Bob,' his voice stopped me in my tracks, 'if there's a repeat performance in Eddathorpe as a result of anything you've said and we get a call from Cary's store, it's not down to the uniforms. You, personally, can go and sort it out!'

Teddy playing consequences, and there were now five chiefs to my solitary Indian on the warpath in connection with this enquiry, at the latest count. Gently, very, very gently even, I closed my divisional commander's door.

Paula laid the statements on my desk, while Pat hovered in the background, the Goodall features suitably grave. Ever since the Rachel Foster debacle he had been keeping carefully out of my way.

'Pat took the statement from a Mrs Margaret Phipps,' she said quietly. 'She and her husband are retired. They live in one of the chalet bungalows on the hill above Ansell's Creek.'

'The Seagull's Nest,' said Pat, 'it takes all sorts, dun' it?' He pulled a face.

I was glad to see that his recent unfortunate experiences hadn't left him totally crushed.

'Come to the point,' I said. I wasn't yet prepared to let him know exactly how far I was prepared to forgive and forget. For the past few days I'd heard little or nothing about him, and I was basking in the relative peace.

'Mrs Phipps has got two little dogs,' he explained. 'Either her or her husband exercise them twice a day, they always take the same route, down the track from the bungalows to the road, turn left along the lane, and left again through the pines onto the beach. Last Thursday, her husband did the morning stint and she went down there in the early evening, around half-six, just after dusk.'

Paula looked at him impatiently, and he hurried on, 'Anyway, she didn't see anybody, but there was a dark green Mini with a hand-painted white roof parked among the pines when she went past with her dogs. She says they barked and yapped a bit around an old boat on the beach, but she called them off and followed the path back up the bluff and went home.'

'Armstrong's boat?' I asked.

'Yeah. Mind you, boss, it might not mean a lot. She's got a pair of those funny Tibetan terrier things, and they bark and yap at everything in sight.'

'OK, but we've had sightings of other cars, surely? What's the significance of this?'

'The statement of Mrs Wendy Pointer,' said Paula. 'She mentions Rachel's Mini, dark green with a white roof.'

'Rachel went missing on the Thursday morning,' I mused, 'but her aunt says that her car stayed put.'

'She left the hotel on Thursday morning,' said Paula stubbornly, 'it doesn't necessarily mean that she went missing straight away. What's to have stopped her popping back to the service road at some time and collecting her car?

'Then she's missing for nearly forty-eight hours, during which time she's killed, and somebody dumps her, using her own car after dark on Thursday, and then they return the vehicle to the service road at the back of the hotel.'

'And manage to put it back in exactly the same spot?'

'It doesn't have to be exactly, does it, boss? Not to a yard or two?'

'One,' I said, 'that pre-supposes that it's somebody who knows where she was staying as well as where she kept her car, and two, if what you say is right, they've got a bloody cheek.'

'Nerve,' said Patrick. Something he apparently admired.

'If it's the same car.'

I thought about it carefully, Rachel had left her aunt's hotel on Thursday, on foot, at around nine o'clock. She'd been found on the *North Star* by Armstrong at around eight-thirty on the Saturday morning, dead. By this time she had probably been dead a minimum of thirty-six hours according to Lawrence's final estimate. Give or take, as our Home Office pathologist had so helpfully said. If Mrs Phipps' sighting was right, she'd been pretty close to colliding with a murderer disposing of a very fresh corpse.

I thought about the shoeless state of the body, the pine needles, the sandy earth. Had she been killed in the wood? The searchers hadn't found any positive signs. In the Mini, then? Possible, I supposed, but very cramped for a struggle. Then again, why not? People managed to have sex, I reflected cynically, in spaces more confined than that.

'Have we got—'

'Her car,' finished Paula smugly. 'Yes, I had it removed to the police garage, just in case. Nobody's touched it so far, other than a quick look through. It wasn't terribly relevant until now.'

'We're a bit behind,' I grumbled. 'When did you take this statement, Pat?'

'Yesterday.'

I raised my eyebrows.

'They're not on the phone,' he muttered, 'and they were never around.'

'Not around on Saturday, or Sunday or Monday either?'

He shrugged, a hint of a whine entered his voice, 'When DI Spriggs gave me the action form, I did it straight away.'

I clocked on to the change of story, as well as Paula's grateful glance at Pat.

'Somebody had the enquiry form in their pocket,' she admitted. 'They left it outstanding. Sorry, boss.'

'You've spoken to that particular somebody, I take it?'

'Yes.'

'And,' I said unfairly, turning on Patrick, 'it wasn't you, for once?'

Miserably, he shook his head. That was unnecessary, and I'd gone too far. Man management on the police force, I chided myself, wasn't what it had been.

I've already said that I like the sausage machine on a murder enquiry, lots of statements, lots of descriptive forms, and above all information, information, information to follow up and file. Although it all sounds thoroughly boring and bureaucratic, it's an article of faith; you'll get there in the end if you just keep grinding on.

Problems do, however, arise: money, for example. Never mind the cost of man-and-woman power, the overtime, the overheads, and the cars. If the enquiry isn't being indexed on little cards, then cross-referenced and placed in something like a big shoebox, there are the computers to worry about. One computer plus all the supplementary bits, anyway, and you're more than welcome to ours.

It was all right back in 1985, or whenever the bloody thing was built. Our computer, it was the all-singing, all-dancing answer to an investigating officer's prayer, way back then. One Central Processing Unit, thirty-eight separate visual display units, and you could even run two or three major enquiries at once without worrying about stuff getting filed on to a paper system and lost.

But times change, the best time to buy a new one is always tomorrow. Not only that, Police Authorities always go red, white and blue every time somebody mentions cash. We are, apparently, due for a budgeted update in our system sometime soon. Sometime about 2005, that is, the wind being behind us and all being well.

In the meantime, being the boss, I'd got a newish VDU. The technicians, however, have to cannibalise bits of hardware and fiddle about with the elderly stuff in the incident room, and all just to keep our enquiries creaking along. At the cutting edge of technology, despite all the propaganda they keep putting out about Britain's modern police force, we are definitely not.

Still, we just had to keep struggling on. I spent a good three hours with my very own (strictly temporary) computer terminal, doing what I should have done before. Relying on your staff is one thing, especially people like Paula who know the system inside out. Leaving them totally alone to get on with it is quite another, although statement skinning and cross-referencing isn't quite my forte.

Not that I did very much more than skim through: four hundred and twenty statements with accompanying descriptive forms, where were you, why were you and what did you do? Not terribly inspiring, I had to admit. Lots of information from the public, though. We were collecting outstanding action forms like confetti, everything from the useless, *I knew Rachel at school*, variety to suggestions about the identity of the killer, complete with name and address. It's amazing what Eddathorpe neighbours will say about one another, the moment they fall out. Somewhere in here, I kept thinking depressively, there could lurk some vital piece of evidence, like the story of the mini that we just weren't tying up.

Lunch was two cups of coffee and a canteen pie, I had them brought in. Crumbs, I am told, are not especially good for keyboards, nor are they any great assistance in improving the performance of screens that keep going blank.

George popped his head around the door about twenty past two, 'You owe me a favour, boss.'

'You mean you've got a prisoner?' I wasn't really being hopeful.

'Yes and no.'

'Try me with the yes.'

'How about Alan Cobden?' he said.

'Not funny, George.'

'It's true, I short-circuited the control room sergeant on your behalf. He was just about to ring you, when I grabbed a set of car keys and took Pat Goodall to Cary's supermarket, instead.'

'Keeping it in the family, huh?' I said gloomily, 'I'm in trouble with Teddy and Pat's in trouble with me. That should have cheered him up.'

'Yeah,' George sounded very chipper, 'I had heard about it. Still, look on the bright side, Alan Cobden is now downstairs in the bin.'

'Why?'

'Theft and false accounting as far as I can work it out. Simon Gell and his little sidekick didn't appreciate you putting them off the scent. Once they'd found that there was nothing doing at Aylfleet, they promptly turned up here. Say what you like about Gell and his attitudes, he certainly knows where to look.'

'OK, he's an investigative genius, what exactly has he found?'

'A wages scam, mainly. It looks as though Cobden, and possibly his girlfriend, have been running Pusser's men, or women, as the case may be.'

'Speak English, George.'

'Pusser's men, they used to do it in the Navy in Nelson's day, non-existent sailors on the books. Cobden couldn't do it with full-timers, of course, they're all paid from the company's wages office, but part-time casuals are left to him. One or two extra check-out girls, a couple of trolley boys extra on the wages sheets, and thank you very much.'

'Evidence?'

'False names and addresses, Tax and National Insurance records. Get a few statements. It's sound but it's mostly up to us.'

'And, according to Gell, that makes him an extortionist, and possibly a murderer as well?'

'Something like that.'

'George,' I said wearily, 'Templeton's blackmailer has just clocked up something approaching seventy thousand pounds, so far. Wouldn't you think he was being a trifle petty if he was conning the company out of a few part-timer's wages as well?'

'Times are hard,' suggested George frivolously, 'and besides, boss, you should never look a gift horse in the mouth.'

Chapter Seventeen

'Well, that's it then,' said George. 'He won't talk to us.'

I glowered at Alan Cobden's retreating back, 'Give him time,' I said, as I watched the civilian custody officer leading the way down the cell passage with our latest victim shambling unhappily behind. 'A couple of hours counting bricks, and we'll probably be well away.'

'Oppressive conduct.' He didn't seem too concerned by the prospect, though.

'He's being detained in custody,' I replied virtuously, 'while further legitimate enquiries take place. Let's have another word with that sidekick of Simon Gell.'

The sidekick, fiftyish, plump, faintly shabby, and barely five foot four, sat in a waiting room while Patrick Goodall laboured on a preliminary statement, mostly for the look of the thing at this stage. It's all very well taking statements of complaint, but it isn't exactly straightforward, even when you're dealing with a minor fraud. Burglary statements are great, so are thefts, indecent assaults, and, comparatively speaking so are arsons and GBH. You've got a time, a date, a witness and an event he can talk about straight off the top of his head. Even piddling little frauds, however, involve a description of the system, an explanation of how it has been perverted, and the production of documents in accordance with the provisions of the Criminal Evidence Act. And that was just for a start.

Pat looked up from his labours when we came into the

room, he sounded frustrated. 'Mr Bentley can't tell us all that much,' he said.

'But you're an accountant, aren't you?' I asked.

The little man looked indignant. 'I'm experienced, if that's what you mean, but I haven't got any letters after my name.'

I sighed and sat down, no need to antagonise him. 'Sorry, Mr Bentley, that's not what I had in mind. You can tell us what's happened, right?'

'Of course I can, but this young man here wants chapter and verse. He wants to incorporate all three copies of the wages sheets, the Tax and National Insurance records, the lot. He reckons that a few false names and addresses, and the Eddathorpe records aren't enough. If he wants to be fussy, he'll have to go to head office for most of the proof.'

Pat, unusually diligent, groaned. 'It's going to take ages, boss. Ron here can tell us all about it all right, but there's loads of stuff to collect to tie it up. It's a trip to Nottingham, and two or three days' work.'

Ron. I smiled a little, at least they were on Christian name terms, so they hadn't fallen out. The problem, however, remained, a couple of days' work taking statements, obtaining all the documents and conducting a proper interview. The trouble was, however, we had a prisoner in the cells, and the custody sergeant's clock was ticking, right now. Besides, from our point of view, the current grounds for arrest were a convenient excuse for a more in-depth chat.

Cobden's detention, though perfectly legal, was hardly an earth-shaking event. You could hardly hold him forever for a wages fiddle. I doubted very much whether Teddy would let us keep him for as much as twelve, let alone the full twenty-four hours without charge. Pump him dry, and do it quick, otherwise our prisoner was going to walk.

George and I exchanged glances, and there was silence in the room for a few minutes apart from Pat's occasional queries, the rustle of statement paper, the occasional grunt and the sound of his pen.

'Just get the general story, Pat. We can produce the documents properly, and take further statements as we go on.'

'Yeah.' The pen continued to travel back and forth.

'I don't want to sound disloyal,' Bentley broke the silence once again, 'but I don't really see what you're playing at around here.'

'Playing at?'

'Sorry, I put that badly, I mean Mr Gell.'

'Would you like to explain?'

Bentley stared at me, apparently torn between exasperation and doubt, 'I would have thought . . .' he said. He fell silent for a few moments. 'Whatever I say is in complete confidence, of course?'

'Of course.'

'I don't want to lose my job.'

'No.'

'He can be very vindictive, you know.'

'Simon?'

'Mr Gell. He thinks you deliberately tried to make a fool of him, for a start. Sending him on a wild goose chase, you know.'

George started to grin, changed his mind, coughed instead and straightened his tie.

'And is this a wild goose chase, too?'

'I didn't mean it quite like that, but in my opinion, you're wasting your time. Just because a person's committed one crime doesn't mean he's guilty of everything else in sight.'

'Innocent until proved guilty?' asked George sententiously. 'Why don't you stop worrying and leave that sort of thing to us? These legal fictions are all very well for juries, but if I see a man scooting off round the corner when a shop's been burgled, and he's got a sheet of previous as long as your arm, it's a damn good indication that he's not just out for a jog.'

'Equally,' snapped the little man smartly, 'if you're working on a crime worth half a million, are you really likely to involve yourself in some petty back-street scam?'

'Depends how desperate you are,' argued George.

'How petty?' demanded Pat.

Bentley, having, in his own opinion at least, demolished George, turned to Pat. 'I haven't gone through this in any detail,' he said. 'I think Mr Gell has jumped the gun. This man Cobden has only been at the store about eighteen months, but just supposing he's been doing this right from the start. From what I've seen so far, he could only have taken three, or at the most four thousand pounds.'

Patrick Goodall looked impressed, 'Top whack?'

'Top, er, whack.'

And our blackmailer-cum-murderer, with the able assistance of the late Rachel Foster, had already clocked up seventy plus. Even conceding that the fiddle preceded the blackmail, once involved in the latter, Cobden would have had to have been either a completely barmy, or a very greedy, very stupid man.

'He's still Rachel Foster's ex-boyfriend,' insisted George stubbornly, 'he works for the complainant company, and from your own enquiries already, you know he's involved in crime.'

Bentley switched his attention back to his statement and shrugged. For a mousy little sidekick he wasn't doing too badly. 'Please yourself.'

It was naughty, very naughty; no office, no chairs, no table, no tape recorder and no formal interview. Just sitting there on the prisoner's hard wooden bed. The custody sergeant, hesitating uneasily in the cell passage outside, shouldn't have allowed it. In his situation I'd have never allowed it myself. The *Home Office Code of Practice*, vulgarly known as *The Green Fairy Book*, makes no provision whatsoever for the informal two-minute threat.

'You can still say anything you like,' said George.

'Or not,' I interposed hypocritically. 'You can still say absolutely nothing, if you wish. But the evidence is there, isn't it? Even if you keep quiet, it's only a matter of time.'

'What you really ought to be doing,' murmured George kindly, 'is thinking about Sam.'

'Samantha? What about Sam?'

'Well,' my detective sergeant sounded regretful. 'What would you think if you were in our situation. It's only logical, is that.'

'You bastards, you utter pair of shits.'

'Aw, come on now, what are we supposed to think? After all, she's your girlfriend, and she *does* work there,' wheedled George.

'I'm going to get a lawyer,' snarled Alan Cobden unwisely, 'and when he gets here, he's going to pulverise you two.'

'It's your decision,' said George, helplessly spreading his hands, 'entirely your decision, Alan; absolutely up to you. We're only trying to put you in the picture, old son. Getting you to see sense, right?'

Alan Cobden brooded for a while.

'OK,' I said finally, 'time's up. If you want a solicitor present, just tell the custody sergeant on the way up for interview when we book you out.'

There was a cough, a shuffle, and the sound of hastily retreating footsteps in the corridor outside.

It was a long, hard day. Alan Cobden was a much harder nut than we were ever entitled to think. 'I didn't do it,' 'I didn't do it,' and 'I didn't do *anything*.' That was his style.

Four and a half hours, one meal and several cups of weak tea later, he was still saying it. A man who could hold on to an absolutely hopeless position, he hardly even perspired. Frustrating for the interviewers, but I had to admit it showed a certain amount of style.

'You ever been in custody before?' asked George, in a pause while we changed the interview tape.

'No, why?'

'You're an absolute natural,' he replied, paused for the statutory two seconds and added, 'not that it's going to do you a lot of good.'

'OK,' I said once we were rolling, and I cautioned him

again. Silly, really, he knew all about not being obliged to say anything, or at least anything useful.

'I want to turn now,' I said, 'to the offences of making unwarranted demands with menaces from Cary's Stores.'

'You what?'

'Blackmail, poisoning the food.'

'Oh, that.'

'You seem to have taken that very well.'

'I was expecting it, and all because of that hysterical git, Simon Gell.'

'Would you care to explain?'

'Why not? None of this is anything to do with me. I am a store manager, right? Therefore I manage the bloody store. I work five, sometimes six or even seven days a week. No sodding overtime, I have to take time off.

'If I'm supposed to have taken cash out of flaming cash machines, perhaps you can tell me how I find the time?'

'On all these days off,' said George smartly. 'You just said so yourself.'

Not the answer to the problem and I knew it, I scowled warningly at George.

'I suppose,' said Alan Cobden sarcastically, 'that you've got a timed record from all these bank and building society machines?'

I nodded.

'For the sake of the taped interview,' he recited, 'I'd like to record that I saw the chief inspector nod.'

I smiled at him, he'd obviously been watching *The Bill*, but there are days when only a sustained burst of police brutality will do.

'You seem remarkably well informed.'

He returned the compliment, stretching his face into a confident, cocky grin. 'You can thank Simon Gell for that.'

I could imagine, it explained a lot. Simon Gell, once he'd captured Cobden, had left the statement of complaint to Bentley, and he hadn't even stayed around to gloat. He'd bailed out, promising a statement later, pleading pressure of work, almost as soon as George arrived at the Eddathorpe store. Silently, I expressed my thanks to the amateur interviewer; the man who'd probably given away our line of questioning and buggered us up.

'For an innocent man, Alan, you seem to have a pretty good grasp of what's going on.'

'I'm far from stupid, and I've had time to think. Never mind messing around with the wages sheets, look at my days and hours of work. Gelly-belly said there'd been loads of withdrawals from the machines, so I admit that some of them may coincide with my time off. Most of 'em won't, and I'll bet you on that; how about a pound to a pinch of shit?'

Clever enough in its way, but I scarcely blinked. 'Which brings us,' I said smoothly, 'to Rachel Foster.' And in strict accordance with the rules laid down in the *Green Fairy Book*, I cautioned him again.

For the first time his overweening self-confidence took a dive. However well prepared he'd been for the interview, he didn't like that. I began to feel happier. In one area at least, Simon Gell had kept his blundering size nines entirely off my grass.

'You may have been at work, Rachel Foster may have been at work, but not all the time.'

'What's that supposed to mean?'

'It means that Rachel was collecting the extortion money from the machines. Rachel was your ex, you work for Cary's, you're on the fiddle, so work it out for yourself.'

'You can't believe . . .'

'Oh yes I can, let's go through your alibi for last Thursday, shall we, the day she died?'

'I've already told you, both Sam and I were at work.'

'Never mind Samantha, let's talk about you. You arrived at work about eight o'clock, from what you said?'

'Yes.'

'And you reckon you were there until about half-six?'

'OK.'

'No, Alan, it isn't OK, I'm going to go through everything

again, and I want details of everybody who spoke to you, saw you for every moment of your day.'

'Why? What's all this about? It's all on my statement already.'

'We know what's in your statement,' growled George, 'but perhaps we don't believe you quite as much as we did when you made it.'

'She was nothing to me, we hadn't been out together for years.'

'Maybe she wasn't your girlfriend, Alan.' I waited to see the relief dawning in his eyes before I struck. 'But that doesn't mean that you weren't her, er, business partner, does it?'

'Screwing Cary's Supermarkets?'

'You've got it in one.'

'Christ!'

'Is that why you killed her, Alan?'

'I didn't kill anybody, I don't know what you mean.'

'You were a bit too keen to tell us all about your climbing weekend, weren't you?'

'This is a wind-up, what the hell are you on about now?'

'Rachel Foster went missing, died, on the Thursday. You tried to play the innocent by going on about your activities from Friday afternoon to Sunday night.'

'You said you found her on Saturday, I'd no idea—'

'You work for Cary's.'

'Yes.'

'You knew her well.'

'I don't deny—'

'She was involved in a plot to get their money, effectively she was a thief, you're a thief and now she's dead.'

'That's madhouse stuff, you're just trying to bounce me into . . .'

'Bounce? That's pretty rich, coming from you. You've given away about as much as an oyster on superglue, so far. We've got the wages records, but you're not a thief, you work for the complainants, you were involved with a woman associated with the blackmail, now she's dead and we're trying to bounce little mister innocent into making an admission. Is that right?'

Ask the questions, get the answers, watch his face. And all the time, I had a pretty good idea that it wasn't going to wash. It was such a tenuous link, and what Bentley had said still festered at the back of my mind: if he was such a super-criminal, why should he still go ahead with a second-rate wages fraud?

'But I haven't done anything wrong!' His voice rose an octave as his face reddened; I wasn't too proud of it, but something was happening at last. He looked on the verge of tears.

'Oh, but you have. Why should we believe you, Alan? We already know you're a thief.'

'And I'm not the only one, am I? Even supposing I am.'

George couldn't wait, 'The girlfriend, eh?'

'What girlfriend?' Wrong question, wrong moment, I thought we'd broken the rhythm and brought him up short.

George was equal to the occasion, however, he backed off. 'Sorry, Alan, I forgot. We do have a choice of two.'

It was the final needle; he was beyond rational self-interest now.

'Samantha? It's nothing to do with Samantha!' he screamed. 'Why don't you go after somebody worthwhile for a change? Bullies! Cowards! What about having a go at the real criminals? You'd never dare to put one of the big bastards like Richard Cary in the cells!'

Chapter Eighteen

'And do you?' asked Paula wickedly.

'Do I what?'

'Dare to put Richard Cary in the cells.' She was, of course, winding us both up. Personally, I'd lock up the Home Secretary, irrespective of Party, given half a chance. But Richard Cary presented us with problems as well as an opportunity. I was being a bit of a dog in a manger, but I wanted to figure out a way of using Alan Cobden's information without getting Colin Templeton and his merry men involved. Besides, I still wanted to search his holiday cottage: ambition is a dreadful thing, once it strikes.

'He might not,' said George depressingly, 'be telling the truth.'

'And then again he might,' Paula smiled encouragingly. 'It sounds good to me. Cobden was a trainee in Cary's Wholesale Cash and Carry outfit less than two years ago, and he says that he knows that Richard was working a nice little scam. A very credible little scam, it seems to me, and now he's willing to tell.'

'It's a very old story,' muttered George. 'Cobden could have made it up. Cheques for payment of accounts come in; Richard stops and then restarts the computer sales ledger printout to conceal their arrival. He steals the equivalent amount of cash, reintroduces the cheques into the banking to balance the books, and there you go.'

'And you only get caught if the auditors ignore the sales ledger, examine the computer log, and go back to the individual client accounts at source. All we have to do is grab the records, and check the computer log for the reruns and the times he was switching on and off.' Paula, our very own expert, now had the bit firmly between her teeth.

'You are,' I said superciliously, 'forgetting one small point.'

They both stared at me incredulously, Paula had been on the courses, George had a natural bent, but there was nobody more computer-illiterate than I was. I usually liked these things explained to me in very simple language, and at least three times.

'Go on, boss,' said George rudely, 'tell us about the technicalities of this big computer fraud and give us all a laugh.'

'Nothing to do with computers: jurisdiction,' I said.

'Eh?'

'Cary's Cash and Carry business is in Nottingham, and we, just in case you haven't noticed, are way out here. What we are supposed to do is hand this one over, and wave Richard Cary and his alleged misdemeanours a fond goodbye.'

'It's all part of our murder enquiry,' suggested George.

'Go on.'

'Richard Cary has allegedly been screwing his old man's company for some considerable time. Therefore, if he's behind the current large-scale blackmail, Rachel Foster was also part of the blackmail set-up, therefore killed her, and . . .' his voice trailed away.

'Evidence?' I asked.

'You don't need specific evidence, just reasonable suspicion to make an arrest, you said so yourself.'

'I'm not talking about arrests, I'm talking about trouble with the Crime Squad, not to mention the Nottinghamshire Police for rubbing our jammy little fingers all over their job.'

'We could always tell 'em how sorry we are later, after we've cleared everything up at our end,' suggested George.

'By that time,' I said gloomily, 'their Chief and our Chief

and the Director of the National Crime Squad will be engaged in a three-sided civil war.'

'*If* we manage to clear it up,' said Paula.

'What's that supposed to mean?'

'Funny about Cobden,' she said thoughtfully. 'He's managed to keep this story under his hat for about eighteen months. I wonder why?'

'But has he?' George grinned cynically. 'Kept it under his hat, I mean? He's the youngest supermarket manager they've got. From trainee to boss in a couple of years. It's not a wonderful job, but he's done far better than most; not only that, he's summoned up the confidence from somewhere to run his very own scam.'

'What, he's successfully blackmailed Richard Cary?' retorted Paula. 'That's even odder, if Cary is as ruthless as you say.'

'I think,' I said sadly, 'that this is one we're going to have to share with our friends and colleagues on the Crime Squad, after all. We haven't got enough, so there's no point in us jumping the gun.'

'Any minute now,' said George to Paula, but meaning me all the same, 'you're going to tell me that we're all on the same side, and that we ought to be working for the universal good.'

'Balls, Sergeant.' It wasn't often she swore, it was all the more heartfelt, therefore, when it came.

'Thank you, ma'am!'

'Of course,' said Paula thoughtfully, 'there is an alternative. Before we hand anything over we can make one final attempt to discover whether Richard Cary and his shenanigans are anything at all to do with us.'

'Search his cottage, anyway?'

'No. Well, not quite yet. Why not go and talk to the one person who *really* knows him? Let's question his estranged wife.'

Around two hundred and twenty thousand pounds'-worth, at an educated guess. One of those late Victorian, marginally faded, gothic-looking houses in Nottingham's Mapperley Park. Nothing faded or old-fashioned about the interior, though. Dark green leather Chesterfield sofas, gold-tooled, green leather-topped occasional tables, a deep shag-pile carpet and a huge brass-fendered gas fire, complete with artificial logs in what Heather Cary was pleased to call the lounge. It was, to my mind, all a bit of a mistake, especially the Chinese cabinet with cables peeping coyly from the back. Not entirely to my taste then, the elaborate chandelier, the wall lights, and a late Middle Kingdom TV.

OK, I was feeling slightly ratty by this time, a touch of sour grapes, and a tinge, perhaps, of the good old green-eyed god. Something to do with the rain perhaps, the grinding two-hour journey with a series of long vehicles on single carriageways in front, and George in one of his bloody-minded moods. Even apart from that, there was still nothing whatsoever going our way. The Scenes of Crime team had examined Rachel Foster's car: a road atlas, a stub of pencil, an out-of-date fire extinguisher, and three screwed-up toffee papers among the dust and gravel on the floor. No fingerprints.

The tyre treads had, however, told us a slightly different tale, sandy earth and pine needles from the track leading through the straggle of woodland leading to Ansell's Creek. Nothing especially exciting, though, it merely confirmed what we already knew.

'Apart from that,' said the SOCO man with an air of perverse self-satisfaction, 'it does tell me that somebody was just bright enough to wipe over the car. Zilch on the steering wheel, nothing on the mirror and even the door handles were as bare as a baby's bum.'

'It's something of an improvement, all the same,' I was feeling slightly bitter and twisted at the time. 'The yobs round here tend to set 'em on fire once they've had their ride.'

'OK, so you're looking for a house-proud amateur,' said the man from Scenes of Crime.

On first acquaintance Richard Cary's wife was something of an unexpected bonus, though. Pretty rather than beautiful, smooth round face, full lips, straight nose and dark hair. She also looked quiet and sensible as opposed to snooty and arrogant on first acquaintance, which made a nice change for that particular clan.

Mid thirties, a year or two older than her husband, perhaps, wearing a pale blue wool dress, a little tight over her marginally over-generous breasts and hips, an expensive-looking necklace of small gold leaves, and a tiny gold watch. No wedding ring, I noticed. Not the kind of lady then to mourn and pine and hang about. Husband Richard was already yesterday's news.

She sat us both down on the stiff unyielding Chesterfield, and following the direction of my gaze on her ringless fingers, she smiled. 'No, I'm not divorced yet, I'm just practising feeling free.'

She'd wrong-footed me straight away, 'I see.'

'I'm sure you don't,' the smile stayed effortlessly in place. 'Is Richard in some sort of trouble? I hardly expected a visit from the police.'

I babbled something about not really, no, launched into the circumstances of the Cary Supermarkets' blackmail, and did my best to give the impression that it was all purely routine.

'I've been seeing Simon, you know.'

'Simon Gell?'

'What other Simon is there, Chief Inspector? He does keep me up to date with the family saga, and I am not, whatever Richard may have said about me, entirely a fool.'

'Then you will also know,' I said quietly, 'that my Force is running a murder investigation which seems to be connected with all this.'

'Connected? In what way?'

'I suppose Mr Gell has told you that our victim, a young woman called Rachel Foster,' said George, 'was detained near a cash machine which had been used to remove money originally belonging to your husband's firm?'

'My husband's father's firm,' she corrected him lightly. 'You must never under any circumstances forget who is really in charge.'

'Meaning?'

'Absolutely nothing sinister, I assure you. I'm just stating a fact. Dear old Maurice is, and always will be, the top dog.' There was nothing specific in either her general attitude or her voice, but something told me that the lady did not hold anything about her father-in-law, apart perhaps from his wealth, as particularly dear.

'But your husband is a major shareholder, as well as being the MD.'

'Major? He holds ten percent.'

'And you are a shareholder, too?'

'You've obviously been doing your homework, Chief Inspector. You should therefore also know that I hold the bare minimum, which entitles me to sit on the Board and draw directors' fees. Er, otherwise known as housekeeping money,' she said.

'I see.'

'Again, I very much doubt it.' She waited for a moment to ensure that she had my full attention and added, 'Being associated in any way with Maurice is like being a minor functionary at the Borgia court.'

'You wouldn't describe yourself as being an active director, then?'

She chuckled derisively, 'No.'

'What happens,' George was exercising his unbridled curiosity yet again, 'if it comes to a divorce?'

Momentarily, her expression froze, none of our damned business, after all, and I waited for the blast. It never came, instead, she breathed out slowly. 'That,' she said eventually, 'is a matter for my solicitor, and it's probably the best question you've asked all day.'

'Money-wise?' persisted George.

'Settlement-wise,' she agreed. 'They can vote me off the Board, anytime they like. But my shares are a negotiable asset when push comes to shove, and I don't see Maurice being keen on an ex-member of the family retaining any part of his precious empire.'

I was puzzled. 'Surely,' I said, 'you only possess two shares?'

'True, but it will be two too many for Maurice, believe me. And they are pretty valuable; the whole share issue only amounts to a thousand, after all. Imagine the asset value of the company, then work out what each individual share must be worth.'

I couldn't, but I was prepared to bet that she knew a man who could.

'Forgive me, Mrs Cary,' George had obviously decided that he was on a roll, 'but how would you describe the relationship between Richard, your husband, and his Dad?'

'Unhealthy, fearful?' She was smiling, it was out before she'd fully considered, and it sounded flip. 'No, sorry, I'm feeling a wee bit grouchy and anti-Cary at the moment, and that was designed to shock. Respectful but wary; very wary, I'd say, on Richard's side. It's Bernard who's scared stiff.'

'Bernard?'

'The second son and Daddy likes to let him know the score. *Work harder, Bernie, your big brother is way ahead. If it wasn't a family business, I might find myself having to kick you out.*'

'As stark as that?'

'Well, no, not quite. But Maurice Cary is building a dynasty, and he can be a very ruthless man. That's part of my problem with Richard, you see, no kids.'

'And so . . .'

'Richard genuinely wants to follow in father's footsteps, and so he tried to take it out on me.' She handed round a small, brittle smile, and uncrossed and recrossed her legs, gently smoothing her skirt as she did so. 'Bit of a tragedy, really, for both of us. Still, too late now, and you don't need to hear about my problems, that's not why you came.'

'What about,' said George disingenuously, 'the youngest son?'

'Tony? So that *is* the reason? You actually did come to dish the family dirt? I don't mind talking to you: not that it's going to do you the slightest bit of good. Maurice has high hopes of

Richard, but Tony is his favourite, and ironically, he's the only one who appears to stand a chance of getting out.'

'He's away at University, isn't he?'

'Aston. Doing a degree in Social Sciences with a view to doing good.' There was a note of admiration as well as a suspicion of derision in her voice. 'He's certainly managed to snooker the old man. Maurice doesn't know whether to boast about his independent spirit, or scream with disappointment and rage because he's determined not to go into the family firm. Maurice wouldn't have minded, I suppose, if it had only been Linda going around doing something daft.'

'Which brings us to the only daughter,' I said.

'Loyal little Linda? Otherwise known as the poison dwarf.'

She waited awhile to let that one sink in before she condescended to explain. 'I can't altogether blame her, I suppose. She's been stuck there in a man's world all her life. Maurice doesn't especially care about *girls*.' She made a tiny moue of disgust. 'She should have gone out and bred a few babies, boy babies for choice, then, according to Maurice, she'd have been of some use.

'Unfortunately for Linda she didn't cotton on. Instead, she's gone around compensating like mad. Daddy this, Daddy that, and whenever necessary, she's Daddy's chief intelligence officer and family spy.'

'That sounds like personal experience talking.'

She hesitated momentarily. 'Let's put it this way,' she said finally, open bitterness in her voice. 'I once confided in Linda, about a couple of, er, hospital visits, shall we say? And Maurice wasn't terribly keen on me as a daughter-in-law after that.'

Even George looked uneasy, but opening other people's cans of worms is all part of the job. Middle class people in middle class houses with middle class ways. It all looks so smooth and easy when you're casually peering into their warm, well-lit living rooms from outside. Sure, Richard had been violent. Richard had been a womaniser, and Richard had dumped his wife. He might also, I had to remind myself, have killed Rachel Foster and poisoned the food in Cary's supermarkets.

And he'd certainly, according to Alan Cobden at least, been cheating the company well prior to all that. Nevertheless, I felt almost squeamish, as if we'd somehow managed to go one revelation too far. There was, however, still the cottage and the money, so I had another go.

'Has he had any recent financial troubles?' I said.

'Other than me?' Simon Gell had obviously been a faithful reporter of conversations. 'Not so far as I know, Chief Inspector, why?'

'Not,' I persisted, 'over the past eighteen months, shall we say?'

'No, I don't think so, and I'm not sure that this is a legitimate line of enquiry. I think you ought to ask him that yourself.'

Well, bugger me, or words to that effect. She'd discussed the state of her marriage, her in-laws, and her chances of pregnancy within twenty minutes of meeting me, but one hint of the unmentionable, cash, and she was prepared to turn all bourgeois and shy.

'No problems?' I persisted.

'Not that I know of, and none to make him threaten to poison the food on his father's shelves.'

'But that's how he'd see it?' asked George.

'I beg your pardon?'

'You said his father's, not the company's shelves.'

Her eyes narrowed, 'You think that's significant? Something in the nature of a Freudian slip?'

'I only wondered,' murmured George.

'I can see where this is leading, I'm not stupid, you know. You're about to ask me about our weekend cottage, and whether Rachel Foster was one of his girls. Anyway, I very much doubt it, a dumpy, semi-employed schoolteacher like that.' Not to mention a liar and a crook, but Heather was still a twenty-four carat snob, as well as speaking ill of the recently, violently dead.

'And how would you know that, Mrs Cary?'

'Know what?'

'Dumpy, I think you said.'

'She was living in this City, and they do publish newspaper photographs around here.'

'She was,' I said cruelly on the spur of the moment, 'not an unattractive young woman. When I last saw her alive, that is.'

She considered me carefully for a moment before she replied, 'You aren't going to make me feel guilty,' she said, 'and I am quite convinced that this young woman's death had nothing to do with us.'

'Us?'

'Nothing to do with either Richard or myself.'

'I hadn't for a moment suggested . . .'

'No, but you're both policemen, don't tell me that the thought hadn't crossed your mind.'

'When,' said George heavily, 'did you last visit your husband's holiday cottage, Mrs Cary?'

'Not since the spring.'

'And the Eddathorpe area, particularly Ansell's Creek?'

'Eddathorpe, the Spring Bank Holiday weekend, just as I've said. This Creek place, not at all.'

'But it's a local beauty spot, it's quite popular in the summer. How long have you and your husband owned the cottage?'

'Four years.'

'Do you still have a key?'

'No, I do not, and even if I did I would refer you to Richard. We may be separated, but this is beginning to sound increasingly tacky, and I am not going behind his back.'

'And you say you've never been to Ansell's—'

'No, and before you ask, I have no idea whether Richard has been there or not, but I can practically guarantee that somebody like Rachel Foster would not feature in his sexual plans.'

'I reckon she's frigid,' moaned George unfairly, once we were safely on the other side of the doorstep. 'Simon's welcome, who on earth would want to get seriously involved with a woman like that?'

Chapter Nineteen

The flat was in one of those converted Victorian warehouses down by the river Trent, very upmarket, with over-landscaped, shrub-infested gardens, and spindly, dangerous looking iron balconies attached to the first and second floor walls. A flock of expensive cars were parked on the forecourt outside. Richard Cary might be maintaining an estranged spouse, but he wasn't exactly down to a crummy bed-sit and a second-hand Skoda, I decided.

'Another lot?' asked the red-haired female who answered the door. She was practically in tears. 'Why haven't you brought him with you? I hope you've come back to apologise, and tidy up.'

'Sorry, I don't understand you,' said George.

'Richard. You thick, or something? It's bloody disgraceful, and I want him back.' My heart sank; so did we. Want him, I mean, never mind the back.

Young, willowy, green eyes, translucent silk top and very tight jeans. Despite the strong Nottingham accent, she was obviously George's type. Mine too; Angela seemed a long way away.

'I'm sorry,' I said, 'Miss, er . . .'

'Weston, Hilary Weston, Richard Cary is my partner, and just for your information, mate, it's Ms.'

Oh, dear.

'We are police officers,' said George inadequately, producing his warrant card, 'but we're not from round here.'

'So that's your excuse! I don't care where you're from; I've had one mob trampling through already and you're not coming in here.'

'You've had a visit from the local police?'

'I've already told you, they arrived a couple of hours ago, and now they've taken him away. You wait!' she added aggressively, her voice rising. 'His solicitor will soon sort you out.'

Flushed, angry, tearful, she was almost the epitome of the maiden in distress. George took charge.

'It's a shame,' he said hypocritically, 'we only came to ask a few questions, and now they've upset you. Where were this lot from?'

'You really don't know anything about it?' She eyed the bulky, middle-aged figure, the thick grey thatch and the sober expression. Suddenly she seemed disinclined to slam the door in our faces, maybe he reminded her of Dad.

'Hilary,' he said impressively, 'we're as surprised as you.'

'You don't sound at all like that Templeton person,' she said doubtfully. 'He was very rude. D' you think I did the right thing?'

'About the solicitor? It's what his family would have wanted, I'm sure you did.'

'You know his family?'

'Chief Inspector Graham,' George waved one graceful, reassuring hand, 'has been working with them. He knows Mr Cary senior pretty well.'

'Oh, I see.' It was more than I did, but I was quite willing to go along with George's old-fashioned diplomacy, it was a dying art.

'It's a bit awkward,' she said. 'I didn't like to ring Mr Cary senior myself.'

'Awkward?' asked George. 'Oh, yes, I see . . . I'm sure it would be all right. It's not as though you were pushing yourself forward . . . taking into account the circumstances,' he said.

You had to admire him, not only had he presented me as some sort of family retainer, he was employing the delicate circumlocutions of a middle-aged washerwoman discussing female ailments with a neighbour over the fence.

'You think I ought to do it, then?'

George shrugged. 'I don't see why not.'

We were there, right out in the open hallway, and there was no chance of giving this particular representative of the Citizens' Advice Bureau a swift tap on the ankle, or even a hard warning hack. It's all very well pursuing your own advantage, but George appeared to be setting out to make life miserable for fellow members of the CID.

'Would you like to come in while I do it?' she asked, looking almost pleadingly at George. It was breathtaking, two minutes with the ageing Rudolph Valentino, and she'd done a complete volte-face.

'It was Richard we really wanted,' said the professional hypocrite casually, 'but then again . . . if you feel you need a bit of moral support.'

I shuffled inside in the wake of my devious detective sergeant, while she continued to open up and chat. I wasn't inclined to spoil his success, but I had the distinct feeling that I, personally, had achieved the lofty rank of his acting police cadet.

'I didn't ring his brief straight away,' she confided, 'I was that upset and confused. Then I had to search all round for the number in his desk. By the time I got around to it, his lawyer already knew.'

'That can't be bad then, can it?' he enthused. 'It's upsetting I grant you, love, but he must have rung from the police station. They are giving him his rights.'

'Yes,' she said doubtfully, 'yes I suppose so, but I don't understand what's going on.'

'What exactly did they say?' My turn at last to make a bid to recover status and earn some of my not inconsiderable pay.

'They had a piece of paper, a warrant thing. Then they searched the study and took all his computer disks away. They were going on about money from the wholesale side of his business, and something about his cousin. Richard wanted to keep me out of it, and I didn't understand too much about what was going on.'

'His cousin, Simon Gell?'

'That's right.'

'Bloody whistle-blower,' I muttered under my breath.

'Sorry?'

'I was just saying, I don't understand too much about it, either,' I said.

The flat didn't look too bad, considering it had been searched. By and large the living room remained its modern, expensively-appointed self. Largely steel and glass tables and chairs, rugs and polished parquet, I noticed, as well as a wheat-coloured suite. There was more than one way in which Richard Cary, domestically speaking, appeared to have started all over again.

The study, a twelve-by-ten box, with a window overlooking the river looked slightly forlorn. Books had obviously been removed from shelves and roughly replaced, a cupboard door had been left open, half a dozen box files containing correspondence had been rifled and a desk diary had been left open on an office chair. Personally, as the proud possessor of a warrant thing, I would have taken the lot.

She went over to the diary and picked it up, 'Business phone number,' she murmured distractedly. 'If you're sure it's all right to ring his Dad?'

George nodded encouragingly, no doubt relishing his role as the new family friend, the purveyor of worldly wisdom and fatherly advice. Personally, I was imagining myself in Colin Templeton's shoes. Our behaviour smacked of treason and I was far from sure.

'Hello,' said Hilary into the telephone mouthpiece, 'I'd like to speak to Mr Maurice Cary, please.'

The phone yakked briefly, there was a pause. 'Mr Cary? Yes, well, my name's Hilary Weston . . . Yes, that's right, I'd like to speak to him . . . It's very important.'

The phone continued to yak, I couldn't make out the words, but somehow, I vaguely recognised the snappy voice at the other end, and I was more than familiar with the tone.

She flushed, 'I sooner speak to him myself, if you don't mind.'

Another burst of sound.

'Yes, I do know who you are. I'd sooner speak to him myself, all the same.' A longer pause this time, followed by an obvious rejection at the other end. 'Very well then, *Linda.*' By now it was becoming obvious that the daughter of the house was in the process of making another friend. 'Just tell him that his eldest son has been arrested by the police, OK?'

Flushed, angry, and inclined to ignore any further conversation, she removed the receiver from her ear and prepared to bang down the phone. It was only then that I managed to hear the latter end of Linda Cary's tinny message, 'They're already at our warehouse,' she said. 'My father's gone to—'

Then she was cut off.

'Bitch!'

'Er,' said George.

'There's a word for people like that!'

I thought she'd already used it, but, 'She can be a bit of a dragon,' I admitted.

'Well, I'd never have thought it. You were only trying to help, and you're practically family, after all,' murmured my detective sergeant insidiously.

'I'm sorry,' she said, 'really sorry that you had to overhear a thing like that. Some people . . .'

'Well,' he said magnanimously, 'they've got the message, anyway. I shouldn't worry about it if I was you.' She was still hypnotised. 'After you've been so helpful, too.'

'Never mind.'

'What did you want to ask him about, anyway?'

'We-ll, we've been having a bit of trouble with one of his managers in our area, you know.'

'Yes?'

'Over on the East Coast.'

'I see.'

'We wondered whether he'd been over there himself on Thursday of last week?'

'Thursday? I can't really tell you. Wednesday and Thursday, he was on business somewhere. He was certainly out of town both days.'

'Ah, you know about the weekend cottage near Eddathorpe, I suppose? Did he say anything, did he stay there overnight, perhaps?'

Her face stiffened, 'No, he came back here, but he was very late,' she said. 'But that Templeton man was interested for some reason, he just kept banging on. Richard seemed pretty upset when they searched his study, and especially when they took the cottage key.'

My first stop was Central police station, where Fairfield greeted the news of Cary's arrest with an irritated snort. 'You should have nicked him yourself, while you had the chance.'

'But it was you who wanted me to be cautious,' I said.

'Well, in my opinion your supermarket manager sounded completely kosher. I was only warning you against information originating with Faithless Frank. Once you heard about the thieving you should have dragged this Cary character inside, straight away.'

'But,' I protested, 'there's no link between Richard Cary and our victim at all.'

'It's not,' said Fairfield sententiously, 'a perfect world.'

'Thank you, sir.'

'It's no use coming crawling round looking for sympathy from me. It's your case, Bob. What do you intend to do?'

'See Templeton,' I said. 'Now.'

I met Christopher Bowyer on the way out. He bared his teeth in something approximating a triumphal leer. Not only had he heard of my present difficulties, he'd only too probably been back to Roger Prentice to scrounge for staff, only to be presented with my *billet doux*. Our relationship had not improved as a result.

'Sex and travel to you, too,' he said over one shoulder as we passed through the outer door.

'You got a new feud going?' asked George. 'Or was that meant to be something about your little note?'

'No idea, probably cracking up under the strain,' I said casually, 'some people are very easily upset.'

Over at the Crime Squad offices, life was definitely on the up and up. Lots of carefully straightened faces, interspersed with one or two innocent smiles.

'Sorry,' said Colin Templeton, 'I'd no idea what you'd got out of this man Cobden. Simon Gell spoke to me direct.'

I was prepared to bet he had. A man happy, no doubt, in a carefully calculated game of tit for tat.

'I tried to ring you at Eddathorpe,' said Colin mendaciously, 'but you were out.'

'Bit of a communications problem,' I said.

'Yes,' he agreed, looking me straight in the eye. 'I must have missed out on your message to me, as well.'

There was a pregnant pause while both of us mulled over our respective positions. Neither believed the other, but for the time being at least, neither of us wanted to rock the boat.

'No harm done.'

'No.'

'Has he said anything?'

'Richard Cary? Not yet, but it's very early days. We've only just seized the wholesale warehouse documents from his old man.'

'Get an order, did you?'

'Yes,' said Colin Templeton. 'From a Nottingham Crown Court judge, first thing.'

Not a lot in common with our bloke, then. A little unfair, perhaps, but I felt like sticking pins in a small wax image of the smiling assassin, His Honour, Judge Ralph Brand.

'A bit of a coincidence,' I said. 'Richard Cary having a weekend cottage within a mile or two of where our body was found.'

'Yes,' he said. 'Got anything else?'

'Only the fact that Cary appears to have been stealing from the Wholesale Division of his old man's firm, and Alan

Cobden, the supermarket manager at Eddathorpe, has been holding it back.'

'Yeah, Gell had apparently got this story from this Cobden feller before he passed him on to you. Then he came straight to us. You managed to upset him, did you?'

'Simon Gell? Yes, very likely, just a bit.'

Semi-sympathetically, Colin Templeton shook his head.

'You're sure you haven't got anything else?'

'I'm not holding out on you, if that's what you mean. We went to see Cary's wife; she doesn't seem to think that Rachel was Richard Cary's type. On the other hand, his girlfriend says he was out of town on business the day our victim was killed. According to her he wasn't back till late.'

'Well, that's something. It's more than she'd say to us. It's hardly enough, though, from your point of view.'

'It's not enough for you, either. As I say, I wasn't holding out, I was just trying to get as much together as possible before we pooled resources, so to speak.'

'Hmm.' That was a face-saver and he knew it. I'd hardly expected him to be convinced.

'Gell could be putting up a smokescreen, himself.'

'True.'

'How's Maurice taking it?'

'I'm expecting a posse of lawyers any minute. It's hate the Crime Squad day; lots of threats.'

'What's your next move, Colin?'

'Speaking to your man Cobden would be ideal, he might be able to pin down some dates or bankings, or something. Save us a lot of paperwork and sorting through. What d'you want, Bob?'

It was horse-trading time.

'Well, being as you're the new key-holder, what about searching the cottage?' I asked.

He stared at me levelly for a moment, sucking his teeth. Suddenly he rose to his feet and grinned. 'Like it,' he said. 'Legitimate enquiries, we can take Cary with us for the search, I can see your man Cobden and by the time the lawyers get here, we'll be well out of harm's way!'

Chapter Twenty

They cuffed Richard Cary, and the Crime Squad took him in their own car while we followed on behind, once I'd made arrangements for our Scenes of Crime department to meet us at the house.

'It's not like the old days, is it?' asked George.

'What do you mean?'

'A nice long car journey,' he said wistfully. 'Plenty of time for a chat.'

'One or two nice little admissions, you mean,' I said sarcastically. 'No nonsense about formal interviews, and having to record 'em on tape. *I wrote it all down in my pocket book as soon as we arrived at a police station, M' Lud!* That sort of thing?'

'Very relaxing, car journeys,' he replied indignantly. 'No need to make anything up, they used to make really damning admissions almost before they noticed they were out.'

'And that's only one of the reasons they stopped us doing it,' I agreed.

George lapsed into silence and concentrated on his driving. It's only barely possible, but I suppose his feelings might have been hurt. His very own DCI was making an implied attack on the integrity of the CID.

It was, however, a very boring journey, our only touch of excitement came at the very end of our trip when the car in front of us took an unexpected left down a country lane, leaving George, who overshot, braking sharply and scrabbling for reverse gear. Richard Cary had apparently informed his captors of a short cut.

The cottage itself was one of those late eighteenth century isolated brick boxes with a slate roof and a wooden porch, typical of the fens. Charming anywhere else if surrounded by trees, but stark, almost intrusive, even after two hundred years against its flat surroundings and the ploughed fields of chocolate-coloured mud.

'Not much wonder property's so cheap around here,' I said as we negotiated the rutted gravel of the drive and pulled up behind the Crime Squad car directly in front of the house.

George grunted, changed his mind at the last moment, and rewarded me with a monosyllabic, 'Yes.' I had not yet been forgiven for my brief essay into crackpot libertarianism, apparently.

On the far side of the cottage, half-hidden by the angle of the building, the SOCO staff had parked their small white van. The Templeton contingent ignored them; strictly my business, I suppose.

'Chief Inspector Graham?' murmured the driver morosely, getting out. Short, balding, early fifties, he looked more like an out-of-work undertaker than a technician in Scenes of Crime.

'They said this was urgent. We've got a lot of calls stacking up, sir, and we've been waiting for ages. Can we get on?'

His companion, younger, hairier, silently hauled their box of tricks from the back of the van, looking equally upset. It appeared that my selfish demands for action had thoroughly spoilt their day. I glanced at George, but he ignored me. What are sergeants for, if not to offer help?

I sighed, it was a toss up between playing the bloody-minded senior officer, and trying to get what I wanted by being nice. I chose the latter, asked politely for a potential crime-scene examination and hoped, vainly as it turned out, for service with a smile.

Colin, his sergeant and the detective constable acting as escort unfolded themselves from their own vehicle, while Richard Cary struggled clumsily to swing out of the car impeded by his handcuffed hands. They were hardly necessary; it was, after all, three on to one. Disapproving of his old enemy, the Crime Squad sergeant, George sniffed.

The detective constable looked enquiringly at his boss. Colin took the hint. 'OK,' he said amiably to the prisoner. 'We're going to take off the cuffs, but if you try to do a runner, I'll chop you straight down the middle, Dickey, mate.'

Silently, Richard Cary held out his hands while the DC fumbled with the key; once released, he gingerly rubbed his wrists. Trouble, I decided, might shortly be looming. It was not the most tactful way to express onesself to the aspiring middle class.

Inside, the two bedroomed cottage was all pine furniture, quarry tiled floors downstairs, and a distant but recognisable sourish smell. Country dream-homes do not always have damp courses, I find.

'Sorry,' volunteered Richard Cary with the air of a disappointed estate agent, 'what this place really needs is a thorough airing and a good fire.'

'When were you last here?' I asked, a trifle too casually for my own good.

'Six, maybe seven weeks ago.' He gave me an equally offhand reply. Damp or no damp, it hardly fitted in with my personal hypothesis, so I took that with a very large pinch of salt.

Conversation lapsed; hands ostentatiously stuck in pockets to avoid contaminating the scene with five perfect sets of police fingerprints, we hung around impatiently while SOCO did their stuff. Deploying the occasional sigh, combined with a little discreet huffing and puffing, Colin and his minions made it perfectly plain that I was wasting their time. The body language said it all: they were merely humouring me, and waiting for the lesser breeds to get out of their way.

'OK, Dickey,' the Crime Squad sergeant finally turned to their prisoner with a kind of semi-jocular familiarity mixed with casual contempt. 'Once the clowns upstairs have finished, why don't you save us all from a nasty chill and give us the rest of the stuff?'

'What sort of *stuff*?' Whatever the man's failings, a twinge of sympathy escaped. The language, the chrome-leather jacket and the thick gold wrist-chain might be impressive in Crime Squad circles, but there was no mistaking Richard Cary's air of studied distaste.

'Papers,' suggested the sergeant, unabashed. 'Copies of the bank and building society accounts, the cash from under the bed maybe, or one or two informative floppy disks?'

'There's nothing here, and for the record I object to this entire procedure. You have denied me access to my solicitor, as well.'

'Please yourself, and just for the *record*, Dick, we've got genuine enquiries to make. We're not questioning you until they're complete, and anyway, your solicitor failed to turn up.'

Personally, I very much doubted whether anybody was going to buy that one. George obviously didn't, he sighed elaborately, and the Crime Squad man gave him a look of pure venom in return.

It didn't escape Colin Templeton, either, so he turned on me. 'I wish to Christ your SOCO men would hurry up so we can get on!'

Beggars can't be choosers, but I would have preferred to do this with a full forensic team, myself. Still, this was a Crime Squad show, they'd got the bit firmly between their teeth by this time and they had an agenda all their own. One tiny piece of evidence relating to Rachel, however, and I was going to stop this little charade dead in its tracks until we'd taken the place to pieces. If that happened, Colin and his case could go to hell.

In the meantime, playing second fiddle to the arresting officer had its advantages. Unworthy perhaps, cowardly even, but if push came to shove, it could go a long way towards protecting my own, and my detective sergeant's, rear. We'd participate in what was, after all, their search; hopefully, we'd get what we wanted, and if things turned nasty Templeton and his cowboys would have to cope with the flak. I too had travelled a long way from the trust and companionship of those happy days of yore.

Eventually, Misery and Hairy trooped back, the latter still toting their metal case. Misery was the obvious purveyor of the bad news. 'Nothing here,' he said. 'If this is a murder scene, it's the cleanest I've ever encountered in fifteen years of experience, boss.'

'Lift any prints?'

'Here and there,' he admitted. 'Lots of smudges though. We'll check for this Foster woman, naturally, but there's not so many marks as you might expect.'

'Has somebody tidied up?'

Too eager, too eager, Robert; Misery was in there like a shot to put me down. He nodded casually in the direction of Richard Cary, 'Nah,' he said, 'shouldn't think so. He's probably got a house-proud wife. Oh, and by the way, I can check the HQ files for you and your sergeant's prints, but I'd like some eliminations from this lot, too.'

The Crime Squad grumbled loudly, they weren't stupid, they'd never touched anything, never had their hands out of their pockets since they'd been in the house. It made no difference. Misery and his colleague produced their magic pad and a packet of chemical-sensitive paper. This was a special favour, apparently: no need on this occasion to roll the nice white Crime Squad fingers over a brass plate coated with thick black gunk.

The ritual over, Colin was determined to conduct an honest search. We all trooped around, complete with prisoner, and searched the place room by room, cupboard by cupboard, drawer by drawer. Six people at a time in each location, and none of the bedrooms in particular were bigger than thirteen foot by ten.

'Too many cooks,' I grumbled, after bumping into Brian somebody-or-other, the detective constable, for the ump-teenth time.

'He's not going to get the chance,' snapped Colin Templeton, 'of saying that we planted something on him while he was absent from the room.'

Richard Cary, seated on the bed, feet tucked up out

of harm's way, managed to raise something of a sardonic grin.

'This is an absolute farce,' he said. 'Besides, I trust you, OK?'

'That's not what you were implying before.' The Crime Squad detective sergeant sounded thoroughly fed up.

'I wasn't referring to you!' said our victim insultingly, and shot him a single, triumphant look. Bad-temperedly, the search of Richard Cary's rural icehouse dragged on.

From our point of view it was beginning to look like a complete waste of time, there were no signs of struggle, no indications that the place had been visited let alone occupied in the recent past. Bleak, damp and recently unloved, set among acres of sweet damn all, Richard's weekend retreat was rapidly assuming the status of my least favourite place.

'Well, I'm frozen,' said George eventually, 'I suppose you wouldn't have the makings of a mashing around here?'

'Not unless you want to go out and milk a passing cow.' The Crime Squad sergeant sounded almost pleased with himself. Another, if pathetic, chance to have a go at George.

'There's a packet of tea bags and some sort of powdered milk in the kitchen,' Richard Cary volunteered. 'It's probably the first sensible suggestion I've heard all day.'

Any excuse to take a shot at the enemy. By this time the Nottingham-based contingent had been reduced to rolling back the bathroom lino, and looking for sellotaped secrets on the undersides of drawers.

George lumbered off downstairs, I heard him tinkering about with a kettle and the banging of an air lock in the pipes before the water began to flow. Bored, disgruntled, the Crime Squad effort began to flag. I wasn't all that pleased with life, myself; I'd seen nothing to suggest that Rachel Foster had ever been around. George and I had put ourselves to the trouble of a seventy-odd mile journey, and all for the sake of a second rate cup of tea.

'Hey, boss!' George's distant voice drifted up the narrow stairs.

'Sounds as though tea's up, aren't we invited?' Now it was Brian, the Detective Constable sounding sour.

'Come and look at this!'

'Don't think so,' I answered the earlier question, but at the sound of the voice from downstairs I began to perk up, and there was something of a scramble for the door, while Richard Cary, prisoner or not, was left to bring up the rear. For the time being at least, he looked totally bored.

Downstairs, laden teaspoon in hand, George bent over the pedal bin fitted into the unit below the sink. 'Good job I didn't drop these on top.' Carefully, he re-deposited a pile of soggy tea bags on the edge of the stainless steel top, leaving them to ooze disgustingly on to the kitchen floor.

'Sweet papers, so what?' The Crime Squad DS had elbowed us all to one side.

I looked over George's shoulder at the almost empty plastic container. I was prepared to admit it, myself; it wasn't a lot. Three or four pieces of yellow cellophane lurking in the bottom of a bucket didn't look much like a major find to me. Still, for the first time in hours George was looking faintly pleased with himself, and Richard Cary, staring uncertainly across at the rubbish bin and its meagre contents, was looking just the tiniest bit blue.

Colin Templeton and his troops were pretty disgruntled, and I knew exactly how they felt. For one thing, Richard Cary's Nottingham solicitors turned very nasty indeed. He had, they claimed, deliberately, vindictively, denied them access to their client who was now eighty-odd miles away, and for no good reason, booked into an Eddathorpe cell.

The police had wanted to search a weekend cottage? They wanted to take a witness statement off a supermarket manager arrested in a foreign force? Rubbish, it all sounded like a series of unlawful, unauthorised delaying tactics to them!

Me too. I wanted to interview Richard all right, but I could see a lot of grief coming our way if Colin didn't take him back pretty smartly to Nottingham and give him access to his legal advice.

'I want a witness statement,' he said stubbornly, 'from this man Cobden, first.'

'Please yourself,' I could see whatever case he had unravelling before my eyes. As for me, one or two bits of cellophane found in Rachel Foster's Mini, even when combined with George's find, were hardly worth a full-scale interview at this stage. I was going to ask the questions, of course, but it was exactly the kind of thing that could be disposed of as coincidence in two minutes flat.

It's always a problem; to talk or not to talk. It's easy enough to grab 'em quick, and take them in, but you lose the impetus if you interview people too soon. It's easy enough to sit people down in interview rooms, and, ever so subtly of course, scare 'em half to death, but the law of diminishing returns sets in if you have to do it more than once. Besides, too much to-ing and fro-ing to no good purpose makes the investigator look a total, incompetent ass.

'Do you want to talk to him?' Colin thought he had me on the run.

'Yes, of course.' I tried to sound a lot more confident than I felt.

'Are you in a position to arrest him for anything?'

'On reasonable suspicion of murder? No.'

'Interview him under caution?'

'Only briefly.'

'Well, then,' he handed me the glint of a malicious smile, 'he's only in your cells for the next couple of hours, buddy, so I suggest you talk to him while you have the chance.'

Not that he got things all his own way, however. Shortly after he'd started to take a statement from Cobden, Thomas Munton, solicitor of this parish, and acting, as he said, as the accredited local agent on behalf of Richard Cary, let me off the hook.

Which is not to say that I was glad to see him. As a matter of principle, I've never been glad to see a solicitor in my life.

Thin-faced, thin-lipped and formally dressed in a navy blue pinstripe suit and waistcoat with the inevitable gold fob, Thomas Munton was nearing the end of a profitable, if unspectacular, small-town career. The suit, the gold hunter, and the pious expression were probably all part of the game. Somewhere beneath the chilly, pious exterior, a character actor was probably raging to get out. The reason, I suspected, that amidst all the property deals, the conveyancing, the civil torts and the accident work, the senior partner in Munton, McLaughlin & Co. still turned out to play the Criminal Lawyer, often for the meagre rewards offered by legal aid.

Not that the offer of a local agency from the Cary family solicitors was likely to leave him poor. That probably accounted for the glint of battle in his eye when he entered the interview room.

'I am truly surprised at you, Mr Graham,' he said, 'and I'd like an explanation, if there is one, prior to seeing my client.'

'I don't quite understand you, Mr Munton, but please sit down.'

That, in my view at least, gave me a ten-point start. He usually prided himself on his urbanity. He sat.

'I have been asked to act on behalf of Mr Richard Cary. Why have you arrested my client?'

'I haven't,' I said bluntly, 'he's been lodged here temporarily by Crime Squad officers following a search of his nearby house.'

'According to my information, he was arrested in Nottingham, denied access to his solicitors locally, and promptly whisked over here to keep him out of sight.'

It was one of those times for a soothing explanation, the deployment of buckets and buckets of smarm well mixed with touches of sincerity and tact. Lots of sincerity, come to think of it; as somebody or other said, once you can fake sincerity, you've got it made. A plea relating to the urgency of the enquiry featured, together with a hint of delay on the part of the Nottingham solicitors. What is more, my out-of-town colleagues hadn't gone in for any unauthorised questioning, perish the thought!

'So he's not your prisoner, then?' said Munton at last, cutting through my latest exercise in bullshit baffles brains.

'Oh, no.'

'And these, er, Crime Squad people are simply conducting a brief enquiry before they take him back?' Imagination, perhaps, but I had the feeling that he didn't like urban Squads with fancy titles. A note of quiet disapproval may have entered into his voice.

'Quite.'

'And you personally don't want to speak to Mr Cary at all?'

'We-ll . . .' I started slowly.

'I thought so,' Munton, having caught me out, relaxed. He seemed pleased. 'My instructions,' he said, with something of a happy gloat, 'are to advise Mr Cary to say nothing to the police at this stage.'

'Isn't that up to your client?'

'His father—' he said, and stopped.

'You're acting for Richard, not Maurice, and his father isn't the one who's in trouble at the moment,' I pointed out.

'Ah,' he hesitated momentarily, then he almost smiled. I could practically see his brain turning over. He was far from Maurice Cary's sphere of influence. Richard, however temporarily, was his client, he therefore intended to exercise his own judgement, and, reluctant as I am to admit it, he wasn't a bad old stick.

'In that case, we'd better be guided by the circumstances,' he said.

Chapter Twenty-one

He did not know, had never met, had never heard of Rachel Foster prior to her death, and that was the honest truth. No, seeing a couple of sweet wrappers in a waste bin hadn't worried him at all. Frankly, he'd simply been fed up by the length of time the search was taking, and he'd been totally bored by the whole event.

Could he account for the presence of the sweet papers in his waste bin, then?

'Somebody, sometime in the course of a weekend visit to the cottage must have put them there.'

'Who, for example?'

'I'm not in the habit of scrounging around waste bins after my guests; don't be so bloody silly,' he'd said.

We'd found similar sweet wrappings in Rachel Foster's car, how did he account for that?

He didn't have to, and he didn't think he'd got anything else to say, but no, nobody else had borrowed his key. We had, however – plenty to say, that is – and we went through the story over and over again. Rachel had been involved in the blackmail at Cary's, that much was clear. He too had been involved in a scam. She'd died within three or four miles of his weekend cottage; there was an apparent link between his kitchen waste bin and the contents of her car. He knew her, didn't he?

'No.'

'Can you account for your movements last Thursday?'

'Why should I?'

'Because that's when Rachel Foster was killed, and your girl-friend says that you didn't get home till late on Thursday night.'

'I was away on business, the only significance of what you're saying is that you've been around to my home badgering her.'

'Can you give an account of your movements, then?'

'When?'

'Last Thursday.'

'This is bloody silly!' He'd already said that, 'Could *you*?'

Could I what?

'Pick a detailed account of your movements last week out of thin air?'

This was beginning to sound like the old run-around. Prisoner versus copper in the old game of cat and mouse. Whenever they turn evasive, it's a pretty good sign. But then, after a cynical smiling silence on our part, he did his best to bugger it all up.

'Thursday,' he said slowly, thoughtfully. 'I was away in South Yorkshire.' He waited once again for me to lead him, and failed. For an intelligent man he wasn't doing all that well, an under-rehearsed story, perhaps. He glanced sideways at his solicitor before he spoke. Munton misinterpreted the message, he thought his client was about to lie.

'You don't have to reply to any of these questions, Mr Cary,' he said. 'In any case, your Nottingham solicitors have already instructed me to advise you—'

'Yes, I know, you've already said that. I've no intention of speaking to the police about the other matter at all.'

Bad news for Colin, then.

'I'd like to remind you that the Chief Inspector is conducting a murder enquiry. He will certainly make sure that his colleagues check everything you say.'

'I know that, too. You're making it sound as though you think I'm going to come out with a load of crap.'

Munton looked up sharply, he'd managed to surprise us both; it wasn't much as obscenities went, but it was hardly the managing directorial style. Munton compressed his lips, and the hint of a flush appeared on his sallow cheeks. He'd obviously thought he was dealing with a better class of criminal, for once.

'If you must know, I was up in South Yorkshire visiting our shops.'

'Times?'

'All day, and most of the evening too.'

'You'll have to do better than that, Mr Cary. As Mr Munton says, we're going to check.'

'To the best of my recollection, I left home about eight. I called at the office, I sorted out some paper work, and I left for Worksop at about half past ten. I spent a couple of hours at our branch in Worksop, then I had lunch. After that I . . .'

'Worksop,' said George pedantically, 'isn't in South Yorks, it's in Notts.'

'It's on the way. I spent most of the afternoon at our store in Sheffield; the manager can confirm it if you like. Then I went over to Rotherham and spent some time in our eight-till-late.'

'Eight till what?'

'It's an experiment we're doing. Like Eddathorpe, it opens at eight in the morning and it doesn't close until eleven at night.'

'Are you saying you were there all that time?'

'No, of course not. I was there until about seven, or just after, I think.'

'And the rest of the evening?'

'Meal again, drink with the manager, a bit of a chat and then I drove home.'

'And these times are right, and you didn't make a little trip in this direction in the course of the day?'

'No.'

And so it went on, round and round, backwards and forwards, Rachel Foster, sweet papers in buckets, business trips. It even got slightly pathetic in the end. Would he, for example, with his thickening body and beginnings of a double chin, describe himself as beginning to look middle-aged? Did he realise that one of the descriptions of a middle-aged businessman opening one of the false bank accounts could well fit him? Had he and Rachel Foster been in it together? At what point did the partnership go wrong?

If he was making business trips to company stores he had

every opportunity to visit holes in the walls at the same time. Coincidental was it, that the blackmailer took money from machines situated in the same area as the various stores, when he was a regular visitor to them all?

'I did not know that woman, I have not been engaged in a blackmail plot against our company, and this is total fantasy on the part of the police.'

'Fantasy, eh?' My detective sergeant was getting tired. 'What about the current reason for your arrest, the scam you worked with the Cary Wholesale bankings eighteen months ago?'

Munton held up one hand, but Cary beat him to it. 'That's it,' he said. 'I've nothing else to say.'

George hesitated momentarily, then he let loose his final blast, 'What happens,' he said, 'to your story when Scenes of Crime identify Rachel Foster's fingerprints in your cottage?'

The silence was deafening.

Or, as Angie said sleepily when I finally got home sometime after midnight, 'It's all beginning to sound like a dreadful mess.'

'Nothing!' screamed Maurice Cary down the phone. 'Nothing links that woman with my son!'

'There is, however,' I pointed out, 'a definite link between Rachel Foster and the extortion of money from your firm. Like it or not, Mr Cary, your son Richard is suspected of having his fingers in the till.'

'There's probably a reasonable explanation,' he said. 'In any case, I intend to write to your chief constable, the chief constable of Nottinghamshire and to the head of the Crime Squad, too. In future the police will have no contact with any member of my family, except through me.'

'I beg your pardon?' The sheer breathtaking effrontery of this one left me stunned.

'You heard me, Chief Inspector, and furthermore, neither you nor Templeton have heard the last of this.'

'None of your sons are juveniles,' I said to him quietly, striving to keep my temper. 'Therefore I have no intention of asking your permission before I interview any of them. And,' I added for good measure, 'you'd be far wiser to consult your solicitor, sir, before trying to impose impossible conditions like that.'

There was what I can only describe as a pregnant silence at the other end of the phone.

'I want my son released.' I had almost forgotten that he was an old man, his voice had acquired something of a whine.

'Of course, but once these things have started, they achieve a momentum of their own.'

'What happens if I withdraw the complaint?'

'Chief Inspector Templeton has a court order,' I replied, misunderstanding, 'and he already has the accounts allegedly relating to your son.'

'Yes I understand entirely, but I'll withdraw the complaint against Mr Purcell, if you want me to do that first!'

So that was it, I was being used as a messenger boy again. Richard Cary was in custody in Nottingham, Peter Fairfield was in Nottingham too, but I was being expected to . . .

'Look,' he said, we were down to pleading now, 'he's not your murderer, he received the blackmail letters, he didn't write them. They're nothing to do with him, as for the rest . . . I'm sure we can sort something out.'

Could we, indeed. I wasn't even angry, he wanted something, he assumed that we wanted something back; in his eyes the Frank Purcell complaint was expendable, and he was a businessman. Time to make a comfortable arrangement between contending parties; an offer, negotiations, followed by an acceptance. A normal, every day contract: nothing like a bribe.

'Why not leave things to your solicitor, Mr Cary? Your son has got nothing to worry about, if he's done nothing wrong.'

He didn't say anything; he didn't have to, an atmosphere of total disbelief oozed down the line.

I'd used, I have to admit, a very old, almost meaningless police cliché. The equivalent of offering Rachel Foster's bereaved auntie a nice cup of tea to assuage the pains of death. But it was either that, or mount my high horse to cut him down. I even felt a twinge of sympathy; the whole ploy smacked of desperation. The poor old bugger was in a panic, and in a blind pursuit of his family interests he'd lost his common sense.

'I'm sorry, Mr Cary,' I said as gently as I could, 'but the outcome of these enquiries do not depend on whether or not you withdraw your police complaint.'

'No, I never expected that.' His voice grew firmer as he outlined his version of the quid pro quo. 'All I'm saying is that Richard is innocent, in those circumstances neither you nor your colleagues need to carry this whole ridiculous business too far. Therefore, if it would help you to concentrate on the important issues instead of wasting resources on inessentials, we could come to some . . .'

'Arrangement,' I said. 'Yes, I see.' Of course I did, I simply wondered whether Charlie Renshaw, Peter Fairfield, Colin Templeton, the troops on the ground and all the members of the subsequent Public Enquiry team, not to mention the massed ranks of the media, were likely to see it in exactly the same way . . .

Afterwards, I rang Peter Fairfield to impart the good news.

'I don't suppose you managed to tape all that?' he said.

'I'm afraid not, I don't have a recording facility on my phone.' Forewarned is forearmed, though, I wondered whether Peter Fairfield did.

'Never mind, do me a statement straight away.'

'You're not thinking of prosecuting him, sir?'

At the other end of the phone Fairfield grunted, it might have been mistaken for a laugh. 'Keeping him quiet, anyway! There's more than one way,' he said confusingly, 'of robbing a blind horse.'

'It's back to basics,' I said, staring gloomily at the piles of statement folders, and preparing for another long, hard grind.

George sniffed, 'Remember what happened to the last feller who wanted us all to do that?'

'Eh? Oh, right, I see what you mean.' I managed a dutiful smile. I didn't feel much like it; prospects were not looking good.

'It could be old man Cary,' offered George.

'Very funny,' I said.

George picked up Maurice Cary's statement and descriptive form from the pile. 'Millionaire grocer kills accomplice in the course of screwing his own firm. I suppose not,' he said. 'Besides, he checks out for the Thursday, so does Bernard. I suppose he *could* be lying. Want us to double-check?'

'Bernard? Yes, for what it's worth, set up some action forms and do the main contenders again. It looks and sounds pathetic, but if we end up getting reinvestigated, it shows we're thorough, helps keep us safe.' I felt ashamed as I said it, wimpish, defeatist, keeping us safe.

'Easily discouraged, boss?'

'We've been at it a week, we've had a look at Rachel's various colleagues, lovers, friends, and we still don't have a lot.'

'I don't know so much about friends,' pondered George. 'She didn't seem to have very many.'

'Nottingham?' I asked.

'One or two; people she had a drink with after work.' He continued to leaf idly through the stack.

'Not even a few close girlfriends, confidantes? A spot of pubbing and clubbing? She was a young woman living alone in a flat for God's sake. A part-time worker, aren't we missing something here?'

'Possibly, but nobody's found any close associates so far,' admitted George.

'What about auntie?'

'I don't see her whizzing around Nottingham visiting the pubs and clubs.'

I treated him to a modified version of the Glare.

'Sorry, boss.' He paused for a moment, contrite, then he added, 'Pat Goodall went round to see her, you know.'

'The soul of tact, I take it?'

'He did all right,' George shrugged. 'Want to know what he found out?'

'The names of her friends?'

He shook his head, 'She didn't eat sweets.' He picked

up a single sheet of statement paper and stuck it under my nose.

Hope springs eternal. 'Forensic,' I said, 'those sweet wrappers we found, I don't suppose . . . ?'

'No fingerprints. One totally unidentifiable smudge.'

Idly, I began to read Wendy Pointer's supplementary statement. 'It says here that Rachel was always on a diet. Maybe she dieted because she was overfond of sweets.'

'Not according to the aunt.'

'Which brings us back to Richard Cary and his cottage waste bin.'

'Coincidence,' suggested George reluctantly. 'After all there's millions of the things around.'

'Waste bins?'

'Sweet wrappers,' he said.

'I don't suppose forensic know the brand?'

'No, but I suppose you want me to ask them, boss. They won't be experts on sweet wrappers, though. I doubt if it's something they come up against every day. I can see you becoming a really popular boy.'

Tough. Besides, it ought to provide some overpaid scientist with a challenge; he might even enjoy having a go at bits of cellophane. Probably make a nice change from his usual business, messing about with fifty-seven varieties of semi-putrid gunk. Equally probably, however, the results would turn out to be irrelevant, information we didn't even want.

'Then there's Birmingham,' I said.

'The school where she was teaching? She left there damn near a year ago, and if you're looking for University friends, where do we start? She'd been gone over two years, and they'll be dispersed all over the country by now.'

'True, but there will still be staff who knew her.' Then, as a kind of inspiration struck, 'Aston's in Birmingham,' I said.

Chapter Twenty-two

There was no immediate trip to Birmingham, however, Colin Templeton called instead.

'He says he'll only talk to you.'

'Richard Cary? You've still got him then?'

'Of course we've still got him, you trying to be funny, or what?'

'Sorry, Col, his Dad's been on the phone to me, that's all.'

'What did he want?'

'Oh,' I replied evasively, 'a spot of whinging, one or two threats. I've already told Peter Fairfield all about it, just in case.'

'OK,' he said complacently, 'but he knows better than to try that sort of nonsense over here.'

'Locked up in the cells at Central, is he?' I'd caught the implication, but I wasn't going to rise to the scattering of that particular bait. I might, in Colin's opinion, be a bit on the soft side for the CID, but you catch fewer flies with vinegar than you do with honey. If Richard Cary wanted to talk to me, at least I had some chance of getting a result.

'Of course he's at Central, where else? But you'd better get your skates on, Bob. Time's running out, and Charlie Renshaw isn't inclined to apply for a magistrate's order to keep him beyond thirty-six hours.'

'Has Cary said anything at all?'

'You can all sod off, and if you think you've got anything on me, prove it, or words to that effect.'

'And can you – prove it, that is?'

'Given time, the documentation's there, it's just a matter of ploughing through. In the meantime, it looks as though we'll have to bail him for the time being. Unfortunate, I'd like to wipe the smirk right off his face, but we'll get there in the end.'

'And what about his Dad?'

'What about him?'

'He's very likely to turn round and refuse to support a charge, despite the fact that Peter Fairfield reckons he's got the black on him, now.'

'Fuck his luck, matey.' Colin was in too much of a hurry to probe into that. 'It's not up to him, the company is a separate entity from the old man, and we can issue witness summonses to make him give evidence any time we like.'

I grinned cynically into the phone; I'd heard that particular song before. 'Theoretically,' I said.

'Theoretically,' he replied smartly, 'you might get your backside over to our fair city, and make your little pal here confess. For one thing, it'd please our beloved leader no end.'

'Oh, yes?'

'He's off to London on Monday. It's Charlie's big day.'

'Big day?'

'The interview for the ACC's job, remember? Stay in his good books and he might give you a leg up, yourself.'

'Oh, yes,' I said cheerfully, 'I almost forgot. From what I hear, it's between him and Clive Jones.'

'What exactly have you heard?' Distinct as it was sudden, there was a certain lack of warmth and enthusiasm at the other end of the line. No note of surprise in his voice, however. The devious bastard, he'd known about Clive Jones being on the short list all along.

'Oh,' I said vaguely, 'he's got lots of administrative experience, and he's well in politically at the Home Office, naturally. Staff Officer to one of Her Majesty's Inspectors of Constabulary, that sort of thing.'

'You reckon he's in with a chance?' So Charlie Renshaw had been a foregone conclusion. No serious thoughts of Jones.

I let the breath hiss slowly, significantly through my teeth.

There was another impressive pause on the line, amidst which I thought I heard the sound of horses being changed in midstream.

'Christ!' Followed by silence. 'Does that mean you won't be applying for Faithless Frankie's job?'

'You have to be joking, not with Jones about.'

'Ah.'

His farewells were perfunctory; he appeared to have other things on his mind. And as for me, I was having a pretty good day already, and it was scarcely half-past nine.

It was far too warm in the interview room, there was even a kind of hot, metallic smell combined with a distant odour of dry dust coming from the old fashioned radiators and pipes which ran along one wall. The same strictly utility office furniture, the same scuffed parquet floors with little or no polish, especially under and around the interview table, worn by generations of shifty, nervous feet.

Nothing different about the place since the time I worked there. Even the off-white paint, the nicotine yellowed walls, and the faint trace of rust wearing through the gloss on the iron-framed windows, looked the same.

Distantly, I could hear a familiar trampling of feet, doors opening and shutting, and a rumble of voices. Somebody on the other side of an inadequately soundproofed wall was unsympathetically telling a city-centre shoplifter exactly how it was. Had I really wanted to come back to Notts? I must have been suffering from a mild case of big-city syndrome at the time. Angie had been right, it didn't take long to cure me of any lingering traces of nostalgia. Just an hour or two reacquainting myself with the realities of life in Nottingham's Central nick.

Richard Cary probably felt the same; he was clean enough,

he'd managed to obtain a fresh shirt and he'd had a shave. He wore, however, that indefinable, slightly tacky, defiantly hangdog air of a man who'd spent the night in the cells. By contrast his solicitor, a florid, broad-shouldered man in his late thirties, with his perfectly knotted tie in the colours of a local Yeomanry regiment, his immaculate double-breasted suit and his air of effortless superiority, was probably fifty points ahead of his client before he even bothered opening his mouth. I felt slightly sorry for Richard, but I doubt whether George, eager to indulge in blood sports as usual, concurred.

My detective sergeant, his face expressionless, chanted the formula, time, date, the details of the persons present, the general rules of engagement, the moment he started the tape machine.

'Yes,' said the solicitor, 'can we get on?' Something to cheer up your average interviewer right from the start.

I cautioned Richard Cary, nodded encouragingly, and sat back and smiled.

'It's your client who wanted to see me,' I said.

'I don't altogether approve of this, I would very much have preferred to see the strength of the police evidence, first.'

'And I, Mr Howe,' said Richard Cary coolly, 'would prefer to sort this out without having to go to court. If one is innocent, I do not see any reason to delay.'

He handed his brief a look that suggested that he was reluctant to be the source of finance for another expensive new suit. For a man in a morally inferior position, he was doing rather well.

'Firstly, I did not murder Rachel Foster, I never knew the girl.'

Girl, she hadn't been a day under twenty-five. I kept on smiling; true or not, it was a little exercise in the politically incorrect.

'I have absolutely no connection whatsoever with Rachel Foster, and I'd like to make myself perfectly clear.'

'Is that all you wanted to tell me?' I asked, making it equally clear that I expected better value for my eighty-mile trek from the East Coast.

'Among other things, yes.'

'Please go on.'

'It therefore follows that I had nothing to do with the attempt to extort money from our company.' Two unsupported assertions, I wasn't convinced. Nevertheless, it wasn't up to him to prove his innocence, lawyers' weasel cliché or not, it was up to the bold gendarme to prove his guilt.

'It was more than an attempt, surely? There is something of a pause at the cash machines at the moment, but the current score is around seventy-two thousand pounds.'

'Well,' he said calmly, 'you needn't look in my direction. Y'know what the supermarket manager said to Simon Gell?'

George looked up, and with absolute certainty I clocked his current thoughts: it was neither the time nor the place for silly remarks. The actress and the bishop could remain at rest.

'He said,' continued Cary, 'that Simon could examine all the times and dates of the withdrawals and check them against the occasions when he was indisputably elsewhere. That would show in the majority, if not all the cases, whether the bank withdrawals were anything to do with him. I can only suggest the same.'

'So he did,' I snapped, 'but then again, you could have been the mastermind hiding behind Rachel Foster, and she could have been your mule.'

Irritating, that. So Alan Cobden had practised his smart remarks on Gell, prior to passing the same story on to me. All the same, it was probably true enough so far as it went, and to nail either Cary or Cobden the problem remained the same: to establish a firm connection between either of them, or both of them come to that, and our victim in the stranded boat. Still, I could always fall back on the good old interview room stand-by, an air of weary disbelief.

'It's like this, Richard, you're *telling* me but you're not helping me to believe you, if you see what I mean.'

'This, Mr Cary,' said Howe, trying once again to spoil it, 'is a complete waste of time. The police are only anxious to find some plausible suspect, and stick him in the frame.'

'Thank you, Mr Howe, I'm grateful.' I'd learned that one from a sarcastic QC in the course of a tricky session in the box. If he could use police slang, I felt entitled to borrow the occasional phrase from one of his expensive, high-powered mates.

Having had his fingers burnt already, he sat back and left the final decision to his client. To maintain his self-respect, however, he still awarded me the lawyerly version of the Glare.

'I suppose you think you can sling any kind of allegation at me, just because you already believe I'm a crook?'

Well, yes, it did help, but I wasn't about to admit something like that, only to find myself being recorded for posterity on the interview tape.

'The discrepancies on the wholesaler's accounts, you mean?'

'Don't tell me that you're turning shy, Mr Graham? The false accounts, the substitution of cheques for cash in the bankings, that's exactly what I mean.'

'Haven't you made this admission already?'

Howe didn't comment, but there was a sharp intake of breath.

'To Templeton's crew? Certainly not.'

'Then why are you prepared to talk to me?'

'To help to clear myself of the more serious allegations, of course. I am neither a murderer nor an extortionist, and, as you are a fair-minded man, I also expect you to see that I'm innocent of criminal intent so far as the warehouse accounts are concerned.'

'They aren't in my possession,' I said, hedging my bets like mad, 'so I'm unable to interview you properly, whatever you may say.'

'You won't need them,' he was speaking with confidence, now. 'Whatever they eventually come up with in the way of substitutions, I will freely admit. I collected various sums of money, I recorded their receipt informally, but I put them to one side. I deliberately failed to enter the receipt of certain cheques, and then I reintroduced them on to the bank credit slips to cover the missing cash.

'Subsequently, I cleared the debtor's outstanding accounts on the computer to prevent the staff chasing them for the apparently outstanding bills. If anybody checked casually, they would have seen that the cheques had gone into the bank. There were one or two complications, but essentially it was as simple as that.'

'But you're still innocent of fraud?'

He even smiled slightly, 'It may all sound slightly discreditable in your eyes, Mr Graham, but yes.'

Howe stirred uneasily, and stared at his client with more than passing doubt, while George allowed a look of simple pleasure to pass over his face, 'How do you make that out?'

'I did not take any personal benefit from this.'

Not a defence. I prepared to pounce.

'I'm afraid I didn't tell you the truth in the first place, the first blackmail attempt took place eighteen months ago. For the good of the company I kept quiet at the time, and . . .'

'You mean,' said George crudely, 'that you screwed the wholesale company, and paid up?'

'Er, yes.'

'Why weren't we told by the banks?'

'The blackmailer used different accounts from the ones he's using now.'

'How much,' I asked, 'do you claim he obtained?'

'There's no claim about it, I salted the accounts he was using with fifteen thousand.'

'Why?'

'It was very difficult . . .' He paused. 'At that particular time there was some suggestion that we were going to float as a public company. It would have been very – embarrassing,' he said.

'Float your group on the Stock Exchange?'

'Where else?' He felt confident enough to give me a glance of studied contempt. 'But we decided to keep the control within the family, in the end.'

'Did your father know about what you'd done?'

'I didn't want to worry him at the time.'

'I don't suppose you wanted to worry any other members of the Board either, huh?' Heavy irony, something George did very well.

'No,' Cary's voice was cold and flat. 'That is absolutely right.'

'Did anybody know?'

'I engaged Simon and his firm to clear it up.'

'He knew about the fraud you were committing?' Bloody Simon Gell.

'Of course not, and anyway, there was no dishonest intent, so it wasn't a fraud.'

Howe stared across at us to see how we took it, he must have known that there was a hole in that particular argument something like a mile wide.

'So to protect Cary's Supermarkets you used another member of the group as a vehicle, by falsifying its accounts and stealing its cash?'

For the first time, he flushed. 'I resent that. I was acting in the company's interests all the time. It was probably a little unethical, I grant you, but it wasn't a criminal offence.'

'So, you dealt with a case of corporate blackmail by paying him off?'

'I engaged Simon to try and stop it. He didn't catch the person responsible but it ceased. To that extent it obviously worked.'

'And what about the latest phase? They're asking for half a million, now.'

'Well, obviously I couldn't . . . and anyway, we called the police.'

'In the end.'

'Surely, we have the right—'

'To do what you like whenever you think it suits you, and play ducks and drakes with the law?'

'Chief Inspector Graham!' Howe jumped in where angels should have feared to tread.

I was ready for him, 'Did you have any part in this?'

'Certainly not! I have only recently heard Mr Cary's, ah, story, and he wouldn't listen to me when I advised him of the attitude you might take.'

'Attitude? The wholesale enterprise is a separate company, isn't it Mr Howe?'

Miserably, I received the tiniest nod from Cary's brief, 'As I say, I did try to explain . . .'

'And each company is a separate entity in law. Therefore, Mr Cary has misappropriated its funds and falsified its accounts for the benefit of Cary's Supermarkets Ltd., which is legally speaking somebody else. Mr Cary, if you were, as you say, acting in the interests of the supermarket company, why didn't you use supermarket money for all this?'

'I used the wholesalers because it was easier to, er, manipulate the cash and cheques.'

'So you literally robbed Peter to pay Paul. If that isn't dishonest, what is?'

'Look, you're just talking technicalities, effectively we're all one firm. I didn't kill Rachel Foster, I'm not into this blackmail business with anybody, least of all her. I only told you all this to show that I've been one of the victims, not the criminal, all the way along.'

'What about the cottage?'

'What about it?'

'What happens if our Scenes of Crime come up with her fingerprints, or anything associated with her there?'

'They won't.'

'And the sweet wrappers?'

'This is ridiculous, you just keep harping on about those.'

'Answer the question, please.'

'For the very last and final time; I know nothing about Rachel Foster, I know nothing about any sweet wrappers and I don't see what it's supposed to prove, anyway!'

'You know very well that wrappers were found in your premises, and similar wrappers were found in her car.'

'Coincidence, for all I know. It was certainly nothing to do with me.'

'Or anybody you know?'

'What's that supposed to mean?'

'Have you lent your key to anybody, a member of your family for example?'

He hesitated. 'No.'

'You don't seem very sure.'

'Not this season, anyway.'

'And before that?'

'They've all been there at sometime or other. I've emptied the bin time after time since then. What do you expect me to do, fill it and leave it for months to stink?'

'No,' I said, 'but it does mean that somebody else could have duplicated your key.'

'So,' he said sarcastically, 'the good news is that I'm off the hook, the bad news is that you're obsessed with sweet papers and you intend to persecute the rest of my family now.'

'The bad news,' I said calmly, 'is that the Crime Squad are probably going to keep on talking to you, and they're almost certainly going to be sending the file involving the family wholesalers to the CPS.'

For the first time his solicitor looked almost happy. 'I did try to warn you, Richard,' said Mr Howe.

Chapter Twenty-three

'You haven't had a day off for a fortnight,' said Angie dangerously, 'and I thought we were going out.'

Wife, child and dog stared resentfully at me across the width of the sitting room.

'Sorry,' I said.

'Sorry,' she announced, 'is not good enough. Where are you going, anyway?'

'Birmingham, to see Tony Cary. I'm taking George.'

'On a Saturday? He's a student, isn't he? Ten to one he won't be there.'

The thought had already occurred to me, but if I phoned for an appointment I'd lose any element of surprise. If, however, he'd gone home for the weekend, he was probably hearing the Gospel according to Maurice, laced with lots of warnings against the wiles of wicked policemen, right now. I wished fervently that I'd gone to see him earlier in the week, but there's only so much a person can do in any given twenty-four hours.

'Sarah won't like it.' Angie wheeled her artillery into position. Sarah was George's formidable, loose-tongued wife.

'Sarah,' I replied heavily, 'doesn't run Eddathorpe CID, or at least not yet, so far as I'm aware.'

'Your name,' said Angela with quiet satisfaction, 'will be mud. Especially if your little excursion turns out to be another complete waste of time.'

'Another?'

'It's the eighth day, now. People are beginning to talk.'

'What you mean,' I said bitterly, 'is that Sarah bloody Caunt is beginning to talk. Maybe I ought to hand the job over to her, then the rest of us can all stay at home.'

'Can't you at least establish whether he's back in Nottingham for a couple of days before you go chasing over there?'

'How?'

'Anonymous girlfriend rings him at home?'

'You're cunning,' I admitted. 'You ought to be in the CID.'

Both child and dog looked apprehensive, but Mrs Angela Graham merely sniffed.

'Don't you think you're just a little old for him?' asked George, as Paula put down the phone.

'Oh, I dunno,' she said, smiling innocently, 'I think I'd prefer a toy boy to a sugar daddy any day of the week.'

George had the grace to look slightly uncomfortable; Paula might be in her thirties, but according to my reckoning her opponent was pushing fifty-four. Therefore today's score so far was definitely one-nil.

She turned her attention to me. 'That was Mummy on the phone,' she said. 'Tony Cary isn't there.'

'Expected?'

'She doesn't appear to approve of me as a potential girlfriend, so she was a bit short with me, but no, he's still in Brum.' She paused for a moment, and looked consideringly at George. 'How old is this Tony person supposed to be?'

He hesitated, suspecting a trap, 'Nineteen, twenty, maybe,' he finally admitted, 'he's just in his second year.'

'A bit on the young side for blackmail and murder, don't you think?'

'If they're big enough, they're old enough, ma'am,' said George. A familiar enough expression, but frequently used in connection with something else.

I think it was being called ma'am that did it; Paula looked quite shocked.

* * *

Lincoln, Leicester, Coventry, or Nottingham, Tamworth, Sutton Coldfield; there was the usual argument about the route. George was the driver so, naturally, George won.

'But I don't know my way through Birmingham,' he moaned. Nor did I.

We were all right until we arrived in Goster Green, where Aston University, looking very much like a mixture of Mid-European prison accompanied by an upended concrete match-box, skulked unlovably next to the Fire Station on our left.

'Pity he isn't there today,' sighed George.

'We could have ripped young Cary out of a lecture room and arrested him,' I agreed, 'just so he could go around publicising yet another fine example of police sensitivity and boundless tact.'

George grunted. 'I can never understand you, boss. We can do that out in the sticks too, y'know; why should the Metropolitan Police have all the fun?'

He plunged into a series of dual carriageway tunnels running beneath the city centre, and more by luck than judgement, we found Edgbaston. That's when our troubles really began. The natives appeared friendly, but the better the district the more they're inclined to misdirect the tourist. They probably do it for laughs; either that, or nobody knew the location of Priory Road.

Once found, however, and it took us a good half-hour, George was impressed. Rich Victorian mansions set in a tree-lined avenue, only the occasional house going slightly to seed. The lines of bells at the sides of some of the doors showed which of them had been divided into up-market flats.

'Pity the poor students,' muttered my disgruntled Detective Sergeant as I sought and found the bell labelled Anthony Cary.

'He's not a poor student, he's already company director, courtesy of his Dad,' I pointed out.

'Bloody tax fraud.' There are times when I fear that the Socialist Workers have been proselytising George.

'Shhhh!' The intercom crackled into life.

'Yes?'

'Mr Cary? Can we have a word? Police.'

'You do surprise me!' A short pause. 'OK, first floor, door on the right at the top of the stairs.'

Tony Cary's flat was comfortable, the furnishings respectable, if slightly shabby, in the traditional oak-and-scruffed-leather mould. Neither the armchairs, nor the dining suite had been assembled with a late nineties student in mind. Even the big glass-fronted bookcase, although it was stacked with brightly-jacketed modern titles, recalled the tastes of an older generation. Only the series of posters depicting science fiction and fantasy figures on the walls, and an impressive chrome and smoked-glass CD stack with its pair of four-foot speakers, relieved the air of archaic gentility.

Tony Cary noted my interest and grinned. 'The majority of paperbacks aren't mine,' he said, 'Sis left 'em here when she finished her degree.'

'She was at Aston too?'

'Nah, nothing so sordid, she was at the proper University at Selly Oak, she managed better A level grades than me. Take a seat,' he added. 'I'm afraid I've lost the tobacco and the Persian slipper, and I'm plumb out of cocaine.'

'You could,' I replied, hesitating only momentarily, 'always entertain us on the violin.'

George looked indignant, then the lights came on. 'Oh, I geddit,' he said. Sad that Tony Cary was a suspect, on first acquaintance he appeared relaxed, the first clan member I was prepared to like.

Slightly built like his father with the family brown eyes and neat, long fingered hands, he resembled his sister rather than his other heavier, self-indulgent looking male kin. Not that he seemed effeminate, although he lacked her watchful air, tightly compressed lips and the inimitable touch of the gimlet gaze.

I gave him my name, introduced George and he waved us both into chairs. 'What can I do for you, as if I didn't know?'

'If you already know,' I said, taking a chance, 'you could save me the trouble of asking, Mr Cary. OK?'

'Number one,' he replied promptly, 'what do I know about the extortion racket at Cary's? Nothing, apart from the current cost to the company and the fact that the bad publicity is putting customers off and driving my father mad.

'Number two, what do I know about a murder victim called Rachel Foster. Answer, absolutely nothing at all.' He waited for a few moments while that sunk in, then he added wickedly, 'It seems a long way to come for so little, chaps; will that be all?'

'Not quite.'

He sighed elaborately. 'I didn't think it was. Are you going to arrest me, or something?'

This sounded all too much like twenty-year-old flip. Somebody had been putting him right about the police, and he'd been practising what to say.

'What about *something*?' I suggested. 'For the time being, at least.'

'How's Richard?'

'He's quite well, so far as I'm aware.'

'Is he out yet?'

'I would have thought you'd have known that, Mr Cary. I haven't seen him since last night.'

'Oh, right. No, I don't know as a matter of fact. I've heard nothing since yesterday evening, nobody's bothered bringing me up to speed.'

'So your father spoke to you yesterday?'

'Linda.'

'Right.'

'I think I ought to warn you,' his tone was still light. 'She doesn't like you, and she really hates this Templeton guy. Taken all in all, she's absolutely gone off cops.'

'Something we're going to have to live with, I suppose.' Heavy-handed George.

'Hey!' He didn't seem particularly upset, but he'd decided to have a go. 'You haven't done much for us so far. One successful blackmail, one unresolved police complaint, a female criminal slips through your fingers and now my brother's in jail accused of bumping her off.'

'Not strictly speaking true. Richard has been questioned, yes, but he was arrested in connection with discrepancies on your subsidiary company's accounts.'

'And that makes everything all right, does it? Anyway, Linda says that our solicitor says that that particular cock's not going to fight.'

I didn't pause to admire the syntax. 'I understand that you won't be joining the family firm?'

'I've already joined it in a sense, or didn't you know?'

'Yes,' I smiled briefly, 'I put that badly, of course. You are a director and a shareholder; you draw directors' fees. But you don't intend to make your father's business your career?'

'That's right. Three out of four siblings is quite enough.' I appreciated that one, a spot of social science speak.

'Don't you find that there's a certain amount of family conflict because of that?'

'Dad, you mean? He wasn't altogether a happy bunny when I – Oh, I get it, big family fall out, resentment of the heavy-handed Papa? Politically motivated junior radical blackmails the family firm?' He sounded really angry for a moment, then he laughed. 'Sure, he took some persuading, and I don't think he's altogether given up hope, but there's no real resentment, not on either side.'

'So you're both satisfied the way things are turning out?'

'I'm more than satisfied, believe me. My father isn't unreasonable, he's generous, and as long as I'm prepared to work, he's equally prepared to let me go my own way.'

'Have you ever been active in the companies?'

'That's not very nice, is it? I'm not a complete drone. I do attend board meetings as a non-executive, you know.'

'Apart from that.'

'Sure, I did a few months with the old man and the others when I left school. Learning the business from the ground up, they called it.'

'And?'

'It wasn't for me, but as I say, there were no hard feelings on either side, so you can forget any ideas you may have about the younger son's revenge.'

He remained calm, perfectly poised and relaxed, the merest whisper of impatience in his voice. I changed tack.

'Can you give me an account of your movements a week last Thursday?' I said.

'Can you?' the answer came back with a snap. 'I've always thought that was a particularly useless thing to ask. How many people can give a detailed account of what they were doing a couple of days ago, let alone sometime in the last ten days? I was here, if that's what you're getting at.'

'Here in your flat?'

'Here at the university, OK?'

'So,' said George, 'you've got a timetable, surely? Tell us about your lectures on a Thursday, that shouldn't be too hard.'

Another elaborate sigh, 'Hang on a sec. If you're going to be pedantic about it I'll have to make sure.'

He went over to his briefcase and a pile of books he'd left carelessly on the floor beside the bookcase, and took out a ring-file.

'Here we are, Social Structure, 10 a.m., a Politics Seminar at 11.15. Psychology lecture two o'clock, case closed.'

'And of course your lecturers will have a record of these events?' asked George.

'Ye Gods! You mean you're going to check the registers? How embarrassing, Tony Cary, master criminal strikes again!'

'It's not all that amusing,' I said mildly, 'Rachel Foster is dead, after all.'

'Yeah, I'm sorry about that, believe me. But I never knew her, and you lot seem to be running around like headless chickens at the moment. Who's been using Richard's cottage, who's been scattering fudge papers, stupid stuff like that.'

'What time did your afternoon lecture finish?' A slightly hostile note introduced by George.

'A one hour lecture, so it finished at three o'clock. I haven't got a helicopter, so I could hardly have got to your neck of the woods in time.'

'You seem remarkably well informed.'

'I think Linda was worried about me, it's quite enough to have one of your brothers locked up. She was putting me wise to your tactics, just in case.'

'You didn't skip a Thursday lecture by any chance?' George was still plugging away.

'No I did not, and the last time I was at Richard's cottage, or anywhere near Eddathorpe for that matter, was sometime around last July.'

'With Richard and his wife?'

'No, by myself as a matter of fact.'

'Asked to borrow the key from him, did you?'

'No need, I had a standing invitation. If I wanted a bit of peace to do some work, or take a girlfriend or even just relax he told me that I could go over anytime I liked.'

'And which was it?'

'Girlfriend, so I wasn't being strictly accurate there, but you can't put me in handcuffs for that.'

'But you say you didn't borrow your brother's key?'

'I'm surprised he didn't mention it. He keeps the spare under a brick beside the drainpipe at the back.'

Now why the hell hadn't we thought of something as simple as that? There was a brief, embarrassed silence.

'Now that's what I call perfect security,' said George.

Chapter Twenty-four

'There's no doubt about it,' said Angie, 'all you need is a spot of gentle bullying and it all works out fine.'

In other circumstances I would have disputed that, threatened a spot of wife-beating, for example. As a domestically enforced rest day, however, Sunday morning had gone rather well, a leisurely breakfast, a gentle family walk in the autumn sunshine, a long and lively ball game with kid and dog to raise an appetite for lunch. No doubt about it, these modern foodie trendies don't know what they're missing; nothing competes with the smell of an old fashioned roast wafting through the house immediately prior to one o'clock.

I was busy rejecting the theatre, the opera and the ballet reviews in the Sunday paper when the phone rang, so regrettably, Angie reached it first.

There was a distant murmur of voices from the hall followed by a typical Angie broadcast, loud and clear.

'Who?' she asked tightly. 'Oh, it's you, is it? I hope you realise that this is Sunday lunchtime, and this is the first day off he's had for weeks.'

It didn't take a genius to realise that somebody senior in official circles was on the receiving end of the Angie version of a hard time. My divisional commander, Superintendent Teddy Baring, she liked. She also liked Paula, and she'd never put the boot into George, besides, he was a fellow-sufferer in this particular case. That left . . .

'It's that man Fairfield,' she said as I reached the hall. No muffling hand, I noticed, had been placed over the mouthpiece of the phone. 'Tell him,' she added, 'that whatever he wants is going to wait until after you've had your lunch.' She is nobody's idea of the subservient or even halfway tactful police wife.

Surprisingly, Peter Fairfield didn't sound even slightly irritated, more depressed. 'Sorry to disturb you, Bob.'

'That's all right.'

Angie raised her eyes heavenward, I thought she was going to shake her fist. Men react differently from women on these occasions, and besides, I'd caught the conciliatory tone of voice.

'Charlie Renshaw isn't available,' he said.

'No?'

'And as for Christopher bloody Bowyer . . .'

Open disloyalty to a colleague, unusual for Peter; neither was he famed for beating about the bush. Something delicate by the sound of it, even personally embarrassing, then.

'It's Frank Purcell,' he said. 'I want you to come over to Nottingham with me, he's probably on his way out.'

'What?'

'He's had a heart attack, a bad one, and he's in the QMC.' The Queen's Medical Centre, the Nottingham University Hospital, but all circumstances considered, Peter was hardly the natural choice for visiting the sick.

'There's nobody else around, his wife rang me. I knew her, too, once upon a day.'

'I see.' I didn't, but it was something to say. Probably something to do with Peter and his long memory, which didn't altogether fit in with his hard man image.

'Well, you've at least met him, Bob. And even if we can get in to him, he's unlikely to want to see me.'

A good question at last, 'You want *me* to go in and see him? Why?'

'Well,' he hesitated. 'Marian says he's on his way out.'

'Yes?' He'd used that particular euphemism once before.

'Perhaps – perhaps we could manage to get him to put in his papers before it's too late.'

'I don't underst—'

But yes, I did. Peter was out to screw the system once again. If Frank, alive, retired, Frank's potential widow was in for something like a hundred thousand pounds in commuted retirement pension, plus her subsequent widow's half. If Frank died in post, there'd be no lump sum, the widow's mite was all she was going to get.

'Reckon you can swing it, boss?'

'It's been done before.'

'OK, pick me up here. Twenty minutes? Maybe half an hour?' Bounced again, I didn't even think; I'd just been cast in the role of the junior ghoul.

Angie stood in the kitchen doorway, a trifle pink, I thought, but for the moment at least, heroically holding her fire.

'What was all that about?'

'Guilt,' I suggested, 'maybe a touch of nostalgia, I believe.'

Detective Constable Patrick Goodall was at it again. Opinionated, totally insensitive, and the proud possessor of a voice whose pitch and intensity was unlikely to do his long-term career prospects very much good.

'Imagine,' he blared, 'the poor bastard's busy clocking his clogs in hospital, and the only thing his wife can think about is ringing the boss at home so she can screw the County Council for cash.'

'What are you on about now?' Paula, at the far end of the incident room, sounded bored. Her lack of interest only encouraged Pat.

'I'm telling you,' he said. 'Frank Purcell's bloody wife. Fancy being married to a woman like that! He has a heart attack, and she persuades Bob Graham to go raving over to Notts with a completed letter of resignation in his sticky little paw so that the poor sod can sign it before he dies.'

'What good is that supposed to be going to do?'

'He's retired, right? He's entitled to commute part of his pension into a lump sum; if he dies on the job she only gets the widow's pension by itself.'

'Anybody who dies on the job,' said a voice in the background coarsely, 'is a very lucky man!'

'The ideal way to go,' suggested another anonymous comedian. 'Shafting Madonna, supping a pint, while watching *The Bill!*'

'Fancy old ladies, do you?' Easily distracted is Patrick; 'Not me mate, not even with yours.'

'As a matter of fact,' I said, appearing in the doorway like the demon king in a pantomime, 'it wasn't his wife's idea. Peter Fairfield worked it out on her behalf.'

Pat recovered at once, 'Is she another of his—'

'You're flirting with death,' warned Paula.

'Don't even ask,' I said.

'I thought that Frank was one of Peter Fairfield's greatest enemies?' Roger Prentice interposed himself between Patrick and his supervisors, saving him from further harm. 'Then he goes paying hospital visits to him and risking his professional neck.'

'Risking his neck?'

'You too, boss. Think what the Cary family are going to say when they find out that you and Peter have been encouraging their victim to slip through their fingers and resign.'

'Come off it, Roger. The guy's in cardiac care. And besides,' I added, Maurice Cary's phone call firmly in mind, 'Peter has ways of keeping old man Cary's mouth firmly shut.'

'The Carys,' said Roger Prentice with gloomy self-satisfaction, 'blame him for all their troubles. They'd probably prefer to see Frank's missus in poverty, and him laid out stiff and stark on a mortuary slab.'

'You know this, do you?'

'I've been hearing things, boss. That lot only pretend to be civilised: remember, I've spent a lot of time over the last week taking statements from their poor bloody employees.'

'I never thought that they were a popular family,' I said.

'Popular? Old man Cary is so mean he'd kill a louse for its

skin. The two older sons are pretty much the same, Bernard especially. They reckon he sacked a supermarket manager a few months ago for dumping some dodgy fruit and veg in a skip.'

'What was he supposed to do with it?'

'Pile it high and stick a discount label on it, of course. I tell you, boss, from what I've been hearing, there's hardly a member of staff who isn't secretly pleased they're in trouble.'

'Yeah,' muttered Pat smugly, 'even the poor relations they employ don't like 'em all that much. Maybe this blackmail thing is just a twentieth century version of the peasant's revolt.'

'I'm glad you've got the message,' I said a trifle bitterly. 'What else do you think I've been trying to get you to sort out for something approaching a fortnight, now?'

'Not the best of days,' said Colin Templeton draining his glass.

'Oh, I dunno, I quite enjoyed seeing Maurice Cary's face.'

'Not your problem, is it?' Colin nodded in the general direction of the barman in the half-empty Vernon Arms to signal a refill. He was studiously ignored. Colin flushed.

'Another bugger who ought to be unemployed,' he said.

'Maurice Cary?'

'You know perfectly well who I mean. It's just not been my day, what with Charlie Renshaw in London for his interview, and your boss turning gun-shy and leaving the bad news to me.'

'Frank was a Crime Squad man, and it's a Crime Squad retirement,' I said. 'Up to your lot to deliver the news, Peter Fairfield was only here so long as there was a police complaint to deal with, after all.'

'And where does that leave you?'

'Sorry?'

'Why did you bother coming over to Nottingham, Bob? All circumstances considered, I wouldn't have put you down as the eager volunteer.'

'Put it down to idle curiosity,' I said vaguely. 'I'm just

another student of human, or rather Cary, nature, Colin, that's all.'

'You're a bit of a sadist on the quiet. You must have known that old man Cary hates your guts; interviewing Richard for murder, harassing Tony, irritating his daughter, being in at the death when his police complaint goes down the drain.'

'Just like you say, mate, it's been a bad day. I just need to cheer myself up whenever and wherever I can.'

'Charlie's big failure, you mean?' He'd obviously been saving that one, but I'd already heard the news; Detective Chief Superintendent Renshaw's London interview had not gone well.

'Clive Jones's success, more like. I always suspected that one day he'd achieve command rank. I hope you're going to like your new ACC.' Mockingly I drained my glass. 'Here's to Clive; the rat race is over, the rodents have won!'

Colin stared balefully at the dregs of his pint; 'I take it that you definitely won't be applying for the Crime Squad vacancy, now?'

'In a word, no. To be honest, Colin, I wasn't all that keen, anyway. I didn't like the way your mate Charlie used you to dangle the carrot when he thought I might be of some use. Once they've got you, them as dangles carrots are all too fond of using sticks!'

He stretched his face, doing his best to ignore the implied criticism, but it was nothing like a genuine grin. 'No intentions of letting bygones be bygones, huh?'

'You have to be crazy, not with Clive!' I paid a brief, unpleasant mental visit to a world in which we, and more specifically Laura, might conceivably have contact with Daddy Jones. Serve in any capacity under Angie's ex-lover? I shuddered: I sincerely thanked God for the Force boundary, and the eighty-plus miles between us. Long, long may they remain!

Colin, however, was thinking other, more personally advantageous thoughts. 'I suppose,' he said hesitantly, 'I could apply for the job myself.'

I gathered up the glasses; he didn't altogether surprise me.

Over-ambitious Colin, and him less than twelve months in post. On the other hand he might even do well, I thought meanly, he could always introduce his new ACC to his brand-new wife.

'Why not? Now that's what I call accelerated promotion, let's drink to that.'

He stared after me suspiciously as I made my way between the tables to the bar. Some people can never take the open-hearted gesture at face value; they're always looking for the hidden trap. I gave a passing thought to Frank Purcell and his advice. Pity he hadn't taken it himself, maybe he wouldn't be ending his career in cardiac care.

Eddathorpe might have its drawbacks, but his advice had been good. Never mind the chancy onwards-and-upwards stuff, I knew where I was better off.

'No offence,' said Eric the barman brightly as I ordered, 'but that pal of yours takes too much upon himself from time to time.'

'You know him, then?'

'Oh, yes, I know him all right. Comes in here throwing his weight about. Another copper, in'ee? Has a flash blonde with him from time to time.'

'That,' I said crushingly, 'would be his new wife.'

Unabashed, the barman winked, 'Her too,' he said.

'More people,' I said sadly, 'know Tom Fool than Tom Fool knows. You'd better have a drink.'

'Half a Guinness, OK? I've been hoping to see you again, ever since you came in the other week.'

'Oh, yes?'

'I've been thinking,' he said.

'That's nice.'

'About your own particular girlfriend, the one who got the chop? I saw your pictures in the paper, she used to come in here.'

'Rachel Foster?'

'That's the one. I'd no idea you were a bigwig. Just like him,' he nodded in the direction of Colin, 'until I saw the photos, I thought you were just another cop.'

I didn't disabuse him about the company I was keeping; it's amazing how you can warm towards the strangest people all at once.

'Regular as clockwork at one time,' he continued, lowering his voice as he leaned confidentially across the bar. I waited, the conspiratorial type, he so obviously enjoyed dragging it out.

'Drink and then a meal, usually on a Tuesday, sometimes on a Friday night as well. The other one paid, of course.'

'Boyfriend, huh?'

'That's one way of putting it, I suppose.' The barman sniggered nastily, 'Your girlfriend was the fem, that's for sure, and by the way she was dressed the other one was definitely playing the chap.'

'That took you long enough,' muttered Colin plaintively upon my return with the drinks. 'Making new friends and influencing people, I suppose?'

'Something like that,' I took an abstracted sip of my new pint.

'OK, so what are you thinking about now?'

I smiled at him seraphically, 'Fudge, and that's just for starters,' I said.

Chapter Twenty-five

'I wish,' said Linda Cary, 'to make a complaint.'

The custody sergeant, pen in hand, looked at us reproachfully and sighed. It's a thankless job, stuck in a windowless, neon-lit room for eight hours a day, frequently badgered by arresting officers, walking the tightrope between constabulary demands and the Home Office-sponsored bible of prisoners rights.

'Oh, yes?' Reluctantly he drew the custody record a trifle closer, ready to write it all down. When in doubt cover your own back by sticking it all on the sheet.

'This lot are just like the bloody Gestapo,' proclaimed the lovely Linda. 'Night and fog.'

'I beg your pardon?' He'd not heard that one before; he settled his belly more comfortably against the edge of the wood and prepared himself. Quite a novel way to complain.

'Are you thick, or something? It's the oldest trick in the book; turn up at the crack of dawn, hammer on the door, and terrify the victim while they're still in bed, then drag them off to the other side of the country while they're still only half awake.'

'We didn't hammer, we rang the bell,' said George.

The Eddathorpe custody sergeant raised one restraining hand in his direction. 'You mean they invaded your bedroom?' he asked, interest quickening and awaiting the allegation of indecent assault.

'No-o,' she admitted reluctantly, glancing sideways at the pair of us. She'd never thought of that. 'They had a woman with them, anyway. I'm saying that they deliberately took an unfair advantage by raiding my flat at an unreasonable hour just to upset me. Then they conducted an illegal search.'

'Ah,' the custody sergeant felt safer now. He obviously distrusted the airy insubstantiality of the Nazi psychological approach.

'What do you mean, *ah*? It certainly invalidates anything they have claimed to have found, doesn't it?' Somebody else had confused the English and American laws of evidence; she'd obviously been watching too many Hollywood cop shows on late night TV.

'And what exactly have they found?'

Slowly, she looked down at the charge office counter and the plastic envelope containing prisoner's property. 'A couple of plastic cards, but that doesn't necessarily mean they belong to me. Anyway, they can't use them now because it was an illegal search.'

'You were under arrest at the time?'

'Yes.'

''Fraid you're wrong, then; they had every right to seize property germane to your case.'

That pulled her up short; germane, it was not your usual blue serge word. 'Oh.' It was only a momentary setback, however. 'I want to talk to my father on the phone. He'll be beside himself, wondering why I haven't come in to work today.'

'We'll contact him. What about a solicitor? You've got a right to legal representation, if you like.'

'That's what I meant, I want to talk to him first. He's a very rich man with a battery of lawyers, and once they get going they'll crucify you.'

I looked from Linda Cary to the sealed plastic bag and back, while the custody sergeant took the threat in his stride. She sounded so loud and cold and confident, but she wasn't thinking it through. The first signs of panic were setting in, and so far as I was concerned, she could call whomever she liked. I nodded to the man behind the counter, and shrugged.

There are, however, times when I would like to gag my sergeant for giving the game away. 'Daddy *is* going to be pleased,' said George.

She looked startled for a moment, then angry and confused. Her thin lips compressed until they almost disappeared, and her brown-button eyes bored furiously into George's face.

'You think you're clever, don't you? I can explain everything to my father, and anyway, he won't believe a word you say.'

'The phone,' said the custody sergeant, reluctant to involve himself in disclosures and thereby become a prosecution witness, 'is over there.'

'On second thoughts I can wait.'

'Would you like to see the duty solicitor, instead?'

I have to admit it; it was my turn to scowl. I wasn't altogether pleased with my uniform colleague. Obey the Home Office instructions by all means, but he'd already asked her once, and this sounded a bit too much like leaning-over-backwards time.

By now, however, Linda had the bit firmly between her teeth. 'Second-rate advice from some small town oik who's probably known these two since they were juvenile delinquents themselves?' she said aggressively. 'Nice try, Sergeant, but I'm brighter than that. No thanks!'

'Sign here, please.'

'I'm not signing anything.'

Glumly, he endorsed the custody record, 'Please yourself.' He turned his attention to me. 'Are you going to interview her straight away, sir?'

'No, I don't think so. I've got a couple of enquiries to make. Besides,' I added virtuously, 'it was a long journey. I think she ought to have had a drink and some breakfast by this time of day.'

'So ought we, and apart from that,' murmured George *sotto*

voce as we left the custody suite, 'it will give her the opportunity of thoroughly inspecting our cells.'

He frequently misrepresents the best of my motives, does George.

Wendy Pointer stared hopefully into my face, 'You've arrested him, then?' she asked.

'Er, well . . .'

Rachel's aunt's face crumpled and she sat down heavily into one of her over-stuffed armchairs, 'It's not more questions, is it? It's not right, you ought to have got somewhere by now. I can't even put her to rest, the Coroner won't release the body. My own niece!'

'I'm sorry, Mrs Pointer, it's not easy, I know, but it isn't straightforward, and potentially the defence might want to do their own, er, tests to confirm . . .'

'The Coroner's Officer explained it to me. The lawyers might want to – to have her opened up again and try to help their client wriggle out of it, if they can.'

Obviously, it wasn't becoming any easier for her as the days went on. Her bulky frame shook and her eyes overspilled while, selfishly, I wished myself a hundred miles away from this latest demonstration of grief.

George, embarrassed, cleared his throat, 'We aren't there yet, love,' he said placatingly, 'but we are getting on.'

'So you *have* caught him? I just knew it was that ex-boyfriend of hers!'

Unwisely, George jumped in, 'Which one?'

'The one whose name I got mixed up, the homosexual, I think.'

'I beg your pardon?'

'Peters,' she said, 'Roy Peters, from what I've heard he's a pouf, and she was the only girlfriend he's ever had.'

'Really, and how do you know that?'

'Asking around; it's common knowledge, apparently. I never really liked him from the start,' she replied.

Common knowledge? Both George and I kept quiet, an in-depth enquiry running, and that little gem appeared to be well known to everybody other than the police. A spot of mutual camouflage; Rachel and Roy; defending themselves in a cruel teenage world, maybe. It did not, however, put Wendy Pointer's target on our particular map.

'Tell me,' I said, sliding away from the subject, 'did Rachel have any particular friends while she was away?'

'Away where?'

'In Birmingham, for example?'

'No special boyfriends, I've already told you, not so far as I know.'

'Any friends at all, females for example?'

George glanced at me from under his eyebrows, but I wasn't going to start a row. Face neutral, voice bland, there was nothing for Wendy Pointer to fasten onto, unless she already knew.

'I suppose, but I don't remember any names. It wasn't something she talked about a lot.'

'What about in Nottingham over the past few months?'

She merely shrugged.

'Would you say she was a very private sort of person, kept herself very much to herself?'

'I don't know what you're getting at,' she sniffed. 'She was always very considerate to me, if she didn't come home at the weekend she always wrote to me regularly with her news. She wasn't in the least secretive, if that's what you mean.'

George was there before me, 'While she was at the university,' he asked, 'where did she live?'

'Half a dozen different places, you know what students are like.'

'Did you keep her letters?'

'N-no,' the question almost set her off again, the tears welled up in her eyes. We'd reminded her of missing souvenirs of Rachel, carelessly destroyed. 'One of your men went over that the other day, he was looking for names. I've still got my address book, though, if that's any good.'

It was. There were five different Birmingham addresses

as it happened. In her final year she'd lived in the flat on Priory Road.

According to the Registrar at Birmingham University the careers of Rachel Foster and Linda Cary had overlapped. The former had done a three-year joint honours course in History and Education, followed by a one-year postgraduate certificate in order to teach. The latter, two years ahead of her, had obtained an upper second in Business Studies and Law.

It's one thing, however, having reasonable suspicion, or even evidence of a sort, but it's quite another to prove your case. They'd gone to the same university, fine. For a time they'd shared the same flat. Later, in Nottingham, a barman had seen them canoodling together, and Linda had slipped-up when she'd talked about 'fudge' to her younger brother instead of 'sweets'.

She'd had the knowledge, the opportunity and probably the motive to put the boot in financially to her chauvinistic old man. Linda had, of course, kept her mouth shut about her relationship with the murder victim, but it's not an offence to fail to volunteer. We had evidence, of course, via two recovered cash cards that she was involved in the blackmail plot in some way, but that alone was far from being enough.

'She's a bloody dyke, isn't she?' said Patrick Goodall indignantly in the midst of the incident room conference upstairs. 'Isn't that enough?'

A distance, physical as well as intellectual, opened between him and his colleagues at this point. It's not like the good old days, a certain amount of left wing, pinko-commie-liberalism, as he puts it, seems to have insinuated its way into the ranks of the late twentieth century cops.

'Listen,' said Paula, 'we're busy trying to sort out a sensible way forward here. You can be so crude as well as stupid at times.'

He glared suspiciously at his superior officer; he even went so far as to open his mouth to make what passed in Goodall circles as a crushing reply. Then he thought better of it; promising careers have floundered for less.

'You've got her, anyway, haven't you, boss?' He tried for a touch of his usual swagger, and failed. 'It's game, set and match to us.'

Linda Cary thought otherwise, and she was not inclined to give in. Once the interview tapes were rolling both George and I grew sick of the sound of our own voices. She let us do the talking, staring at us through dark, appraising eyes, giving yes and no answers with long, frustrating intervals in between.

'And now,' she said at last, 'you're beginning to realise why I didn't tell you that I knew Rachel Foster before. I knew you'd jump to conclusions, I knew you'd persecute me because you always thought the blackmail was an inside job.'

'But you did know Rachel Foster at university?'

'I don't deny it,' she said.

'And during your last year you even shared a flat?'

'Correct.'

'You were lovers?'

'Subtle, aren't you? Not that our sexual orientation is anything to do with you.'

'You knew one another at Birmingham, and your friendship was resumed once she left the city and came to Nottingham, OK?'

'OK. Just remember that I don't have to take any snide remarks from you.'

'Remember the words of the caution,' said George flatly. 'If you have a proper defence, now's the time to tell.'

Momentarily the thin lips curved. 'So it may harm my defence if I do not mention something I later rely on? But what happens if I don't have any confidence in you as questioners? If you're insulting me, for example, by making irrelevant comments about me, just because I'm gay?'

'We've done nothing of the sort.' It wasn't a bad move, and George was taken aback.

'That's a matter of opinion,' she said. 'Just now, it all sounded very prejudicial to me.'

Clever, I had to admit; as a complaint it would hardly stand up, but she was trying to put us on the defensive, and if she succeeded she could turn the interview around. Trying to make the opposition behave as though they were treading on eggs wasn't totally new, but it was an excellent ploy.

'You're entitled to your opinion,' I said calmly, 'but we're the only interviewers you're going to get. Perhaps you ought to reconsider having a legal representative to look after your rights?'

'How very pompous.' She was still in there batting, 'In any case, I'm legally trained.'

No, not exactly, madam. You're no experienced solicitor; you've only got a joint degree. Besides, and I kept the old proverb strictly to myself, the lawyer who defends herself has a fool for a client.

I ignored the insult, 'As long as you're sure,' I said. 'I want to show you these cash cards, the first was recovered from Rachel Foster's home. She had used it to obtain money from one of the accounts set up on behalf of your father's company. These two similar cards were found in your flat this morning, they've all been used to blackmail Cary's Supermarket chain.'

'Yes, so I understand.'

'I believe you probably obtained these cards in false names about eighteen months ago.'

'No, they're nothing to do with me. Besides, from what I hear a man originally obtained them.'

'Richard told you that?'

She shrugged, 'A fat, middle-aged man, wasn't it?'

'Or a somewhat effeminate looking man. Did you dress up as a male for the purpose?'

She compressed her lips into a thin straight line. 'As I say, you two are a pair of sexual bigots, and they're nothing to do with me.'

'Then how do you account for possessing them?'

'Only two of them,' she corrected. 'Easy, I took them off Rachel to prevent any more damage being done. I kept them hidden because she was a friend, and I didn't want her prosecuted.'

'And when did you commit this act of charity?' George stepped in, he can't resist the occasional sarcastic touch.

'Well, it must have been a few days before she died.'

'The week she died?'

'I think it was the week before.'

'And you did this because you were friends?'

'Yes.'

'To stop her getting into further trouble?'

'That's right. I know it was wrong, but it was a dilemma; I was torn between my duty to the company, and saving a friend.'

'Your, er, lover to be precise.'

'Either you're a proper bigot, or you're trying to throw mud to prejudice a jury against me. That's it, isn't it, if the truth be told?'

'Let's stick to the point; how did you find out about Rachel's, er, activities in the first place?'

'I put two and two together, naturally. I remembered her questioning me about the company from time to time. Then I suddenly realised that her lifestyle had improved dramatically over the past few months.'

'Seventy-two thousand pounds worth of improvement?'

'If that's the final figure, yes.'

It was all good knock-about stuff; even leaving aside her original panic stricken comments to the custody sergeant about tainted evidence. No real foresight of consequence here, as the lawyers say.

'All that money, and you still decided to keep quiet for the sake of your friend?'

'That, and I didn't want to disappoint my family. If I'd betrayed her, the nature of our friendship would have come out. My father is a very old fashioned man.'

'So you didn't take back the money?'

'Well, I confronted her, of course. She was very upset, and she said most of it had gone to repay her debts.'

'And all this happened in the week before she died?'

'Yes.'

'Not too bad, Linda, not too bad at all. But there's no truth in it whatsoever, is there?'

She looked at me blankly, 'You've no right to say a thing like that.'

'It's a complete load of tripe. The blackmail plot was your idea from the start. I suggest you obtained the cards, recruited Rachel, and she either got greedy or you quarrelled. You came over to Eddathorpe on the Thursday afternoon in your own car, you met her, and both of you went off in her Mini, probably to your brother's cottage.

'That's where your so-called confrontation took place; you had a row, and you killed her. You probably recovered and destroyed the Retton cash card, too. After that you used her car to dump her body at Ansell's Creek. You returned it to the service road at the back of her aunt's hotel, before picking up your own vehicle and driving away.'

'That's all very neat,' she said. 'The only problem is, you haven't got a scrap of evidence, and not a word of it is true.'

'What about the sweet wrappers?' I asked. 'We found wrappers at the cottage, and there were wrappers in Rachel Foster's car.'

'So what? There must be millions of them about, and you haven't even established that I eat sweets.'

'No, but when you spoke to your younger brother on the phone you slipped up. You were supposed to be reporting the details of Richard's interview with the police. We talked about sweet wrappers, you specifically mentioned fudge.'

'Well, yes.' She hesitated momentarily, but then she recovered and went on. 'I admit it, I guessed you meant my fudge. I do eat it, but I've been to the cottage lots of times, and of course as a friend of Rachel, I've frequently been in her car. I must have screwed up the odd wrapper at sometime when I've been with her and dropped it on the floor.'

She sat back and looked at me contemptuously as if total

victory had been secured. It's amazing how people in trouble can only see things from their own point of view.

'Linda,' I said almost gently. 'Money was collected on some of those cards, including these, well after Rachel Foster was dead. You admit having two of them, what happened to the rest?'

'I don't know what you're talking about.'

'The card,' I said patiently, 'she used on the Sunday morning at Retton prior to her arrest for one thing. And what about the cash from the machine?'

'I don't know anything about any other cards. Nor the cash,' she said.

'We recovered an empty envelope she'd addressed to herself from her Eddathorpe room. It was franked locally, and delivered on the Wednesday before she died. I believe that it contained the cash card and the money she'd obtained and posted immediately before she was caught. I suggest that you saw her the next day, and those were the items you took from her. Is that why you had the row?'

'I never saw any money, and I never had the other card.'

'But you did see her, didn't you? Did she get cold feet following her arrest, was that it? Maybe she got rid of the card herself because she was scared, and she didn't want to go on?'

She looked at me blankly, so I continued. 'Apart from that, the story about her surrendering two cards sometime during the week before she died is nonsense, isn't it?

'The blackmail went on, culminating in the poisoning of the company customers, right up to the day before she died. She wasn't even in Nottingham at that time, and anyway, if you'd found her out, what would be the point of her going on?'

She straightened slowly, there was silence in the interview room apart from the creak of her chair and the almost imperceptible hiss of the tape. She rubbed the fingers of one hand across her eyes and shook her head before staring me full in the face.

'All right, I saw her, but I didn't mean to kill her. It was more or less an accident,' she said.

Chapter Twenty-six

'She started the first scam nearly eighteen months ago,' I explained, 'when she obtained the cash cards, screwed the company and collected fifteen thousand pounds. Richard kept the news from the old man by milking the wholesale company, and that spoiled her game.'

Fairfield grunted, and examined the interview transcript, shifting uncomfortably in his chair.

'And you say she obtained the cards from the banks while she was dressed up as a man? Sounds a bit far-fetched to me.'

I shrugged. 'There's no evidence to suggest there was a third person involved, and anyway, it's Colin Templeton's problem rather than mine. We've got the murder; they've got the blackmail. It seems like a fair division of labour to me.'

'So long as it's not a case of too many cooks,' said Fairfield curmudgeonly to the last.

'Sorry?'

'You've found two of the bank cards plus a third at Rachel's flat, you've got a confession of sorts, but there's still a lot to do. If you and Templeton start pulling in opposite directions, a decent defence could make sure that both your cases drop right through the gap between you.'

'Colin's all right now,' I said optimistically. 'I stole a bit of a march on him, that's all.'

'You went across a Force boundary, you arrested a prisoner, you searched her flat and then you took her all the way from

Nottingham to Eddathorpe without so much as a by-your-leave to the local force. Some march!'

'Notts police don't care,' I said hopefully, 'it's a Crime Squad case.'

'No,' Fairfield grinned wickedly, 'but I know a man who will!'

'Charlie Renshaw?'

'ACC Jones. Is that why you did it, to raise two fingers in the general direction of the new Crime Squad boss?'

'Sir,' I said indignantly, 'I was only doing my job.'

'Nice one, Robert,' the grin acquired a cynical twist. 'If the bugger turns nasty, you can always stick to that.'

There's no point in arguing with Peter; he puts the worst possible construction on whatever his subordinates do. I simply shrugged.

'I suppose you realise,' he continued, 'that you're both going to have your work cut out to prove all this?'

'Colin should be OK with his blackmail,' I protested. 'We can show a long-term relationship between Linda Cary and Rachel Foster for a start. We can prove Rachel's involvement with the blackmail plot, and our recovery of some of Linda Cary's suspect cards. Linda must have stashed her share of the money somewhere, and Colin Templeton's outfit are working on the asset recovery side of their case right now.'

'And what about your murder?'

'Well,' I replied slowly, 'it all ties up. The relationship, the blackmail, Rachel getting greedy as well as scared, and the meeting between them on the day of her death. Linda claims that they had a few drinks together earlier in the afternoon, then they went to the cottage where they had a row over the division of the loot.

'Linda seemed to think that her little friend was getting greedy, and Rachel demanded a bigger and better share from the money they'd already obtained. That's when she was thumped, and what with the alcohol they'd both consumed, and so on . . .'

'She ended up dead, and Linda disposed of the corpse.'

'Yes.'

'So there's no forensic evidence, there aren't any independent witnesses and you're relying on Linda Cary's version of the whole thing?'

'There's the blackmail plot, the cards we recovered, not to mention the fact that Linda volunteered the information that both she and Rachel were half boozed,' I protested. 'Our murder victim would have scored eighty on a blood/alco-test, and I never told Linda anything about the drink in the corpse. And then there was the slip-up she made to her brother about the sweets.'

'You're going to rely on her younger brother as a prosecution witness?' asked Fairfield incredulously. 'Besides, the sweets versus fudge story is only a minor incident along the way.'

'She still confessed.'

'To a so-called accident, or so she said. I'm disappointed in you, Bob; I'd have thought you'd have got her to admit to a straight killing in a row over the Retton money, and the return of the card.'

'Just as you said, sir, we're relying on her for a lot of it, and anyway, it's not a perfect world. We're home and dry on manslaughter, at least.'

'Then why charge her with murder?'

'They can always reduce it,' I said with dignity. 'The final decision is down to the DPP.'

'To her father, more like. Once he starts chucking money at lawyers, they could easily end up charging *you*!'

'She doesn't want to know her father. You ought to read the tape transcript, boss, and see the things she said. Trodden on, undervalued; the brightest member of the family having to act as a glorified office girl, and being forced to play second fiddle to his precious boys. She's totally obsessive, I even feel quite sorry for the old man.'

'I don't.' Fairfield lifted his head, his mouth tightening. 'I don't feel sorry for any of the bastards, it's bloody obvious you haven't heard.'

'Heard what?'

'It happened in the early hours of this morning. Frank Purcell is dead.'

'But—'

'Stress brought on that heart attack, Bob. He'd still be with us now if that bugger hadn't harassed him and made his life a misery with his continual complaints.'

Cautiously, I studied Fairfield's face. His expression was bleak: no more feud, then, no more Faithless Frank. No detectable irony, either, and I hardly dared call it hypocrisy for once. All coppers stick together, and all outsiders are allowed to take the blame for everything, whatever the state of play. However illogical, Peter Fairfield meant exactly what he said.

'Frank should have been looking forward to his retirement,' he concluded coldly, 'and all because of Cary and the antics of a couple of pervy females, the poor old feller's dead!'

Colin Templeton had been right, a vigorous old dinosaur with a nasty tongue, and far too much flesh on his bones.